By DAWN KIMBERLY JOHNSON

Audible
Biting the Christmas Biscuit
Broken*
Button Down*
Come Clean
Fishbowl
Good Question
Grand Adventures (Anthology)*
Higher Learning (Anthology)*
Home*
Juicy Bits (Anthology)*
One Constant
Reverie
Right on Time
What Happened to Larry Alan?
Winter Rescue
Yes, Darling

*Available in Paperback

Published by DREAMSPINNER PRESS
http://www.dreamspinnerpress.com

.

RIGHT ON TIME

Dawn Kimberly Johnson

Dreamspinner Press

Published by
Dreamspinner Press
5032 Capital Circle SW
Suite 2, PMB# 279
Tallahassee, FL 32305-7886
USA
http://www.dreamspinnerpress.com/

Right on Time
© 2014 Dawn Kimberly Johnson.

Cover Art
© 2014 Catt Ford.
Cover content is for illustrative purposes only
and any person depicted on the cover is a model.

ISBN: 978-1-62798-691-5
Digital ISBN: 978-1-62798-692-2

Printed in the United States of America
First Edition
May 2014

To Scheherazade and Sacheen. Thank you.

PROLOGUE

Goodland, Kansas - September 2020

DR. CHARLESTON Meeks waited in silence next to Odette Leaundra. She stared straight ahead, back ramrod straight, jaw set, eyes flinty and focused, just like any good soldier. As a team leader she had worked closely with his son during the boy's time as a temporal agent, but all that was coming to an end now.

She shifted in her seat, obviously not relishing his proximity. He glanced at her out of the corner of his eye. An attractive woman (a grandmother, if he'd heard right) with unblemished dark skin and high cheekbones; she was fit, strong, and intelligent. But she didn't seem to care for him, and he'd never understood that. Why the animosity? Women usually liked him, or at least he thought they did. Maybe he'd been wrong all these years. He glanced at her again. *Nahhh.*

Having more important things to worry about than the prickly woman on his right, the doctor sighed and turned his attention to the members of the oversight panel at the front of the room. A number of men and women sat behind a long desk that ran the length of the wall at their backs. It was raised a bit, allowing them to look out over—and down on—the assembled.

The doctor's Restore Point Program was about to be defunded and for no better reason than what he considered some religious mumbo-hoo-ha. Judging from some of the members' comments, he had nearly reconciled himself to things not going his way. He hated when that happened. Their concerns were hardly new to him as he thought back over the proceedings thus far:

Should we do this just because we can?

We have no idea what might come of these manipulations.

Who are you, sir, to rework God's plan?

Coming from a prominent United States senator, that last one had left the doctor speechless, mouth agape. As far as he was concerned, there was no God, but... if there were, surely he or she had given him the intelligence to theorize and bring to fruition the RPP. Right?

The program was far from common knowledge among the populace, or even many in government, therefore the review was taking place deep underground, in a conference room of the main RPP facility. The members of government who were privy to the existence of the program had reviewed all mission reports on their data tablets via temporal-safe storage before traveling from DC to listen to Meeks make his case.

He sat in front of them, suffering through their questions, many of them the same questions he'd dealt with years ago, right before RPP's launch:

Why not go back and kill Hitler?

Why not go back and save Kennedy?

Why not stop the towers from being taken down?

The doctor had patiently explained, once again, that even if they could somehow overcome the technology's thirty-year window—ceiling, limit, whatever—intervening in any one of those events would cause ripples in the timeline that could undo the very fabric of their current reality. His team simply didn't have the capability to extrapolate from altering something so significant. He'd gone on to detail the successful lives of the people they had saved and the contributions they or their offspring had made to the world, but then came the inevitable:

What gives you the right to decide who to restore?

This was a touchy question. One or two of the committee members had lost children or spouses in accidents that could have, theoretically, been prevented. It was an alluring prospect. Who among them wouldn't want a second chance to be in the right place at the right time, or to go back and make a better decision than they had?

There were times Dr. Meeks, himself, regretted how he and his wife had been too busy and myopic in their scientific pursuits to see the struggles of their only son. Junior had only come out to them recently, just before his thirtieth birthday, and the doctor wondered every day how their relationship might have been closer over the years if the boy had felt comfortable enough or safe enough with them to come out sooner. It had hardly cost them his life, but he knew it could have if things had gone terribly wrong.

Dr. Meeks explained to the panel that a person chosen for restoration had to meet specific criteria. It had to be someone the temporal extrapolators deemed "a potential," or most likely to make a positive contribution to our existence, before RPP's Major Operations sent a team back in time to save that person. The financial cost for each step, not to mention the power required to operate the Portal, meant that the selection had to be precise and they'd only get one shot at it. That had wounded some of them. To suggest that a senator's child, who had drowned in a neighbor's pool at four years old, didn't make the cut, was a stinging slap to the face.

"What about Barnaby Rosenthal?" a member of the panel asked suddenly.

The doctor adjusted his glasses, cleared his throat, and said, "What of him?"

"According to this report," the member said, tapping his tablet, "an agent went back to save his life repeatedly."

"Yes, sir."

"Why is that?"

"An agent—"

"Your son," another member stated.

"After saving the life of the targeted 'potential,' my son accidently saved the life of one-year-old Rosenthal. It was a split-second decision. He—"

"Gave you an opportunity to *experiment*."

"Well…." He shifted in his seat as the panel members stared at him, waiting for him to continue. "I wanted to determine the outcome of multiple restorations on one subject. Since Rosenthal was supposed to die at such a young age, he was the perfect test subject." They continued watching him, and he tugged at his shirt collar. "If you'll recall, I did receive approval from this panel before proceeding."

Yet another panel member peered at the report on their data tablet and said, "After the accident, Agent Meeks time-stepped a total of four more times for Rosenthal, correct?"

"Yes, ages six, fourteen, eighteen, and twenty." Dr. Meeks left out the unauthorized step his son had made in early January 2013 to prevent Rosenthal from marrying a woman who was lying about carrying his child. It was all very "daytime drama" but hardly life threatening. Happy-life threatening, maybe, but…. He'd spotted the details in temporal-safe storage before an oddly *targeted* electromagnetic-pulse event had wiped it out along with all record of who had been scanned into the facility that day. He was certain that Sato girl had something to do with it, but he couldn't prove it. She was too smart for her own good, that one.

A rather somber member of the panel, who sat to the far right side of the giant desk and who had been silent up to that point, asked, "That's one unlucky young man, wouldn't you say, doctor?" The woman had a commanding aura about her. Meeks noticed all other heads turned toward her, deferring to her. She was a lovely, cultured-looking woman, who wore her fifty-odd years well.

She had a graying blonde hairdo that looked hard enough to protect her from falling debris at a construction site. Her eyes, set into a heart-shaped face, were a vibrant green—he suspected contacts—and filled with intelligence and calculation. The doctor felt himself being measured as Sen. Penny Collard stared him down, or tried to.

He set his jaw. "I'm sorry? I don't understand."

She leaned forward, clasping her beautifully manicured hands on the desk, and peered at him. "If you had multiple opportunities to come to his rescue," she said, her voice deep, musical, and richly southern, "it would seem he wasn't meant to be here, would it not?"

Hours later, when they adjourned without a decision (they would "be in touch"), Dr. Meeks and Leaundra rose and headed for the door.

"I didn't like the sound of any of that," he whispered her.

"Then you'll like the sound of this even less," she said, passing him her data tablet. He quickly scanned the report on the screen, then looked into her eyes in shock.

"Don't tell Junior… yet," he pleaded.

CHAPTER 1

Chillicothe, Ohio - June 1993

IT WAS simple foiling the robbery. My two step-mates were hardly even necessary to spook the guy into changing his mind. But then, it was nice to have all the bases, and doors, covered. Most people can tell when someone is watching them, staring at them. And if the focus of your attention is up to no good, he feels it even more intently. Our stares alone sent him running for the door, which my colleague politely opened for him. If we hadn't stopped him, young Miranda Colton would be dead, the victim of a nervous and highly agitated novice bank robber, who was just looking for cash for his next fix. After he fled, we left the bank quickly, two out the back door, me out the front. I heard a woman scream just as a stroller blew past me, heading for an intersection. The woman was sprawled on the ground. She scrambled to her feet, leaving her shopping where it lay, and gave chase, but she'd never catch it in time. I acted without thinking it through—the implications, the consequences. I darted after the stroller and caught the handle right before the back wheels left the curb. I looked in to check the baby, and a pair of large, chocolate-brown eyes looked up at me with wonder. I smiled, and my alarm sounded.

Goodland, Kansas - October 2020

"IS THAT it?"

"That's it, Mee—Charleston," Leaundra corrected, tapping her tablet and closing his file. "You're officially retired."

"Thanks for meeting me here, ma'am."

"It's as good a place as any, and it's not like you can set foot back in headquarters."

True. As a temporal agent, Charleston Meeks Jr. had absorbed his share of temporal energy, and couldn't take any more… well, not and survive, anyway. They sat at a wrought iron table on the patio of Brick Corner Café. A giant red-and-white-striped umbrella kept them out of direct sunlight, but as a cool October breeze disturbed his hair, Charleston would have welcomed a little warmth. Midday pedestrian traffic passed by their little spot as folks enjoyed a lunchtime stroll in that sunshine he longed for. "Join me in a drink?" he asked.

"Bourbon and Coke."

Charleston signaled for their waiter, and an actual flesh-and-blood man rushed over to take their order. It was a nice change from those floating, automated service bots gaining popularity with the larger restaurant chains. As Charleston looked the man up and down, he appreciated the benefits of making a human connection wherever possible. The waiter was young, slender, and attractive, with dark wavy hair and soft brown eyes. He reminded Charleston of someone. He offered them both a warm welcome and dazzling smile before entering their order in a data tablet and rushing off. Letting his gaze linger, for a few moments, over the waiter's retreating backside, Charleston then turned and searched his former superior's dark eyes.

"I feel a question looming," he said.

She smiled, transforming her normally stoic countenance. Her dark skin remained flawless, even after their years working together, after years of him making her want to yank her hair out. "I feel I should ask what's next for you, but I'm fairly certain I know the answer to that."

Charleston grinned. "Are you against it?"

"Would it matter if I were?"

"No, but I value your opinion." Charleston looked toward the street at the SUV idling by the curb. "I'd like to hear your thoughts."

"Your… *encounters* with Rosenthal were hardly the makings for a stable relationship." He had to give her that. "You've spoken to him, what, four times? And always in times of crisis?"

"I hear you, but I have to try, don't I?"

"Do you?"

"*Your drinks, sir,*" an automated server announced, having snuck up on their table. It hovered there and had been virtually silent in its approach. *So much for the ambience*, he thought. He predicted the infatuation with automated servers would die off soon. He removed their drinks from the tray and passed Leaundra hers as the bot floated away, pausing by another table to assure the patron someone would be right with them.

"Ma'am, after my father forbade me to time step again, you pitched in and made it happen. You broke the rules for me. You must have understood on some level what Barnaby means to me."

Leaundra sipped her drink and shook her head. "Uh-uh," she said, "I helped you because I don't like your father." She wouldn't meet his eyes. "Reminds me too much of an old boss. Always thought he knew everything, what was best for everyone." *Yep, sounds like Pop.* Charleston watched her closely for a moment. She turned and looked him in the eyes. "You're not sure where Rosenthal is, if he's attached, if he even *wants* to see you."

He reached into his back pocket and retrieved a brochure his father had given him at his birthday party three weeks ago. "I know he'll be at this art opening next week in Bend, Oregon."

He'd received that information and numerous other thoughtful gifts at the party, but the one he cherished most was a portrait of him Barnaby Rosenthal had done. Dr. Plumb, the woman who measured the effects of time travel on him and other agents, had presented it to him. The painting proved he was clearly still on the young artist's mind, just as Barnaby was on his. Charleston tried to keep his voice nonchalant.

"As for the rest, I've got someone working on that." He smirked, but it was his turn to avoid her gaze.

Leaundra raised an eyebrow. "Really?" He nodded but remained mum. "Charleston," she began softly, "what you're planning has never been attempted before. You're seeking a relationship with an RPP subject. It just doesn't seem like a good idea." With a well-practiced motion, she paused to drain her glass as Charleston just began sipping his drink. "Look at it from Rosenthal's perspective. You saw him three weeks ago, but it's been seven-or-so years for him."

He winced. Right again. He had no idea what he'd say to Barnaby. He knew what he wasn't supposed to tell him (covert government operations and all), but he considered that more of a guideline than a ticket to twenty years in federal prison. Would he walk up to Barnaby's front door and knock? Pretend none of it had ever happened? Could they start something together right here in 2020? What would Barnaby tell his family? He grinned and sighed. *I'm getting ahead of myself.*

His last step to "save" Barnaby had left him literally falling apart, and recuperation had taken some time, during which a friend and colleague had been busy on his behalf, digging up whatever she could about the artist. Speaking of said colleague, at that moment Jeri Sato strode up to their table, the ever-present cherry lollipop in her mouth. She looked around and startled the couple at a nearby table by commandeering their extra chair, dragging it over, and dropping into it, effectively joining the conversation.

"Hey."

"Hey," Charleston and Leaundra said.

Jeri grabbed Charleston's drink and downed it, then delighted them with a long, drawn out grimace. "Bleh!" She withdrew her lollipop and frowned at it as if it had betrayed her. "Okay," she said after catching her breath and putting the candy back in her mouth, "I have the info on Rosenthal."

"How's it look?"

"Sato. Charleston," Leaundra said, getting to her feet, "I'm going to leave you to this. Plausible deniability and all. Plus there's some shit going down at RPP I have to deal with."

Charleston snorted. He didn't think he'd ever heard her curse before. "Really? What's happening?"

She paused as if considering what to say but clearly thought better of it and extended a hand to him instead. "By the middle of next week, you'll be fully back on the grid, son. Best of luck."

Jeri was oblivious, busy typing on her tablet as he bid his former team leader farewell. She walked to the waiting SUV, and the soldier behind the wheel whisked her away.

Back on the grid, huh? Charleston Meeks Jr. would soon be out there for any and all to find. As a temporal agent, he'd enjoyed virtual anonymity, existing enough to pay bills and own property, but not enough for his name to show up in any web searches beyond Goodland, Kansas— nongovernment searches, that is. With his retirement, nearly his entire history would be searchable on the Internet and appear to any and all who wanted to find him. The details of his federal service would remain suspiciously vague, however.

He leaned back in his chair, stretching his legs out in front of him, the picture of relaxation, while at his side sat Jeri, sucking on her lollipop like it was the last one on Earth and unconsciously bouncing her legs with pent-up energy.

For the short time he'd known her, this was her default setting. Always several steps ahead of everyone else, nothing in this world seemed to move fast enough for her, and she was forever in danger of being bored. In sharing her reasons for helping him complete an unauthorized time step, she'd said, "I don't have enough to do, and that usually leads me into trouble."

He smiled as he watched her work on what appeared to be a standard-issue, though bright purple, data tablet, but he knew she had probably added memory, encryptions, code-breaking software, and God knew what else to it. She had named it *Alohomora*.

"Okay, here's the rundown," she said, ready to give her full report on the man Charleston was desperate to see again. "After your last Rosenthal step, at the church—"

"I remember, Jeri."

She glared at him. "Don't interrupt me. Talking it out helps me keep track of things."

"Sorry."

"Since then, Rosenthal *did* go to art school and earn his degree as he'd planned, but...." Charleston raised an eyebrow as he watched her quickly scan the data on the tablet. "Well, he had a rough time of it."

"How so?"

She sighed. "The first year or so, he did well, but after that he began to struggle."

"But he's so talented—"

"—and depressed and a possible alcoholic and temperamental and a loner and... did I say depressed?"

"Aw, hell...."

"You're still interrupting. Now listen. He *is* a successful artist— albeit one clinging to the older mediums—but more importantly, at least to you, there haven't been any stable, long-term relationships over the past seven years." She tapped her tablet and scrolled the page. "His longest relationship to date is the one he's in now with—Oh, oops," she said, looking at Charleston. "Sorry."

"It's okay. Go on."

She looked back at her tablet. "With Rossom Bailey."

"What the fuck is a Rossom?"

"He's a model."

"Of course he is." Charleston sighed.

She studied the tablet. "Mmm, he's lovely…," she mused, then gave her candy an obscene suck as she yanked it from her lips with an audible pop. She glanced at him and grimaced. "If you like the type."

She turned the tablet toward him, and he rolled his eyes. "What type?" he asked. "The beautifully perfected type?"

"The type with dicks."

Charleston chuckled bitterly and turned his attention to the people rushing by (now in the opposite direction of earlier), their lunch hours apparently over. The sunshine wasn't as pleasant, seeming harsher now, glaring and uncomfortable. "Well… if he's happy, then I guess—"

"Looks like the portrait Plump—"

"Plumb. Her name is Dr. Plumb."

"—got you was one of the last," she continued. "He stopped including paintings of you in his shows about two years ago. Around the same time he…."

"What?"

She glanced up from her tablet. "Was hospitalized for 'exhaustion.'"

"Exhaustion?" Charleston frowned. "Are you saying he had a nervous breakdown?"

Jeri shrugged. "There aren't any details available for the general public, but I could probably dig up his medical records… maybe even doctor's notes?"

"You can do that?"

"Chuck, I can do just about anything with a hot spot." She reached out and pretended to snatch a handful of air. "It's all out there for the taking. You just need to know where to look."

"Isn't that illegal?"

"What's your point?"

"Don't call me Chuck."

CHAPTER 2

Chillicothe, Ohio - April 1998

BARNABY GIGGLED as the blue, superbouncy ball with gold speckles tried to escape him, but he caught it just in time, diving on it with both hands. He had plopped down in the aisle where the bright packages of toys sat right at child level: Army men, water pistols, Play-Doh, cheap plastic trucks, and the super balls. His mommy had promised him one toy, and after she'd told him to stay put as she wandered away to do her shopping, he'd promptly pried open a package, already thinking of the ball as his.

He bounced the ball again, and this time it did escape, bouncing higher than his head and disappearing around a shelf at the end of the aisle. He ran after it but stopped short when he discovered a very tall man holding it out to him.

"That's mine," Barnaby said.

"Is that so, little man?"

Barnaby nodded, his eyes wide with uncertainty, just before he reached out for the bright blue ball shifting quickly between the man's fingers. Then came the fear, fear that twisted his tummy, that stole his breath, fear that he couldn't see his mommy, couldn't call to her. He didn't want to go with the man, so he fought as hard as he could. Barnaby fought and kicked and tried to shout, but the man covered his mouth. He was too big, too strong, and Barnaby was so small.

The sunlight blinded him for a moment as the man carrying him burst through the door to outside. Then Barnaby fell to the ground, scraping his palms and knees. Another man was there, and the two big men fought. Barnaby scooted closer to a big, smelly Dumpster and tried to curl himself into something smaller, something they'd forget about, wouldn't see. The new man was just as scary as the first, and Barnaby cringed when he shouted at him to go inside, to find his mother.

He jumped to his feet and slipped by them as they struggled. What he wanted most at that moment was to find her, but once he was back inside the store, he paused and turned back. He peered around the door. They wouldn't see him if he just peeked with one eye. He saw the new man hit the bad man hard, and the bad man fell and didn't move. Then the new man fell, and Barnaby was sad. He didn't want him to fall, to be hurt, but he was.

Red stained his shirt, spreading beneath his hand as he pressed it to his side. This red wasn't like the scratches on Barnaby's knees or his palms. This was a lot more.

Barnaby must have made a noise because the new man looked up at him and smiled—then he disappeared, and Barnaby was scooped up into his mommy's arms. He clung to her and began to cry. They cried together.

Bend, Oregon - October 2020

"WAKE UP! Barnaby, wake up!"

The sharp sting of a slap drew a gasp out of him, and Barnaby opened his eyes to find Ross leaning over him, gripping his arms painfully and shaking him.

"Okay! I'm awake," he said. "Let me go." He fought down his disorientation and looked around at a blurry room. The faint odors of acrylic paint and brush cleaner hung in the air. *Oh yeah.* He was in his studio—or "the garage" as Ross called it. Bathed in sweat and wearing nothing but cargo shorts, Barnaby sat up straighter on the old sofa in the corner. He flinched a bit as the chill of the concrete floor bit into his bare feet.

"You were shouting," Ross said, backing off.

Barnaby unconsciously reached out to his right to retrieve his eyeglasses from the tabletop and slipped them on, bringing his surroundings into focus. He looked up at Ross, who stood there, arms crossed over his chest, watching him with a familiar expression of disapproval on his perfect face. What was it this time? He didn't know if Ross was perturbed by his old-fashioned eyewear, their recent breakup, the fact he'd been painting drunk, or the nightmare. Only Ross could disapprove of a nightmare.

"What was I saying?" Barnaby asked weakly.

"*Shouting*, Barn. You were shouting." Ross looked him over and sniffed. "Christ, you've got paint all over you," he said, reaching out to help Barnaby up. "It's a good thing I decided to come by early, or you would have slept through dinner and possibly your own show." Ross grabbed him by the belt and attempted to undo it—not for any pleasant endeavor, but simply to tighten it so it would better hold up his pants. "I thought you were going to move away from this medium. These old techniques don't sell as well. I've told you that."

Barnaby wriggled free, slapping Ross's hands away. When he looked affronted, Barnaby softly said, "Yes, I remember." He grabbed an old T-shirt and slipped it on, then slid his feet into a pair of tattered flip-flops. His head pounding, his mouth cottony, he gazed about him until he spotted the bottle and short glass by his easel.

"Then why are you still working with—"

"Because," he said, whirling on Ross, "if you'll remember, *I* said I like working with acrylics even if they don't sell as well as the bio-generated pieces. I like having my hands in there, Ross, stained, tired, and cramping afterward. And apparently, the gallery and the people attending tonight like that work too." The heat in his voice apparently brought Ross up short because the man stared at him for several moments. "What was I shouting?" he asked in a gentler tone before draining the glass and sighing as the warmth spread through him.

Ross met his gaze. "'Bad man,'" he whispered, and Barnaby looked away, nodding. "You'd better go have a shower," Ross said in wounded-voice number two. "We're meeting Coral and India in an hour." Barnaby winced when Ross turned to look over the new piece he'd finished before his nap. It was another portrait of a certain man, a man he hadn't seen in years, but a man Barnaby still thought about, dreamed about, and wanted. Ross's expression soured. "And you're telling the girls about our breakup, not me," he said as he continued into the house and slammed the door behind him without another word.

"Shit!" Barnaby flopped back down on the sofa and ran his fingers through his wavy, dark hair. He shouldn't have snapped. After all, they'd agreed to remain friends. He'd make it up to Ross somehow. He seemed to be doing that a lot lately, thinking of ways to make something up to Ross, which was one of the main reasons they'd decided to call their romantic attachment quits. He lifted his glasses and rubbed his eyes.

Bad man. He concentrated and could just about grab a thread of the dream, but it slipped away. He replaced his glasses and looked at his latest painting. He smiled at the image of the familiar face and instantly felt calmer. His subject wasn't male-model beautiful—not like Ross, who had long, lustrous chestnut hair, chiseled features, a perfect dimple in his chin, and intense, sometimes unsettling, green eyes—but his subject often felt more real to Barnaby. He was a few years older than the two of them, with kind blue eyes, a mischievous grin, facial scruff, longish dirty-blond hair, and broad shoulders. In the painting, the stranger stood menacingly over the crumpled figure of a… bad man.

During the twelve months he and Ross dated, there had been many portraits like it (Ross growing to hate each and every one), always of the same man, standing tall and proud, like some sort of superhero. *Isn't that what he was? What he is?* Maybe Ross didn't think he could measure up. *He couldn't, can't*, Barnaby thought.

There was one person who understood his obsession with his blond hero. Donald, his stepfather, had seen Charleston actually disappear right before his eyes in the anteroom of their local church seven years ago. But he'd suffered a massive stroke a year later and, before that, really hadn't been too keen to discuss what he'd seen. Through therapy, both physical and otherwise, Donald had come back about 85 percent, but there were some gaps in his memory, and Barnaby never discussed with him what they'd witnessed, afraid it might upset him and hinder his recovery.

All Ross knew, all the rest of his friends and family knew, was the man in the painting was important to Barnaby, but none of them ever missed the opportunity to ask about his origins. He wished they'd just accept his compulsion to render the image as a tiny aspect of his adorably quirky nature. He wished they would do the same about his drinking and apparent inability to make a relationship work. Hell, he was a tortured artist. Trouble came with the territory, didn't it?

Staring at the image he'd created from memory, Barnaby felt as though he could almost reach out and touch him. *Touch Charleston, my one constant.*

"Have you spoken to him yet?"

"No, Mom, I just got here. I'm checking in at the B&B."

"But you've called him, right?"

"Uh, nope." The silence on his Bluetooth link lingered. "Mom?"

"Why not, dear?"

Charleston thought about it, went through all the plausible reasons he could give her, but he decided on the truth. With a heavy sigh, he said, "I have no idea what to say." He accepted his room key—*an actual key, made of metal and everything*—thanked the desk clerk, slung his bag over his shoulder, and headed for the stairs. "I can't just call him up and say, 'Remember me? Let's meet for a drink? It's been too long.'"

"Good point."

"I'll figure it out, Mom." He reached the second floor and slowly walked the hall looking for his room.

"I thought you would have worked all this out on the flight out."

"I haven't even worked out what to wear to the art show tonight." He smiled at the sound of her chuckle.

"A deep blue shirt would bring out your eyes."

"Mom—"

"I'm just saying. I missed out on doing this with you for years, getting you ready for a date."

"Sorry abo—"

"No. I'm not fishing for an apology. You don't owe me that. We're good." More silence stretched between them. "Do you hear me?"

"Yes, ma'am." A 7 on a door matched his key, and he awkwardly slid it into the keyhole and turned it, feeling and listening in wonder as the tumblers did their magic. Bethany's B&B worked hard to maintain an old-fashioned atmosphere, hence the metal key instead of keycards or a voice activation system to gain access to the rooms. The door unlocked, and Charleston smirked at the novelty, then entered the room.

"Whoa!"

"What is it, dear?"

He stood in the doorway not certain where to let his gaze settle. Polka dots, stripes, patterns, and florals assaulted him from nearly every cloth surface in the room. "This room is...."

"What?"

Despite the riot of clashing patterns around him, he stepped inside and tossed his bag on the king-size bed.

"Let's just say I think they got a discount on fabric selection from some archival warehouse in town." The owners had obviously selected decor randomly for the bed linens, curtains, and carpet, without any knowledge of how to create a soothing room atmosphere.

His mother's soft laughter tickled his ear. "Either that or their décor simulator is on the fritz," she said.

He looked around for the simulator control, but there wasn't one.

"So… a blue shirt, huh?" he asked her with a grin.

"Trust me, dear."

He laughed as he crossed to a window and drew the flower-patterned curtain aside to look out over Colorado Avenue. The late afternoon sun bathed the street as the citizens of Bend went about their business. "Is Pop around? Let me say hi."

"Um… your father's still at work, dear."

Charleston frowned and let the curtain fall shut. "Why so late?" His mother didn't answer. "You there?"

"I don't know what's going on, but your father's been on edge the past week or so."

Charleston unzipped his bag. "Could you ask him to call me? No matter how late, okay?"

"I will, dear. Good luck tonight."

"Thanks, Mom."

He ended the call and unpacked a few things, then took his shaving kit into the en suite and hung up his charcoal-gray slacks on the closet door. He glanced at himself in the full-length mirror in the corner and reached up to tug at random strands of hair, lamenting the fact he hadn't taken the time to get a haircut. He tossed gray socks and a blue cashmere sweater on the elaborate bed bench and wondered if he had time for a nap before he had to get ready. *Ready. Ready for what? Ready to surprise Barnaby at his art show? Ready to ask him if he still or ever wanted me?* Nerves had his stomach in knots, almost like he was going on a blind date, which, in essence, he was.

Despite the riot of clashing patterns around him, Charleston decided a nap was a must. He stretched as if trying to touch the dreary popcorn ceiling—*I didn't think they made that shit anymore*—dropped facedown on the luxuriously comfortable bed, and closed his eyes against the chaos. He toed off his shoes and, just like he'd done for the past month or so, soon fell asleep with Barnaby on his mind. Images of his open, kind face, large dark eyes, smile, and thick wavy hair played through his thoughts like a well-worn and favorite film.

CHAPTER 3

"HEY," RICO Katch said, slapping the shoulder of the lovely brunette on his right. "Heads up."

Benni Kaan looked up from the digital comic on her tablet and watched two men weaving their way through the evening crowd in downtown Bend. She switched screens to review data on their target's known associates as the two men paused in front of their vehicle, checked both ways, and crossed the street.

"There's our boy," she said, her voice sounding as though her throat had been ravaged at some point by something caustic. "Looks like you heard right."

Katch had tapped Barnaby's phone a week ago and heard plans for this dinner date they were witnessing. The two of them had been physically tailing the artist for only three days when they got the call from their boss to grab him.

"Who's that with him?" Katch asked.

"Boyfriend."

"Nice."

"Yup."

"Looks like they're headed into Elliot's…. Good turkey burgers."

"Yup."

"We do them both?"

Kaan shook her head slowly as her silvery gaze tracked the couple. So far this job had been like any other before it. Get to know the target's habits, schedule, and practices. Gather as much data as possible and then move in and pick him up, or wipe him out, as the case may be. "No one is *doing* anybody. Boss just wants to talk to him."

Katch grimaced in confusion. "She hasn't wanted to talk to the others."

The "others" were several random erasures they'd completed over the past month, people with the only thing in common being a powerful woman wanted them gone. She was willing to pay, and handsomely, so those people were no more. Kaan had ignored the tickle of warning in the back of her mind. There was usually a pattern to a number of targets from the same client, but looking over the data on their most recent erasures, she couldn't identify anything linking them.

"Says he's special," Kaan explained. "We'll grab him, toss him in the back—"

"Seat or trunk?"

"—and deliver him for a little chat." She turned her hard gaze on Katch. "Got it?"

"Got it." A few heartbeats later, Katch asked, "What about the boyfriend?"

"If anyone gets in the way," Kaan said, "we break them."

She caught a grin ghosting over Katch's face and began to worry, once again, about her partner's apparent excitement over the prospect of violence. During the years they'd been working together, Kaan could remember a number of times where Katch's temper had threatened the success of a job. The young man needed watching, but Kaan was good at that and had settled into the role of keeping the goal in focus and bringing Katch back down to a professional mindset. As hitters, wet workers, mercenaries… whatever people wanted to call them, they had a perfect record of getting the job done, and this time would be no different.

"THERE THEY are," Barnaby said as he spotted their friends, Coral and India, sitting against a wall of windows in the far-right corner of the restaurant. Elliot's was hardly busy this early on a Friday evening, and Ross waved off the hover-hostess preparing to shepherd them to their seats, but not before snatching four menu tablets from the device. They crossed to the back of the room quickly, weaving around the tables that were set simply with salmon and white linens over dark wood. The short, modern candleholders on each cast a warm, romantic glow over the faces of what few diners there were at the moment. When Ross and Barnaby reached the other couple, they kissed each of the women on the cheek before sitting.

"Sorry we're late," Ross said, with a sideways glance in Barnaby's direction.

Coral snorted, and Barnaby blushed. "Uh, yeah," he said, shaking out his napkin and placing it in his lap. "I sort of got caught up."

"Creative fever again?" India asked as she began looking over the menu Ross had given her.

"Yes," Ross answered for him.

Coral toyed unconsciously with one of her holographic earrings—a naked silver fairy fluttering just below her left ear. "You're having a show tonight, and you can't take a break from painting? What was it this time, or need I ask?"

"Same old mystery guy," Ross said with a sigh as Barnaby tried to ignore Coral's critical stare. They each punched in their drink orders.

"He's not a mystery," Barnaby said as he eyed the grilled halibut with mango-avocado salsa.

"He's a mystery to *us*, dear," India teased. Ross chuckled lightly, and Coral continued to scrutinize Barnaby, but he ignored them all. They were amused by his obsession with a man they didn't believe existed. His stepfather knew—had known—Charleston was real, but he was in no condition to back him up anymore, and at this point, Barnaby himself was starting to have doubts, evidenced by the rise in his intake of alcohol over the years.

When Barnaby's phone vibrated, he glanced around the table, knowing the old thing annoyed his friends (what, with duct tape the only thing holding it together), but India and Ross were absorbed in discussing a certain persnickety photographer hired for their photo shoot in LA in a couple of days, and Coral was still looking over her menu.

He pulled the phone from his pocket to examine the message and was startled to find numerous alerts for an old Google search he'd set up for "Charleston" with his estimated age and general description. The closest he'd come before this was a sixty-five-year-old doctor in Kansas, some contractor for the government, but there had never been any pictures included. That didn't matter, though, because his Charleston was nowhere close to an AARP member.

Now, however, there was hit after hit about him, and it appeared his mystery man's last name was Meeks. No longer an unknown, his life was suddenly laid out in detail—birthdate, education, old class photos, degrees, jobs, hometown, all of it—none of which had been there an hour ago. Then Barnaby landed on a photo of Charleston during his military service and his heart stuttered in his chest. *There you are.*

"Uh...." Barnaby rose to his feet. Everyone at the table looked at him, perplexed. "Order the grilled halibut for me, will ya?" he asked of no one in particular. "I'll be right back."

Before anyone could ask, Barnaby was rushing away from the table and out the front door. He dropped onto a bench in front of the restaurant to surf the Internet in peace. Being October, the night was a bit cooler than he'd dressed for, but it would still be comfortable for a little while. Adrenaline had his skin warming, tingling at the thought of Charleston virtually appearing in front of him. Not the way he'd like, but it was so much more than he'd seen up to this point. *This is proof, isn't it?* But even as he thought it, he realized not everything on the Internet was proof of anything.

It was still early, but the pedestrian traffic had increased, with folks shopping or picking up takeout on their way home from work. Barnaby was vaguely aware of them but more intent on absorbing any and all information about his long-lost hero. He grinned at a high school photo of Charleston and then at one from college.

Charleston had blinked in and out of his life numerous times, the last being his almost-wedding in January, a couple of weeks before his twenty-first birthday. Charleston had seemed ill, barely able to talk or stand, and Barnaby and his stepfather had rushed him into the anteroom of the church where Barnaby had held him, touched him, memorized his scent, learned his name, and kissed him.

Then Charleston was gone. Again.

Despite his disappointment, Barnaby had faith he'd see him again. After all, that's the way the man rolled. His modus operandi was to come to Barnaby's rescue. But he didn't return, not for seven years, not since that wedding fell apart. What if Charleston were gone for good or hadn't made it safely back to... wherever he'd come from?

After ditching his lying bride, Barnaby had fled Ohio to study at The Northwest College of Art and Design. He'd made and lost friends, found and lost lovers, and now he was a fairly successful artist, living as far away from Chillicothe as was continentally possible—Alaska being too cold and Hawaii too expensive.

There had been some rough patches along the way: experimental drug use, heavy drinking, which he was working on getting under control, and putting himself in risky situations repeatedly. His therapist helped him figure out he was unconsciously trying to force an appearance of his mystery man, so Barnaby had ended that behavior and come out of rehab ready to continue his career.

He was a bit wiser but still filled with longing—longing that translated into one painting after another. For everyone else in his life, that got old fast, and despite shutting up about his memories of the man (*you see enough uncomfortable glances aimed your way, you start keeping things to yourself*), Barnaby had never really let go, had never stopped hoping Charleston would reappear.

"WELL, LOOKY there," Katch said, nudging Kaan. "Looks like we won't have to go in after all." They watched Barnaby for a few moments and then glanced at each other. They came to a silent agreement, exited the car, and crossed the street. "Lot of witnesses," Katch muttered, his gaze darting around the very public street.

"We'll use our words first," Kaan growled, but then, in a much friendlier tone, she said, "Excuse me, Mr. Rosenthal? Barnaby Rosenthal?"

Barnaby looked up at them; his large brown eyes appeared annoyed with the interruption, but he said, "Yes?"

"May we speak with you for a moment?"

Kaan saw the young man's eyes go wary as they sat on either side of him. "Just so you know," Barnaby said, as his gaze returned to his phone, "I'm not interested in doing any interviews or talking about Rossom, so if that's what you're after, you can save your breath, folks."

Katch and Kaan glanced at one another over Barnaby's head, then up and down the sidewalk before Katch pressed the muzzle of his gun into Barnaby's side. "We're not what you'd call 'folks,' kid."

Barnaby drew in a sharp breath and straightened abruptly. "Wha—"

"Shhh," Kaan warned with a threatening grin. She pointed across the street. "See that SUV over there?" Barnaby nodded. "We're going to walk over there and go for a ride."

Barnaby snorted, and the two strangers looked slightly taken aback. "No."

"What?" Kaan said, blinking rapidly.

"You two sound like something out of an old mobster movie, and I'm not going anywhere with you." Barnaby stood suddenly and walked back into Elliot's without a glance back, leaving Katch and Kaan sitting on the bench alone. Katch stood, took a step toward the door, thought about it, and sat back down, looking at Kaan questioningly. Kaan simply stared at the entrance of the eatery and grinned, feeling impressed, amused, and surprised. That didn't happen to her very often. She'd be sorry to see the kid go.

"What's our play?" Katch asked.

"Later," Kaan replied.

CHAPTER 4

Chillicothe, Ohio - November 2006

THE WIND *bit into me as I stepped from the shelter of the trees and onto the road. I had to walk about a hundred yards to reach the bridge where the boy stood contemplating the river rushing by beneath him. I approached slowly, wincing when the cold stung me again. I paused as Barnaby ran off down the road to recapture some papers that had been liberated by the November wind, and as he collected them, I reached the bridge undetected.*

I knelt to examine the boy's dropped sketch pad and discovered it filled with beautifully detailed drawings of the people Barnaby Rosenthal loved. I lingered over a drawing of the boy's mother. She still resembled a young Anne Bancroft and had aged beautifully since I'd seen her in Seney Road Market eight years ago. As I fingered a letter the boy had written to his parents, a letter that said, among other things, good-bye, his voice shattered my reverie.

"Hey, leave that alone!" the boy shouted as he ran toward me. I had to fight not to smirk as Barnaby's indignation cooled when he caught sight of how large I actually was, but it didn't stop him from snatching the sketch pad from my hands. I kept my voice calm and told him how talented he was and how he shouldn't waste it.

"You don't know me or what I am."

Dr. Plumb had warned me this step would require a bit more finessing, but whatever I said had to ring true. So I spoke the truth.

I told him I knew exactly what he was, that he was "a teenage boy in a small town who thinks he's all alone, that there's no one like you anywhere, that your family would hate you if they really knew you." I told him there was "a big, wide world out there filled with so many others similar to you, but at the same time there is no one else quite like you in the world. We are, each of us, unique, and that should be celebrated, not tossed away. I know it doesn't seem that way in this tiny town or from a pew at your local church, but it's the truth. I've seen it. I've lived it."

I could see in his eyes he wanted to believe me, but doubt poured off him as he told me he didn't think he could face school or his best friend, who wouldn't come near him now. I didn't lie to him then, didn't fill the air with platitudes. I told him it would be difficult, that he would have a hard few years, but he could get through it. Then, wrapped up in sharing my own experience, I slipped up and mentioned his name, and he called me on it. But I covered by saying I saw his name on the letter he'd signed, which he seemed to buy.

I checked my watch. Time was nearly up, so I finished by telling him to stay strong, that he was fine just the way he was created, and to never forget that. Headlights swept the area, drawing his attention just as my alarm sounded—and I found myself back in the Portal room, disoriented and dizzy as usual.

Bend, Oregon - October 2020

A SOFT but insistent beeping woke Charleston from his nap. He rolled over and tried to get his bearings, then glanced at the clock on the wall and saw he'd overslept. *Jesus*, he thought, as he sat up on the bed and glared at the recreation of a big, black, clunky 1940s phone on the bedside table. It sat there, silent as a brick. Then the beeping returned, and he grabbed his Bluetooth.

"H-hello?" he said, securing it in place.

"Junior?"

"Pop?"

"You sound horrible, son."

"A bit jet-lagged, I guess."

"Is Rosenthal all right?"

Charleston smacked his lips together a couple of times, not liking the taste in his mouth one bit. *Shower*, he thought. *I need a shower and... toothpaste.* He looked around the room, then rubbed his eyes. "Huh?"

"Your mother… told me to call you. I thought something was… wrong." Charleston noticed the hesitation in his father's voice, and he responded with just as much uncertainty.

"I… wanted to know why you were working so late."

"Oh."

Charleston waited, but his father didn't continue. "Pop?"

"Yes?"

"Why were you working so late?"

"Well—"

"Wait," Charleston said as his father's previous question flashed in his mind. "Why did you ask if Barnaby was okay?" In the silence that followed, Charleston could almost hear his father struggling to find the right words. "Tell me."

"We've… lost some people, Junior. Restored subjects."

"What do you mean 'lost'?"

"Long before you'd ever heard of Rosenthal, an outside oversight panel was established for RPP. It's one of the reasons I had to get approval for the Rosenthal experiment."

"I remember."

"The makeup of the panel has shifted over the years, and we've been getting pressure from a certain senator. Says she's there to 'rein us in.' Thinks what we're doing, what we've done, goes against God's plan or some such nonsense. Anyway, I attended a hearing recently where RPP was suspended, pending further review."

"Sorry, Pop. I can understand how that would upset you."

"It's not that, Junior." The doctor sighed. "I'd honestly begun having my doubts about what we were doing. However, I've learned that, of the twenty-three people we've restored over the years, five of them have died in the past sixty-or-so days." Charleston heard computer keys being struck. "Causes are listed as heart attack, anaphylaxis, car crash, drowning, and in-home invasion." Wide-awake now and with a sense of urgency washing over him, Charleston leaned over and slid his shoes on quickly, then looked around for his jacket. His father added, "We currently have no proof, but my gut tells me something's… *off.*"

"Who's 'we'?"

"It was brought to my attention by Leaundra's team, and for the past few days, I've been reviewing her reports as they come in. She's currently tracking earlier subjects, trying to ascertain their status." Charleston relaxed a bit. Knowing his former team leader was on the case reassured him, because investigation and intrigue weren't exactly his father's forte. "I should have heeded recommendations to keep a closer watch on them, but the funding wasn't there, and the whole point was to restore them and let their lives play out as they would," Dr. Meeks said.

Charleston heard mumbled words over the receiver. "I'm sorry, Pop, what was that?" he asked.

"Nothing. I was speaking with your mother. She wants me to tell you to be careful and that we love you."

"Love you too. Listen, I'll call you from the car." He grabbed his jacket, headed out the door, and locked it behind him before rushing to the stairs. He reached the small lobby and gave the desk clerk a quick, insincere grin before pushing through the doors leading to the street. He unlocked the car as he ran toward it, hopped behind the wheel, and backed out of the lot, careful of the meandering pedestrians on the sidewalk. As he put the car in drive and headed up the street, Charleston tapped a button on his steering wheel. "Call Pop."

"*Calling*," a deep, masculine voice announced from the SUV's speakers.

"Hello?"

"Mom?"

"Your father's on another line with that little Jeri girl, dear."

"Do you know anything about this senator, the one who's been giving Pop grief?"

"Just a moment, dear." The phone muted, apparently so his mother could shout to his father in his office at the back of the house. When she returned, she said, "It's a Senator Collard from Texas."

"Thanks, Mom. I'll talk to you later."

"Wait!"

"Yes?"

"Son... be careful, please. Your father tells me people are... people are dying."

Charleston took a deep breath, his gut clenching a bit, and said, "I promise, Mom." He pulled up to a stop light and gunned the engine impatiently. "Please tell Pop I'm going to find Barnaby, and I'll be in touch."

"Yes, dear."

With a tap of his thumb, he ended the call. With another tap, he activated the car's Internet link. "Search Senator Collard," he said. "Audio read out."

"*Searching,*" Sexy, Deep-Voice Guy announced.

"WHAT'S UP with you?" Ross asked as he snatched two flutes of champagne from an automated serving tray, rented and programmed for the art show, and gave one to Barnaby.

"I don't know what you mean." Sniffing the drink and frowning, Barnaby then placed the glass on another passing tray, sending it on its way to the other side of the room. He needed a strong drink not a pretty one. *Bourbon. Yes, that would do it.*

"You've been distracted since dinner. Looking over your shoulder," Ross said as he straightened the artist's lapel, much to Barnaby's annoyance. "And why did you duck outside? Who were you talking to?"

Barnaby shook his head at the buzz of questions coming from his ex and quickly walked (with Ross on his heels) to the bar, where he scored a bourbon and acknowledged a few encouraging smiles from the art patrons gathered for his show. Ross's gaze drilled into him as Barnaby gulped the warming liquid. Despite all appearances and his quick thinking, he had been shaken by the encounter outside Elliot's. He was hardly used to strangers pulling a gun on him. That had only happened once before, if he remembered correctly.

"Barnaby...."

"I hope they all return next month for the benefit."

"Who?" Ross asked, thrown by the change of subject.

Barnaby gestured at the guests around them. "Them. We're showcasing artwork by LGBT youth in a charity show the first of November. The benefit will help raise money for homeless kids, who, as you know, are still mostly LGBT, especially in the smaller towns."

"Save your spiel, Rosenthal. Why did you go outside at dinner?"

Uh-oh, he's calling me by my last name, Barnaby thought, trying not to laugh. "I had to check something on my phone...."

"The beast is still working?"

Barnaby nodded.

"And?"

He shrugged. "And a couple approached me...."

Ross blinked and narrowed his lovely eyes, his full lips thinning. "Someone tried to pick you up?"

Ignoring Ross's incredulous tone, Barnaby said, "Not exactly. However, I resent your shock and disbelief. I think I look pretty darn good." He adjusted his glasses, feigning indignation.

"You're beautiful. You know that," Ross said softly.

"Not next to you."

"So we'll arrange an industrial accident for me, shall we? Then can we give it another try?"

"Ross—"

"Never mind." Ross huffed. "Tell me about these people who approached you."

When he finally met his ex-boyfriend's uneasy gaze, he whispered, "It was a man and woman." Ross frowned and Barnaby continued. "Now don't freak out, but one of them had...." Ross raised an eyebrow, waiting. "One of them had a gun. Hell. They probably both did."

"A gun!" Several heads turned their way.

"Shush!" Barnaby smiled nervously until the patrons had returned their attention to the paintings on the wall.

Ross stepped closer and gripped Barnaby's arm tightly, leaning in to growl in his ear, "Why didn't you say something earlier? We should have called the authorities. What did they want?"

Barnaby extricated himself from Ross and glared at him. "I took care of it." Ross appeared doubtful and was about to protest, when India strolled up to them in all her dark, long-limbed beauty.

"You two aren't fighting, are you?" she asked in a slightly accented voice Barnaby knew wasn't legitimate.

"Of course not," Ross said, smiling tightly and brushing his hair back off his forehead, a calmer expression falling into place.

"Uh-huh." India nodded, clearly not believing them for a second. "Barnaby, these are magnificent," she said, looking around the room and gesturing at the walls with her slender champagne-bearing hand. "I actually think these older mediums are starting to grow on me, but," she added quickly, shaking a finger at him, "don't tell Coral I said so." She laughed lightly at her little joke and sipped her drink, her dark eyes sparkling like the heavens in the glare of the gallery lights. Barnaby grinned when he realized she was wearing Starlight contacts, created to mimic a rural night sky. Well, he figured those were better than having her eyes surgically altered for the effect.

Coral had been "seeing" India for about six months and talking about her for two months before that, but Barnaby hadn't understood the attraction until recently. Obviously India was beautiful—tall and brown, flawless and regal—but her public face had seemed so phony at first. His gaze flicked sideways. *A lot like Ross.* Maybe it was a model thing.

It wasn't until he and Coral had planned a movie night for just the four of them, that he truly understood how well India fit his friend. The model had shown up at his door sans makeup and in sweats, dressed for a slumber party but just as stunning as ever. That was who Coral went home to every night, not the twinkling, vapid diva before him.

He and Ross really didn't fit unless they were fucking. Inside the bedroom, he liked the way Ross took charge, but it was another story outside it. Barnaby never seemed to be fashionable enough, exciting enough, interesting enough, or *interested* enough in the things Ross cared about. Barnaby and Coral were two artists out of time, clinging to textiles and acrylic paint, or "dusty stuff" as Ross called it.

Apparently his ex's shallow ran bone deep. It was fairly easy to end things. After all, they made it a year. Wasn't it time? Ross was in town less and less, preferring the speed and distractions of Los Angeles to the sleepy beauty of Bend. *That's us*, Barnaby thought. *He's fast and distracted. I'm sleepy and beautiful.* He chuckled quietly and slowly wandered away from his friends while they were caught up in conversation.

"Your paintings are quite compelling," a gravelly voice said close to Barnaby's ear.

He paused and glanced down at the hand on his arm. It was a strong hand, a woman's hand with a sensible manicure. No color, but shiny, possibly a touch of glitter. When he looked up into the silvery, strange gaze of the woman who'd approached him outside the restaurant, his eyes widened in surprise.

"Hello again, Mr. Rosenthal," she said, smiling sweetly. "I'm Benni Kaan, and right over there"—she pointed—"standing and chatting with your friends, is my associate Rico Katch."

A deep sense of unease ran through Barnaby as he watched his friend Coral introduce Katch to Ross and India. The thug towered over the group, but smiled warmly at each of them, shaking their hands. Then his gaze lifted to Barnaby's, and the threat was silently communicated.

Barnaby sighed. "Okay, where do you want me?"

"This way, please."

CHAPTER 5

"EVENING, SIR," the bartender said brightly, catching Charleston off guard as he entered. She and her bar were stationed directly to the right of the entrance to nab all comers. Obviously, the gallery owner believed a drink in hand might help shake loose some praise and open some wallets.

"Evening," Charleston mumbled absently as his gaze swept over the room and the faces of the crowd in search of a pair of chocolate-brown eyes set in a handsome, pale face, topped with.... What? On Barnaby's almost-wedding day, Charleston remembered his hair had been short, but in the seven years that had passed for Barnaby, he might have let it grow longer. *Maybe Rossom likes it long.* Charleston frowned.

There was no sign of Barnaby, but Charleston spotted his pretty boyfriend and quickly crossed the room to him, excusing himself through the meandering horde. "Rossom Bailey?"

Caught in the middle of taking a sip of champagne, Ross appeared a bit startled, but when he looked at Charleston, he gasped, aspirating his drink, and began to choke. "Y-you... you're...."

Charleston pounded on his back a bit harder than necessary. "Where's Barnaby?"

"Y-you're—" A wracking cough interrupted Ross's efforts to speak.

"Is everything all right here?" Coral asked as she approached, looking into Ross's contorted, but still beautiful, face.

Ross looked at her with wide eyes, then back at Charleston. "He's... he's the g-guy... in the... in the p-paint... in B-Barn's—" Ross wheezed. Coral studied Charleston for a moment before India appeared at her elbow. Rather than acknowledge their apparent interest in him, Charleston continued to look around the room. Still no sign of Barnaby.

He took a breath to calm himself. "I need to speak with Barnaby."

"Barnaby's paintings? Are you certain, Ross?" Coral asked, ignoring Charleston's statement and peering even harder into his face. Ross nodded rapidly. After all, he'd been looking at paintings of the man for a little more than twelve months.

"Holy shit!" India said, staring at him.

Exasperated, Charleston turned away from them, looking over the crowd again. He spotted the entrance to the restrooms and took off in that direction. The men's room was bright, opulent, and decorated floor-to-ceiling in ceramic tile that resembled blond hardwood. The overhead lights bounced off the reflective surfaces throughout the room, momentarily blinding him.

"Barnaby! Barnaby Rosenthal, are you in here?" he shouted. "Barnaby, it's Charleston. Answer me!" Silence followed. Then someone cleared his throat, flushed a toilet, and hesitantly exited a stall. The man, wearing an expensive, tailored gray suit, nodded curtly and walked to the Clear Clean station to wash his hands, all the while watching Charleston in the mirror suspiciously.

Charleston began checking under the remaining stalls, and in the last one found two pairs of feet. He knocked... hard. "Barnaby?"

"No Barnaby here, buddy."

"Open up! Now!"

The door slid out of sight to reveal two men—one much older than the other, both disheveled, their pants undone, lips kiss-swollen, and pupils blown. One blond, one balding, neither of them the man he was looking for. The stall door reappeared and reestablished their privacy.

When he turned away from the door, he found the other patron had left and been replaced by Coral, Ross, and India. They looked at Charleston in wonder as if he were some mythical creature brought to life.

He could see who the models were: Ross and India were both tall, slender, and painfully attractive. Not that Coral wasn't also lovely, but she had an air of the Earth-bound, rather than the ethereal. She wore comfortable, flowing clothes that accentuated her curvy figure and flat shoes. Her short hair shone bright as a copper penny, and her pale skin was rosy about the cheeks, and not from any blush she had applied.

"I'm sorry, folks," Charleston said. "I know you have questions, but right now we need to find Barnaby. I think he's in trouble." That seemed to get their attention, and he saw a spark behind Ross's eyes as the man stepped forward.

"Barn told me two people approached him outside the restaurant earlier this evening. He said one of them had a gun."

Coral and India's heads snapped toward Ross in shock. "A gun?" they asked in unison. Then they both looked back at Charleston, a bit more accusatory this time, all wonderment gone.

"Do you have a gun?" Coral asked.

"I do not."

"We were just talking to Barnaby minutes ago," India added. "You remember, pet?" She turned to Coral. "We were all talking when you came over and introduced that big guy to us."

Coral shook her head, her gaze never leaving Charleston's. "Barnaby wasn't with you."

He felt a rising panic, much the same as when Barnaby was six and being snatched from a grocery store and moving further beyond his reach every second. "We need to find him now."

"I'll take the front entrance," Ross said, rushing out the door.

"We've got the rear," India said, grabbing Coral's hand and tugging her along behind.

Charleston followed them. "Are there any other exits?"

"Automatic door, back of the warehouse… entrance marked On Deck… that way," Coral shouted over her shoulder and gestured with her free arm as she tried to keep up with India's long-legged stride.

Charleston nodded and ran in the direction Coral had indicated. As he weaved through the crowd, he kept checking faces. Suddenly Ross's voice filled the air above the gallery-goers. "Ladies and gentlemen, has anyone seen our much lauded artist? We have a… an emer—issue that needs his attention. Anyone? Barnaby? You out there?"

Charleston found his way into a darker hallway running behind hulking white dividers, just outside the glare of the gallery proper. It was quieter in the hall, and he tried to slow his heart and breathing, listening for any sounds out of the ordinary. He paused by double doors leading into the storage area and pressed an ear to one of them, but he couldn't hear anything. He gently pressed his finger to a button on the right door, cracking it open only wide enough to allow him to slip in quickly.

He immediately felt a dramatic temperature drop, and no sound from the gallery gathering reached him once the door snicked shut behind him. *So no one will hear me if I scream.* He grinned wryly. Instead of trying to pierce the darkness with his gaze, he closed his eyes and counted to ten. When he opened them again, he noticed dim light strips running along the baseboards of the walls and between a set of towering shelves on his left. He took one step and froze as distant voices within the room reached his ears.

"I'm glad you didn't try to pull another smart-ass move like you did at the restaurant," a gravelly voice said. It sounded like the guy had rocks in his throat.

"Yeah, well that really only works the once"—a wave of relief washed over Charleston as he recognized Barnaby's voice—"unless I'm dealing with a particularly stupid individual."

"Aww, honey, you think I'm brainy."

Charleston moved forward, tracking them by their voices, since what illumination there was didn't quite reach them. Knowing the exit was at the back of the warehouse, he assumed that was the direction they were headed—directly opposite of where he stood.

"What can I say?" Barnaby said. "In only a few hours, you improved your approach, threatening my friends the way you did. Well done. However...."

"Yes?"

"It *is* my show. They'll notice I'm missing."

"Not before we're gone." The sounds of a brief struggle reached Charleston's ears. "Fuck, kid—get up!"

"I can't see where we're going. Let me straighten my glasses, please."

"What is it with people? Why the hell wouldn't you get corrective surgery?"

"Some people prefer the classics."

"Yeah, *old* people."

"You're rushing through here like you have cat eyes or something."

"Or something. Now behave. When my partner gets here, we'll go have a chat with my boss."

"Who's your boss?" Barnaby asked.

"You'll get an introduction, don't worry."

"Then what?"

"Then you'll talk."

"Then what?" Charleston heard an exasperated sigh from the thug, and he grinned at what Barnaby was doing. "Ya know, most fans just attend a showing or contact my agent."

"My boss doesn't strike me as a fan of the arts." Though muffled by the bricks of the building, Charleston heard what sounded like two quick taps on a car horn from the other side of the room. "There's our ride, kid."

Charleston ran forward into the darkness just as a bright light appeared along the bottom of a large, opaque glass wall. Very soon he could make out the silhouettes of two struggling figures—the much larger one with a gun… and long, straight hair.

That's a woman?

"Kid, give it up, will ya?"

When his footsteps alerted her to his presence, Charleston didn't slow down but sped up, shouting "Let him go!" as she swung the gun toward him. Briefly forgotten in favor of a larger, more immediate threat, Barnaby dropped low and threw the woman to the floor with one fluid sweep of his leg.

Nice move, Charleston thought as the gun went off wildly with a whiny *pfft*. Barnaby hopped up and blindly grabbed Charleston by the arm before dragging him behind the set of shelves to their left.

"Katch, get in here!" Kaan shouted.

Charleston followed Barnaby to the wall, and they ducked behind shelves that were heavy with sculptures, pottery, paintings, weavings, and crates of other display pieces, past and future.

The gallery hosting the Rosenthal show clearly had an affinity for traditional pieces, otherwise there'd be bio-generated creations present too, their faint glow possibly illuminating a bit more of the darkness surrounding them, which would not be a good thing right now. From what Charleston had been able to see upon entering the warehouse, there were similar shelves running the length of the wall on the right, while the center area of the warehouse was more spacious, allowing a vehicle, be it van or truck, to enter for deliveries.

Charleston had to get Barnaby out of the room and back in the gallery, among people who weren't wielding guns, among witnesses. Once he accomplished that, he'd be able to ascertain what threat loomed over the other restored subjects, but he intended to keep Barnaby right by his side until the danger had passed. For now they needed to concentrate on working their stealth and avoiding the imminent danger before them.

He tugged on Barnaby's hand, still warm in his. "Barnaby—"

"Shhh!" Barnaby whispered, crouching down and pulling Charleston with him. "I appreciate your help out there, but we have to get back to the entrance, to the gallery and people." *No shit, Sherlock*, Charleston thought, grinning at the back of Barnaby's wavy brown head. "Try not to knock anything over, and stick close—Hey, how did you know my name?"

Charleston braced himself for their reunion, but before Barnaby could turn to look at him, their attention was captured by a car door slamming. They peered through the shelves to see a large, powerful man enter the warehouse. Katch, if Charleston had heard right. The headlights from the vehicle silhouetted the two thugs. The woman was tall and impressive, clearly not someone to be dismissed. He glanced to his right and spotted the entrance to the gallery, now faintly illuminated, as was a good portion of the room, by those same headlights.

"He still in here, Kaan?"

"Yeah, he's here… somewhere." From where they hid, Charleston could see Kaan's eyes narrow as the woman slowly scanned the shelves on the left side of the room. "He's got someone with him. I heard"—Kaan froze, her eyes widening, seeming to look directly at their hiding place—"footsteps." Charleston started to whisper something, but Barnaby silenced him by holding up one finger to his lips as he kept his eyes trained on Kaan.

When Kaan's gaze moved on, they both released the breath they'd been holding, and then Barnaby turned to grin at him and share a moment of silent victory, but instead he seemed to stop breathing all over again.

CHAPTER 6

Chillicothe, Ohio - August 2010

I REMEMBER I was rushing. I had to withdraw cash from my savings for a trip to Stucky's Pawn and Collectibles. They wouldn't take checks, and I needed that locket for Connie's anniversary gift. We'd been dating six whole months, and the portrait I'd done of her for her birthday two months before hadn't seemed to wow her like I'd hoped. Her mother loved it, even had it framed. But this locket would dazzle her for sure. And I had to keep her dazzled, right? Because my friends kept talking about how lucky I was, how they couldn't understand why Connie Bramble was into me.

What they didn't understand, didn't know, was how not into her I was. Connie was great. She was pretty and funny and smelled wonderful, but aside from that? Yawn. I think she liked me because I was what her mother called "a real gentleman, who never got too handsy."

I'd meant to get to the bank earlier, but Donald had some work he needed help with, and I'd rushed over before the bank closed. Everyone else seemed to have the same fear because the place was packed, and the line hadn't moved for quite a while.

Then I saw him, a familiar face by the door. I held my breath as his eyes searched the room. He's looking for me, I thought, and then our eyes met. I couldn't move and just held his gaze. I don't know how long we stood there staring at each other, but I told the guy behind me he could go ahead, because more than anything—more than the locket, more than keeping Connie dazzled—I wanted to be next to my stranger. It had been four years since I'd seen him, four long years.

I stepped out of line to go to him, but the guy behind me threw his arm around my neck, and suddenly there was a gun pressed to my head. It seemed to me as though the screaming and chaos would never end, and I focused across the room... on his deep blue eyes, how serious they were... how frightened.

I tried to calm myself as he spoke soothingly to the gunman. And after a few exchanges, the guy actually let me go! I went directly to my stranger's side, and he stepped in front of me while continuing to talk to the robber. He talked him right out the door.

I spun my stranger around and demanded to know who he was, but he pulled me into the bank manager's office, where we could talk in private. I told him I'd seen him before. I had foggy memories of Seney Market when I was little, memories of being scared. I told him about my plans for art school, about wanting to see the world he'd told me about on the bridge that November night four years ago when he stopped me from doing something beyond stupid. But with this whole Connie thing, wasn't I still being stupid?

My stranger smelled good too, even better than Connie. And he felt—I fisted his shirt in my hands—he felt even better, hard and strong and large in front of me. Substantial. Significant. I wrapped my arms around him, afraid he'd vanish on me again, and he looked at my lips. For a moment I thought he might kiss me, and I thought that would be just about heaven. But I felt him tense, and then he pried himself free of me.

He was telling me something like good-bye when the police banged on the door, startling me, and when I looked back, he was gone, my hands were out in front of me, gripping nothing. I let the police in. I answered their questions, but I lied about my stranger being there. Who would believe me?

I never picked up Connie's locket, which wasn't a great disaster as she didn't remember our anniversary anyway. We spent the evening picking over day-old lasagna my mother had made and seeing some movie starring DiCaprio that I would never figure out, even if my mind hadn't been filled with wonder about a man I would never forget.

Bend, Oregon - October 2020

GAZING OUT of the dim shadows around them was the man Barnaby had been dreaming of for years, in the flesh, his lips twisting in a sardonic grin. But then the humor and warmth in Charleston's deep blue eyes suddenly shifted to pain as Barnaby convulsively tightened his grip on his wrist. *Don't let go*, he thought. *No matter what, don't let go.*

The need for silence prevented Barnaby from whooping for joy but not from gripping either side of Charleston's head and bringing their lips together fiercely. Barnaby tangled his fingers in dark blond hair as Charleston, after overcoming his initial shock, quickly sank into the kiss, reaching out for Barnaby and fisting his suit jacket to pull him closer. The heat of Charleston, his strength and scent and taste, wrapped around Barnaby, every detail assuring him that he was not hallucinating, that this man was real and alive and in his arms.

They paused, rested their foreheads against each other, and tried to pant silently. Near tears, Barnaby couldn't stop grinning and sneaked several quick pecks to Charleston's lips. *Seven years*, he thought. *Please don't disappear on me again. I... I couldn't take it.* He leaned back a bit to look into Charleston's eyes and watched his gaze gradually drift down to Barnaby's lips. Charleston licked his own, dry from their desperate breathing, before gripping the back of Barnaby's neck and pulling him in for more.

If not for their cramped positions and armed thugs on the prowl nearby, Barnaby might have taken Charleston right there—below a large, pink-and-green ceramic nightmare by Luau Pickney and next to a glorious California landscape painted by Catalina Higgenbotham. A well-aimed bullet could rid the world of the Pickney and would probably miss the Higgenbotham altogether. *Woo-hoo, over here, behind this giant, pink, two-headed bunny with gangrene*! Barnaby chuckled softly at the thought but sobered quickly when he heard voices.

"Stand at the back," Kaan directed, "but keep an eye on that door, there. I'll...." She stopped talking and circled her arm, indicating she would search the room. "We want the kid alive. The other guy? You spot him? Put a bullet in his head." Katch nodded and held his gun, also silenced, at the ready.

Barnaby glanced over his shoulder and pulled away from Charleston to watch Kaan begin her search. He soon turned back and, through gestures, explained *she's starting over there*, which Charleston nodded to in understanding. Then Charleston did his own pantomime, laying out his plan to distract the two of them toward the rear of the big room while Barnaby escaped through the door to the gallery. Barnaby immediately frowned and shook his head vigorously.

"No way are we separating!" he whispered angrily.

Charleston pulled Barnaby against him, placed his lips against his ear, and whispered, "They have guns; we have none." Barnaby shivered as the hot breath tickled the shell of his ear, but he pulled away and looked at Charleston, determined.

"You'll disappear aga—"

Charleston placed a finger against Barnaby's lips. "Babe, I'm here to stay."

All Barnaby really heard was "babe" before Charleston gave him a peck on the lips and rushed along the wall toward Katch at the back of the room. Barnaby came to himself, wanting to shout after him, but it was too late. He reluctantly inched his way to the right, closer to the gallery entrance.

CHARLESTON SILENTLY moved along the wall, his fingers grazing the rough surface as he focused on catching the gunman off guard once he reached the back of the room. He carefully navigated around crates, some open, most not. He chanced a glance behind him, fearing Barnaby might have disobeyed his order and followed him, but he didn't see him.

He smiled as he recalled the way Barnaby had taken down Kaan, his movements fluid and precise, like he'd had some training. He accepted that Barnaby and those who cared for him would have questions, but he was quickly realizing he had a lot of questions of his own for Barnaby. Something along the line of "What have you been up to for the last seven or so years?" Not so much the stuff Jeri had filled him in on, but more of the personal story, the one not kept in a public record.

He paused to listen to the sounds around him and, expecting the idling SUV to cover any noise he might make, stepped to the edge of the shelving, and peeked around it to see where Katch was. The second Charleston realized the gunman wasn't where he was supposed to be was the same second he felt the muzzle of the gun pressing against his temple. *Well, fuck!*

"Where's your little buddy?"

"Right here, pencil dick!" Barnaby ran forward and rammed the ears of the ceramic bunny into Katch's gut, making the gunman stumble backward but not fall. Charleston grabbed the guy's gun hand, pinned it to the wall, and kneed him in the nuts. Katch's breath whooshed out, ending on a pitiful whine, and the gun slipped into Charleston's hand just as a bullet pinged off the metal shelf nearest Barnaby's head. Charleston spun, shoved Barnaby to the ground with one hand, and took aim with the other.

Kaan stood in the aisle between the shelves, her black suit, gun, and menacing stance making her look like every clichéd movie villain Charleston had ever seen… well, except for her long silky brown hair, her curvy figure, and her eyes. They seemed off somehow, seemed to reflect the ambient light in the room. A bullet slammed into the wall behind him, singeing his left ear and damaging his Bluetooth as it sailed past. Charleston recoiled, hissed, and dropped low to return fire, but the gun in his hand wouldn't shoot.

Fuck! *Bio-registered*!

Bio-registration of weapons was slowly rolling out across the country. Funny the first civilian he had run into with one would be a criminal. For the most part, it was an option for law enforcement and former military, but maybe both Katch and Kaan were former members of those organizations. The technology was beginning to trickle into the homes of gun-safety nuts too. The weapons were pricier, of course, which tickled the NRA and gun manufacturers no end, since they were the ones who had invested heavily in the technology and registration.

For all those years spent fighting and lobbying against any advancement in gun-control laws, the National Rifle Association had been busy behind the scenes, working on bio-registration, making ready to lead the way when the tide in America turned in significant numbers. For some strange reason, folks didn't mind the NRA having them in a database.

With bio-registration, handguns and some assorted rifles could only be fired by the person who first activated it, and only they could unlock the weapon for use by someone else. The technology was expected to make the public a bit safer.

The stories of some kid accidentally shooting himself or a sibling with Daddy's gun would be on the decline soon, and tracking down and prosecuting a suspect who had used a BR weapon would be much easier with a clear biological trail to follow. Match the bullet to the gun, match the gun to the owner… done and done. Of course, there would always be someone out there constructing a work-around, some way to cheat the system, but it was all so new that those cheats probably hadn't been uncovered yet.

At the moment Charleston just wished the technology had never happened, wished he could fire Katch's gun as easily as the thug could.

"Go!" he ordered Barnaby.

With Kaan's bullets chipping away at the wall and raining dust on them, Barnaby did as he was told, scrambling to his feet, staying low, and skirting out the open warehouse door and into the alley. Charleston moved to follow, but Kaan raced toward him, firing. She moved fast for a big woman. Katch had finally recovered enough to grope for Charleston's ankle, but he got kicked in the teeth for his trouble.

As Charleston slipped into the alley, a searing pain pierced his shoulder, and he fell, spinning and landing flat on his back. He stared up at what little of the night sky he could see above the buildings around him as he clutched his arm against his body and hoped Barnaby was blocks away by now. *We didn't have enough time.* He chuckled sadly at the irony. But Barnaby wasn't blocks away.

Charleston saw him standing just to the left of the warehouse exit, his back flush against the wall of the building, and both arms raised above his head, holding what could only be described as some kind of metal shield. It was elaborately detailed, with raised circular portions where it had clearly been heated and hammered by hand. It was gorgeous. And the pure, clear tone that emanated from it when it connected with Kaan's skull as she ran into the alley hung in the air like a toll from some ancient French bell tower. Stunned, Kaan went down like a bag of rocks.

CHAPTER 7

"LET ME see," Barnaby said as he dropped to his knees beside Charleston and tugged at his right arm, but Charleston held firm and shook his head. A low groan emanated from Kaan, and both men stared at the prone woman in alarm. Barnaby stood and went to Kaan, leaning over her to retrieve her weapon, which he shoved in the back of his belt. "Let's get the hell out of here." Together they got Charleston to his feet and steadied him. "Gallery?" Barnaby asked. "Or take their car?"

Charleston swayed a bit before saying, "It's probably LoJacked. They could track us. This way." Charleston staggered forward, and Barnaby followed. "M-my car's a couple of blocks west." He swayed again, but Barnaby was right there, holding his arm, supporting him. Barnaby steered him backward, propped him up against the wall of the neighboring building, and began searching his pockets. "Wh-what are you doing?"

Barnaby didn't even look up as he said, "You're in no shape to drive. I'm looking for…."

Charleston grinned and nodded as Barnaby dangled his car keys in front of his face. "It's print-registered," Charleston warned.

"Good thing we're together, then," he said as he grabbed Charleston's uninjured left arm and dragged him forward and finally out of the alley. "Just don't pass out before we get there, otherwise—Oh shit! You're bleeding so much."

"It's not that bad, really," Charleston reassured, but Barnaby scoffed at that.

A large number of people were still out, shopping and partying, and some glanced worriedly at the two of them, at Charleston's bloodied arm, and at the expression of concern Barnaby knew was plastered all over his own face. The night air was cool on his skin, but the fear and adrenaline kept Barnaby warm.

"Tell me you've got a first aid kit in the car," he said as they walked quickly along the sidewalk, dodging various clusters of Bend residents. Charleston nodded. "Okay. Good... good," Barnaby said, scanning the crowd restlessly as they hurried forward. "Once we get somewhere safe, I'll patch you up, and then you've got some questions to answer."

He tightened his hand on Charleston's bicep, and he thought he caught a grin on Charleston's lips at the contact. He found it difficult not to smile himself, which was strange considering their current situation. This man he clung to *was* bleeding badly as he steered him along the sidewalk. Barnaby had just gotten him back, and he wasn't prepared to lose him so soon. There was no room in his head to worry about Ross, Coral, and India, and what they must be thinking. He could only focus on the guy who was becoming harder and harder to guide up the street.

"There!" Charleston said suddenly, pointing. Barnaby saw a black SUV hybrid parked at the far corner in front of Goody's Ice Cream. They crossed in the middle of the street, flinching at the cacophony of screeching tires and honking horns. Barnaby propped Charleston up against the driver's side of the vehicle and grabbed his right hand, then dropped it quickly when he realized how bloody it had become from his oozing shoulder wound. He shuddered, gripped the left thumb instead, and pressed it against the print reader.

He opened the door, helped Charleston into the driver's seat, and shoved him beyond to the passenger's. Barnaby wiped his brow with his sleeve and glanced around them. No one seemed to be paying them any attention, even though he felt as though every move they made screamed suspicious. He climbed in after Charleston and shut and locked the door. Then he unconsciously adjusted the seat forward to fit him and peered through the tinted windows at the people of Bend going about their pleasant night. He examined their expressions, but they appeared oblivious to the terrifying events he'd just been through.

Barnaby gripped the steering wheel, closed his eyes, and sighed as he relaxed against the headrest. He wanted to start the night over. No drinking, no bad dream, no argument with Ross, no guns, and no danger. He glanced at Charleston. *But yes to you, to all of you.* In the distance he heard sirens, and they were coming closer. He straightened in the seat, then leaned over and secured Charleston's seat belt, before doing his own.

He glanced at the man himself and noted how pale and sweaty, yet still strangely attractive he appeared. Charleston's eyes were closed, his longish hair plastered to his head and across his face. Barnaby almost reached out to brush the hair back or to trace a finger over his lips and feel the soft warmth there, but he resisted.

It was a good thing, because Charleston chose that moment to open his eyes. He reached forward and pressed his thumb against the glove compartment, unlocking it, and withdrew a small blue box.

Fighting down his urges in favor of a more pressing issue, Barnaby shoved in the key, grabbed Charleston's left hand, yanked it over to unlock the ignition, and started the car.

"*Welcome back, Mr. Meeks,*" the GPS said. "*Destination, please.*"

"I got this, hot stuff," Barnaby said as he switched off the system. He backed out, then headed to the next intersection at a reasonable pace before turning right toward Mirror Pond. "Any preference on where we should go or what we should do? I take it the authorities are out of the question?"

"Certain authorities, yes," Charleston said softly. "Gunshot wounds are tough to explain, and the longer we're talking to the police and being entered into the system, the easier it will be for those guys to find us." Barnaby kept his eyes on the road as Charleston talked, but periodically glanced over to see how he was doing. He watched him inhale an antibiotic mist from the first aid kit and pop a painkiller. "I think it's a through and through," Charleston explained with a groan as he gingerly touched his shoulder. "But I'm going to need you to clean and seal the wound. Can't use the healing accelerant until it's cleaned."

Barnaby grimaced but said, "No problem, once we're safe for the night." He wondered what, if anything, was happening at the gallery. Were his friends safe? Did Kaan and Katch elude the authorities? Were they out on the streets right now, looking for them, possibly following them? Barnaby glanced in his rearview mirror again but saw no vehicle similar to the one he'd seen in the alley. He didn't want to stop and just park in some shaded area. He would feel too much like a sitting duck, but as they began their third trip around the same few blocks, he asked, "How about where you're staying?"

Charleston shook his head. "I don't know if they know who I am or not. If they do, they'll be able to track me back there. We need somewhere that can't be linked to either of us."

Sitting at a stoplight that was becoming very familiar, Barnaby started feeling like he was leading a tour of Bend's more charming features. The shops and streetlights, even some of the people, were beginning to look familiar to him, so when the light changed, he suddenly sped up and turned a corner.

"What?" Charleston asked.

"I'm sick of wandering and waiting, and you bleeding. I know where to go."

Sometime later, after pausing briefly on the Bill Healy Memorial Bridge to send Katch and Kaan's weapons to watery graves, Charleston and Barnaby drove down a quiet residential street comprised of large homes that sat on the bank of the Deschutes River. Charleston watched drowsily out the window as they drove up to a sprawling brick ranch surrounded by a low, stone fence with a white-picket gate set into it.

After Barnaby parked the car at the rear of the house and got out, Charleston reached for the door handle, but his shoulder protested, and he bit off a hiss. The painkiller in the kit had hardly made a dent, but he fought to not show it. As he waited for the throbbing to end, he opened the door with his other hand and asked, "Where are we?"

"The Mitchner's place… Coral's parents. They're in the Bahamas this month."

He looked the massive house over and could practically hear the price ringing up in his head. Charleston slid out of the car. "You might want to call your friends; let 'em know you're okay before someone places a trace on their phones."

Turning to face him, Barnaby paused on his way to the door. "Are you serious?"

"Very." Barnaby frowned, and Charleston tried to look innocent as he said, "I need to fill you in on a few things."

"No shit."

Barnaby stepped up to the back door and pressed his left thumb to the voice recognition pad. "Barnaby Rosenthal," he stated, and the door opened. Once inside the house, Charleston waited in a darkened kitchen while Barnaby called out "Lights," which illuminated the area they were standing in.

"I house-sat here last year when the Mitchners and Coral were both out of town and… I needed some space from…." Barnaby didn't finish but tossed the car keys on the kitchen island and kept walking toward the front of the house. Charleston watched Barnaby's lean form walk away from him for a moment, the tailored suit hanging on his body in just the right way. A smile played on his lips… until his shoulder twinged.

Barnaby shed his suit jacket and turned to beckon him. "This way, Chuck."

Wincing at that name, he followed dutifully. The spotless, charcoal-gray slate of the kitchen floor became a rich, dark hardwood that creaked beneath his feet as he entered the front hall. He joined Barnaby at the door of a small powder room tucked beneath the stairs, where the lights had come on automatically, anticipating their entrance. Barnaby gestured for him to enter and have a seat on the closed toilet lid.

He did as he was instructed and watched Barnaby move around him—filling the sink with steaming hot water, peeling off Charleston's jacket, then unbuttoning his shirt before sliding it off his uninjured shoulder. Barnaby paused to grab two clean towels from the shiny metal racks behind him, then looked into Charleston's eyes. "This is going to reopen the wound and probably hurt like a motherfucker."

"Understood," Charleston said as his eyes fixed on Barnaby's lips.

"Let me just… get…." Barnaby reached over him to the medicine cabinet above the sink, and his shirt pulled free of his pants, placing his bare midriff directly in Charleston's face, close enough to kiss. He fought down the urge to grip Barnaby's waist and pull him forward to taste his skin. "I know there's more antiseptic in here some—Ah, got it!"

Barnaby set the medspray down on the sink and unceremoniously tore Charleston's shirt from his shoulder, ripping open the bullet wound, front and back. Barnaby cringed as Charleston's howl shook the walls of the tiny washroom.

"Fuck!" he bellowed, trying to catch his breath, then looked up in shock at Barnaby's wide innocent eyes.

"Sorry," Barnaby mouthed as he pressed the two clean towels against the entrance and exit of the wound.

"If you're sorry, why are you trying not to laugh?"

"I'm not," Barnaby said as he fought back a grin, his eyes dancing with amusement. He removed the back towel and misted antiseptic into the wound. Charleston hissed in response, trying to pull away. "Hold still," Barnaby ordered. "Let me finish. Then I'll clean off the dried blood and apply the Mend Accelerant and SkinSeal." He poked and peered at the wound. "I think you're right about it being a through and through. Not much other damage. You should be good as new, or close to it, by tomorrow, if the blood loss doesn't hit you too hard."

Despite the occasional lean forward to sniff Barnaby's hair, Charleston forced himself to sit still as the surrounding areas of his wound were carefully cleansed with hot, soapy water. The two of them were in such close quarters it was all he could do to resist grabbing Barnaby and taking him against the wall. If his shoulder wasn't injured, he might have tried it, so a small sniff now and then wasn't so bad, right?

With his eyes averted and all his concentration on opening the Mend Accelerant lifted from the car's first aid kit, Barnaby provided the perfect picture for Charleston to gaze at: the line of his jaw, a nibble of his bottom lip as he tried not to spill any of the gel, the puff of air from his mouth to blow a lock of hair out of his eyes….

Suddenly Barnaby drew back and looked into Charleston's eyes. "What are you doing?"

Mesmerized for a moment by the long, dark lashes against Barnaby's pale skin, by his full, kissable lips. "Nothing," he said as innocently as possible.

"Were you… smelling my hair?" A smirk played at Barnaby's lips.

He sat perfectly still beneath Barnaby's scrutiny and said nothing. There was a calculation in those dark eyes now, a calculation that said "careful how you answer." After several more moments of looking Charleston over from head to toe, a subtle shift occurred in Barnaby's gaze, heat replacing suspicion. Then he was in Charleston's lap, straddling him, capturing Charleston's lips with his own, tangling his hands in his hair. Barnaby clung to him, ground against him.

Finding his arms suddenly full of passionate artist, he fought to keep up with the urgent energy coming from Barnaby, but he certainly wasn't complaining. His shoulder was, but he wasn't. He moaned and steadied Barnaby's jerky, needy movements and sank into the moist heat of the kiss. He lost himself in the faint scent rising from Barnaby's heated skin, buried his nose in the man's hair as he nipped at his neck before finding his lips and tongue again. With the hand on his uninjured arm, he gripped Barnaby's slender, muscled thigh and thrust against him, pulling a groan from Barnaby. This passion was preferable to the suspicion that had poured off the artist a moment before.

Then it ended suddenly as Barnaby pulled away and leaned back, leaving Charleston with a swimming head, lips plump from the onslaught, hair more tangled than usual, and an ache in his crotch that briefly eclipsed his shoulder. He took several seconds to find and collect his wits again before gazing at Barnaby and seeing the heat had been replaced with doubt and sadness.

"Where were you?" Barnaby whispered. "I waited. I missed you… so much."

"I… I—" Charleston's inarticulate attempt brought a wall slamming down between them, effectively cutting off the glimpse he'd had into Barnaby's heart, into his need.

The artist stood abruptly. "Let me take care of this, and then we'll find something to eat. I'm starving."

CHAPTER 8

BARNABY HAD thought once the adrenaline wore off, Charleston would drop where he stood, but he was apparently made of sterner stuff. He certainly looked it, sitting at the kitchen island, shirtless, and scarfing down two grilled chicken paninis, iced tea, and a slice of key lime pie. Charleston Meeks was glorious: just enough hair on his impressive chest to scream man but not beast, broad shoulders, rippling biceps, six-pack abdomen. Barnaby straightened his glasses nervously, wanting so much to reach out and touch again.

After watering the plants on the patio and in the living room, Barnaby returned to the kitchen, made himself a southwestern egg-white omelet, and stood across the island from Charleston, simply eating and watching him breathe. *In and out. Chest expanding, then deflating.* Periodically, Charleston would unconsciously lift his right arm and work the stiffness out of his shoulder. Barnaby could watch that all night, could almost detect Charleston's heartbeat within his chest. He was real. Alive. Warmth and flesh in front of him. Their brief encounter in the powder room had proven that. He'd felt him... *all* of him.

Charleston's blond hair just barely brushed his shoulders, and stubble was dusting his square jaw. He studied the man's handsome face, his kind blue eyes, and pensive expression. Barnaby grinned. He remembered that face or at least had impressions of it throughout his life, here and there. Suddenly the man looked up at him, and Barnaby schooled his features to uninterested.

"This is great, but it's a lot of food for house-sitting."

"Coral's mother stocked the place with my favorites before they left. She thinks I'm too thin."

"Nah, you're perfect," Charleston said around a mouthful, without lifting his gaze from his plate.

Stunned, Barnaby blinked a couple of times, then grinned slyly and leaned forward, elbows on the island, chin in his hands. "Am I, now?" he asked, fluttering his eyelashes.

"Did you call your friends?" Charleston asked, ignoring the bait.

"Yep. Used my phone. Kept it short. Reassured Coral. She'll pass what little I told her on to the others, and I told her I'd be in touch and not to worry."

"You didn't tell her—"

"—where I was? No. And before you ask, yes, I removed the SIM card and tossed it and my phone in the garbage."

"If Coral's in town, why are *you* house-sitting?" Charleston asked.

"We're splitting duties this time. I sign for packages, talk to and water the plants, while she keeps Lwaxana at her place."

"Lwax-what?"

"Lwaxana. The dog, a black Lab, actually, who will eat the pillows off the sofa if left to her own devices." He tapped his fingers on the island and glanced around, not sure what to say next. There were so many questions flying through his head. "More tea?" he asked as he poured more for himself.

Charleston shook his head and appeared lost in thought. "I guess you have questions."

Mmm, gorgeous and psychic.

"A few."

"I'm not sure what to tell you."

"How about the truth?"

"The truth is… problematic."

"Usually is." Barnaby sighed. "Why don't you start with tonight's dynamic dark duo?"

Charleston frowned. "I believe they were taking you to see Sen. Penny Collard. You know her?"

Barnaby wracked his brain, wondering if he actually knew the names of any senators. There were a few who were tripping through his mind. Then… he remembered an article he'd read on a flight last year about a senator who was lauding a new group of right-wing religious conservatives. And here he'd thought most of them had died out.

"I know of her, I think. The religious harpy, right?"

"That's her."

"What's she want with me?"

Charleston didn't answer right away, and Barnaby kept his gaze locked on him. "I'm not certain."

"Bullshit." Charleston grinned, but Barnaby didn't. "You have some idea, or you wouldn't have shown up like you did."

"I wasn't—" Charleston's Bluetooth activated, dancing across the island's granite surface like a wounded, angry bee—a big-ass bee. He seemed startled for a moment but then snatched it up. "Yes?" His gaze flicked to Barnaby as he placed it at his ear. "He's with me... at the moment.... Katch and Kaan...." Barnaby watched a series of emotions play across Charleston's face: shock, disbelief, fear, fury, and then he tensed as Charleston leaped to his feet. "That's insane.... Are you sure?" He looked at Barnaby again. "Well, if Jeri says so... I need to tell him... yes, *everything*.... No. He stays with me...." Barnaby smiled at that. "Pop? Pop, you there?" Charleston swore and ripped the device from his ear to slam it on the island.

Pop?

Charleston stared at Barnaby for several seconds. "You might want to have a seat."

Oh fuck.

"Do you remember me?" Charleston asked. Barnaby frowned. "From when you were six?"

"Six?"

Charleston waited, then said, "The bad man?"

A wave of heat rushed over Barnaby, and a buzzing began in his ears. He became light-headed as images from twenty-two years ago swamped him, images of Charleston, looking just like he did now, fighting with another man—the "bad man."

"Th-that was you?"

Charleston nodded.

"That's. Not. Possible," he whispered as he blindly reached for a kitchen stool and slid it beneath him before his legs gave out.

"You okay?"

"Y-you... you look the same. That's not p-possible." But he knew it was possible because he remembered it. He'd seen Charleston fight the bad man. He remembered Charleston yelling at him, ordering him to go inside. He remembered peeking around the door and seeing blood. He remembered Charleston vanishing right in front of him.

"Remember the bridge?" Charleston continued.

He nodded. This memory was clearer, being one of his favorites: the dark, swirling, icy water of the river passing beneath the bridge, the frigid air biting through his coat, his drawings scattering down the road on the wind, and him running after them, gathering them up, then turning to see the stranger standing by the railing where Barnaby had been standing just moments before. Charleston had looked the same, though he was dressed in winter clothing. And he had said such kind and encouraging things to Barnaby.

"You told me you knew what I was, who I was," Barnaby whispered, awe heavy in his voice.

"Okay, do you remember—"

"You in the bank, stopping that gunman? Yeah, I do. And, of course, the church." Barnaby looked over Charleston, head to toe, as if he were a hallucination. "How?"

"My father, Dr. Charleston Meeks Sr., is a genius in temporal mechanics. He and his team discovered a way to bend space, allowing the creation of a worm—"

"Your dad built a time machine."

"Uh… yeah." Charleston frowned but continued. "Years ago he started a program where a small team would step back no more than thirty years and stop the death of one person… just the once. Until recently, I was one of those temporal agents." Charleston paused, as if he were waiting for Barnaby to start laughing in disbelief, but it didn't happen. "We called it the Restore Point Program."

"Called?"

"It was shut down, defunded, but I had to retire anyway. There's a limit on the number of times an agent can travel back, and you were my last few trips." Charleston ran his hand through his hair, and Barnaby watched it fall beautifully back into place. "I cut it pretty close."

He remembered how ill Charleston had seemed when he appeared at the church, but Barnaby thought he had located a flaw in the story, and his eyes narrowed. "You said you saved someone just the once."

Charleston appeared uncomfortable, not meeting Barnaby's eyes and shifting on his stool. "I made a mis—broke a rule, and it resulted in me accidentally saving you as a baby."

Barnaby's eyes widened. "The stroller!" Charleston nodded, chewing his bottom lip. "Mom told me about that, about the stranger who saved me. Said she never got the chance to thank him—*you*."

Charleston got up and left the kitchen, motioning for Barnaby to follow him. "My stopping that stroller allowed my father to study the effects of repeatedly restoring someone at different points in their life."

He watched as his lifelong hero stopped in the bathroom to collect his shirt, but before Charleston could slip the bloody garment back on, Barnaby turned and went to the hall closet.

"Hang on, Chuck." He knew something was happening. There was an urgency in the air around Charleston. "Coral's dad keeps a gym bag in here," he said, throwing open the door. "You can't wear that shirt out." He dropped to his knees, shoved a couple of raincoats out of the way, reached into the back of the closet, caught a toppling golf bag before it brained him, and pulled out a dark blue satchel. He upended the bag, spilling its contents on the floor, and quickly began sifting through them. "Here." He held up a black Marines sweatshirt. It was massive. "I think this will fit. Leslie's a big guy."

"Thanks," Charleston said, taking the shirt and slipping it over his head. Barnaby noticed only a slight wince as he raised his right arm. "I don't suppose Mr. Mitchner has any weapons stored here."

"Of course. An arsenal. But they're all—"

"—bio-registered."

"Down to the last Beretta, and they're locked away. Sorry. He's serious about gun safety." He grabbed his suit jacket and followed Charleston as he headed for the back door. "So you were saying? Something about repeatedly stepping in to save my ass?"

"That's why you kept seeing me."

Barnaby unconsciously slid his jacket on. "So I'm not supposed to be here," he said softly, slowing to a stop.

Charleston whirled on him. "No! Don't ever say that!"

Barnaby held up a hand and ticked off his fingers as he said, "The stroller, the bad man, the bridge, the bank, the—" Barnaby frowned in thought. "Was my life in danger at the wedding?"

"Uh… not exactly." He raised an eyebrow as Charleston looked everywhere but at him. "But I thought…. She was lying to you. She wasn't pregnant."

"You broke the rules again… for me."

"I had a little help from some friends," Charleston said with a shrug, and Barnaby grinned crookedly. "We need to go. We're meeting up with a team of operatives in Eugene."

"Operatives? You have operatives? For real? Like black-ops badasses?"

"Yep… well, those we have left. No funding, remember? Pop and my former team leader are organizing everything, calling in favors." Charleston paused and reached out to cup Barnaby's cheek. He didn't pull away but felt himself leaning into it. "I know this all sounds like insanity to you, and we don't have all the facts yet, but it looks like someone is having restored subjects deleted."

"Murdered," Barnaby said flatly, a chill rushing through him.

Charleston turned away and grabbed the keys off the island as he went. Barnaby followed, pausing to command, "Lights off. Lockdown in fifteen seconds." The light went out as they exited and closed the door behind them.

"We're playing catch-up because we didn't realize how ruthless and batshit crazy some people in power still are," Charleston said as he hopped into the SUV.

As Barnaby climbed in, he asked, "You're good to drive?"

"Yep."

"Why Eugene?" he asked as Charleston started the car.

"There's a restored subject there, Miranda Colton—Lazarus now that she's married, with a family… three kids."

CHAPTER 9

Chillicothe, Ohio - December 2012

I OPENED my eyes to darkness. Something brushed my face, and I recoiled and banged into what felt like a wall. For several heart-stopping moments, I thought I'd gone blind, which was entirely possible since this was my final step. Maybe I'd pushed the limits too far, and my body was falling apart, making me pay for it. But I couldn't fail. This was my best chance, a chance given to me by my colleagues: Plumb, Lancaster, Leaundra, and Sato. The biggest surprise in that group was Dr. Hiram Lancaster.

He was a tall, thin, Barney-Fife-looking black man who always appeared to have recently sucked a lemon... at least in my presence. I thought he was uncomfortable with my being gay, but turns out he was only jealous I lived openly when he'd chosen to play straight. When I confronted him, he admitted he didn't regret his choices because they had brought him his daughter.

Despite our differences, he'd helped give me this chance with Barnaby, but how could I find him in a strange place and in the wrong year when I couldn't see? I took several deep, calming breaths and listened. Nothing. I reached out to my sides, and my fingers brushed clothing... heavy fabric... coats! I reached beyond them, and my fingers brushed walls on either side of me. I was in a closet. I stepped forward, feeling my way along the wall until my hand touched wood and I bumped a knuckle against a doorknob. I grasped it, turned it, and was literally, but momentarily, blinded by light flooding in from a hallway.

Okay, I'm not blind, not really, not yet. I stumbled into the hallway, and the floor beneath me tipped, throwing me down. I lay there, waiting for the spinning to stop. When it lessened, I pulled myself to my feet, clung to the wall on my right, and stumbled forward, toward the blurry, colorful *shapes at the end of the long hall. I clumsily navigated through a cloud of burbling women smelling of various perfumes and hairsprays.*

They weren't happy with me, but I had to find him, had to stop this wedding. I shouted for him as I burst into the sanctuary. The floor tilted again, but I managed to keep my feet. Several large, angry men rushed toward me, and behind them, at the front of the room, I saw him. Barnaby stood there watching, his brown eyes filled with wonder and confusion again. My head spun, I said something, and the next thing I knew, he was holding me, cradling my head in his lap, and stroking my hair.

We were in a darker, smaller, quieter room. My tie was loose and jacket gone. All I saw was him. I heard others talking, discussing me, but I had to tell him, warn him. "Don't marry her," I said as I fought through a full-body shudder. It felt like I was coming apart. Maybe I was. I heard the word "ambulance" and shouted, "No!" Barnaby stroked my face and asked me my name. I could see fear in his eyes—the fear of losing me. I told him my name. He kissed me. And everything went black.

Bend, Oregon - October 2020

CHARLESTON COULD almost feel the temperature in the car drop as the realization of what he'd said swept over Barnaby.

"A family?"

"Yes," he said, pulling out onto the road.

"A family that wouldn't exist if…."

"Exactly. In 1993 we stopped her from being shot during a bank robbery—strangely enough, the same bank where you were almost shot."

"And the same bank where you stopped my stroller and me from getting obliterated. Maybe it's built on a burial site or something," Barnaby mumbled.

Charleston chuckled and hit a button on his steering wheel, activating his GPS. "Direct route to Eugene, Oregon. Visual only." The windshield flickered, and a ghostly map of their location appeared on it, not obstructing their view of the road as a tiny, blinking red dot crept along to show their progress.

After several miles of silence, Charleston spoke up. "Are you okay?"

"Just trying to not think about what you've told me, that some lunatic is planning to murder three children...."

"Because she thinks we fucked with God's plan."

"Like I said... lunatic," Barnaby said, fighting back a yawn.

"We've got two-and-a-half hours," Charleston explained. "Why don't you get some sleep?"

"There's no way I could sleep now."

"Suit yourself." Charleston tracked their progress and sped up a bit.

"I'm confused," Barnaby said.

"I'm not surprised."

"Why did you show up without a weapon tonight?"

"I don't normally carry one. In RPP we don't delete people, only restore." Charleston frowned in thought. "That's the company line, anyway, and I didn't initially plan on coming to your rescue."

"Then why are you here?"

Charleston watched the road, trying to think of a response that wouldn't make him sound too vulnerable. Failing miserably, he opted for the truth. "I just wanted... to check on you, talk to you, get to know you without some disaster breathing down our necks."

Barnaby slouched in the seat and turned away to stare out the side window as the shadowed terrain rushed by. "Well, that worked out great, didn't it?" he asked softly.

Charleston looked at him, and wanted to reach out and touch him in some way that would reassure him, please him, but he resisted and instead asked, "So, where'd you learn that move?"

"Huh?" Barnaby glanced back at him. "The leg-sweep thing? Self-defense class." He sat up straighter in his seat and faced forward, curling one knee up under his chin. "I figured I couldn't rely on you to always save my bacon, right?" Charleston didn't know what to say to that. "So," Barnaby continued, turning sideways in his seat to face him, "where have you been for the past seven years while I braved the dangers of this world without you?"

Charleston cleared his throat. "You should put your seat belt on."

"Yeah, yeah. Explain yourself, Chuck."

"Please don't call me that."

They fell silent, and during those few moments of quiet, Charleston could practically feel Barnaby's dark gaze boring into the side of his skull. Finally, he sighed. "It's only been a bit more than a month for me," he explained as he spotted the onramp for US-20 W. "This year, 2020, is my present too."

Barnaby turned forward in his seat again and, after half a mile, said, "So you were in my arms, telling me your name, kissing me in the church—"

"Uh… you kissed me."

"—just five or six weeks ago?"

Charleston nodded. "By my experience, yes."

"So," Barnaby said softly, "you haven't really had time to miss me or… or wonder about me?"

Charleston gathered his thoughts as he drove. Keeping his gaze riveted to the road ahead of them, he said calmly, "Ya know, they warned me about the risk to me"—he glanced at Barnaby—"of becoming attached to you. What we did in your case was new, so we didn't really know what might happen."

"And what happened, Chuck?"

"Every time I left, I wondered about you, Barnaby… missed you." He glanced at him again. "Think about it. For each time step, I knew the next time I saw you, you'd be different. I would return to find you older, or possibly lost to me. At first you were just a cute kid with a lot of fight in him. Then you were a troubled, but talented, teenager. Yet there was still strength in you. You stood your ground in front of me that night on the bridge. And at the bank, you stayed calm, counted on me, trusted in me. That's the day I knew."

"Knew what?"

He looked at Barnaby for several moments, the road ahead of them thankfully clear. "I knew I *had* become attached. And I began to worry, because what was just a blink for me was years for you, years where you would have earned a wealth of experiences, possibly fallen in love… and maybe forgotten me." Watching the road again, Charleston could feel Barnaby staring at him. "What?" he asked, wrinkling his brow.

"Forgotten you?" Barnaby said, turning back to his window. "That wasn't a possibility, Chuck."

Warmth spread through Charleston at those words. It heated his face and moved downward through his chest, out to his fingertips, his crotch, and all the way to his toes. "Well, I did see your paintings of me, so I knew on some level, I was on your mind."

Barnaby snorted. "Yep. You could say that." Then he sighed and continued. "So tonight you wanted to see me to... what, ask me out or something?"

Charleston didn't speak for several seconds as he stared at the little red dot moving slowly across the map on the windshield and then at the dark road beyond. "Barnaby," he began slowly, "I don't know how you feel or where you are with that model—"

"His name is Ross."

"—but I found you tonight because... I didn't want us to be apart a moment longer." He looked at Barnaby to gauge his reaction. There was none. No smile. No frown. The man simply stared at him with his large dark eyes. "All this other stuff?" Charleston said, gesturing. "This was just me being in the right place—"

"Right on time," Barnaby finished.

KATCH GRIPPED the steering wheel with one hand until his knuckles went white. With his other hand, he held an ice pack to his mouth. Kaan tried not to grin at the rage pouring off her partner in waves as she examined her backup gun. One benefit of being mercenaries was they were rarely lacking in weaponry.

"You need to calm yourself," she said firmly. "We can't have any fuck-ups, got it?"

"Got it."

But Kaan could practically hear Katch grinding his teeth, the ones he had left anyway. Mysterious Hero had kicked at least three out of his head, one of which was still unaccounted for. Kaan smirked, expecting it to turn up again in about twenty-four hours.

"I can hear you laughing at me," Katch groaned.

"No. Not laughing, but I'll admit to some amusement."

"There won't be anything amusing about what I do to that prick when I get my hands on him."

"I have no problem with that, but Rosenthal is our priority. He needs to be secured before you have your fun."

"Understood."

Kaan glanced at her tablet and continued to track the bright green dot as it moved along several miles ahead of them. The tag she'd placed on Rosenthal's jacket shortly after entering the warehouse would keep him within reach.

Earlier, Kaan had come to, roused by Katch leaning over her and speaking urgently through the nightmare of his damaged, bloody mouth. As sirens blared their approach, Katch spit a great gob of blood onto the ground before climbing behind the wheel and speeding away into the night. Kaan wasn't worried about leaving DNA at the scene because neither of them were identified in any database on the planet. A second benefit of being mercenaries was, though their DNA profiles might show up at various crime scenes around the world, there were no names to match them to. They were ghosts.

They had entered a parking garage and waited until the authorities moved on, then made their way to Rosenthal's location only to see the two men exiting a lavish home on the other side of the Deschutes.

Kaan had instinctively hooked her hand in her partner's belt as Katch moved to exit the car and shoot Mysterious Hero between the eyes. "Not here. Residential neighborhood. We'll get them on the road, some lonely stretch." She'd spoken soothingly, like one would to calm a tormented child, or, in this case, wounded animal.

"They could be headed for the cops."

"If they wanted cops, they would have waited near the gallery," Kaan had explained. She was surprised their target hadn't run around the building and headed right back inside. Maybe there was something he or his friend had to fear from the authorities. Being questioned, possibly booked, *would* put them in the system, and the system was like a flashing neon sign to the senator and any other hired guns she had at her disposal. Kaan suspected Senator Collard was connected throughout the country and not a woman to be toyed with.

Now, as the darkness whipped past them, Kaan sensed a minute change in their velocity and said, "Slow back down, Rico. I know you're eager, but—" She turned to look at her partner and waited until the man looked at her. "—if you mess this up, you'll be swallowing the rest of your teeth."

In the dim light of the front seat, Kaan clearly saw Katch grow pale, and the car slowed. She turned back to stare through the windshield. The night came alive for her with the secretive activities of Northwest wildlife: a bunny dashing from bush to bush unaware of the hawk watching from a tree on the hillside or the coyote on the prowl. That bunny wasn't long for this world, one way or another. She saw it all. Her implants had taken some getting used to over the years. Learning to activate and deactivate them reflexively to avoid temporary blindness had taken some practice, but she was a quick study.

"How close?" Katch asked, his hand wringing the leather of the steering wheel.

"We're two miles behind." She stared at her partner's hands, saw the tension in his shoulders, and clocked his breathing. She turned back to watch the road and sighed. Katch would require watching.

Shortly after checking in with their employer, Kaan worked out Rosenthal's destination. It wasn't difficult after learning about a scheduled purge in Eugene. *Apparently Mysterious Hero is all about saving everyone tonight.* A different contractor had been hired for that job. It involved kids, so someone of a certain "mindset" was required.

Kaan had heard something in their employer's voice when she described to Collard the man who had come to Rosenthal's rescue. The senator didn't elaborate, but it was clear to Kaan—a fifteen-year veteran in wet works—the man was no mystery to the senator. She wished they'd been fully briefed. Kaan didn't like secrets.

Chapter 10

Despite his prediction of sleeplessness, Barnaby woke an hour later, blinking the sleep from his eyes and uncertain where he was. For several moments he gazed out his window as the night rushed by and flashes of memory from earlier swam around in his thoughts. He rolled his head to the left and smiled at the sight of Charleston behind the wheel. A sudden thrill flooded him at realizing he hadn't simply dreamed their encounter. The man was really back in his life—but for how long?

He noticed a candy bar in Charleston's hand and watched him carefully peel more of the wrapper back to get to the goodness, while keeping control of the steering wheel. He watched silently as Charleston finished it off, chewing, taking pleasure in the chocolate, his tongue darting out to lick the sticky sweetness from his lips. By the time Charleston had sucked his fingers clean, Barnaby was suddenly torn between two very different types of hunger.

"When did we stop?" he asked quietly.

"Hey, you're awake." Charleston beamed at him, prompting Barnaby to grin. "About thirty minutes ago. I had to get some fluids in me and some food."

"Food, huh?"

Charleston glanced at him sheepishly, chocolate guilt in his eyes. "I bought a couple of subs," he elaborated, "chips, and some Electro-Life—"

"What flavor?"

"Uh… grape and cherry, I think." Charleston hooked his thumb at the backseat, and Barnaby turned to reach for the bag but couldn't quite get it. He removed his seat belt and scrambled over the seat. He unpacked a sandwich, grabbed a bag of chips and a bottle of the cherry drink, and returned to his seat in front. He unwrapped his sub and took a big bite, then caught Charleston smirking at him.

"Wha?" he asked around his mouthful.

Charleston shook his head and chuckled. "Nothing. Just glad you're here."

Barnaby felt himself flush, but concentrated on eating. He hadn't realized how hungry he'd been as he chewed and swallowed two more slightly smaller bites and moaned. The bread was fresh and still warm, the turkey tender, the lettuce and tomato crisp and flavorful, the sharp bite of the cheese bursting in his mouth—all had obviously been produced locally, no traveling hundreds or thousands of miles to the store. Barnaby shook his drink and popped the top, then took a couple of gulps. *This is almost better than sex.* He glanced at Charleston. *Almost.*

"Ya know, I'm surprised I'm this hungry. We just ate an hour or so ago."

"Probably the adrenaline from earlier," Charleston explained. "If you're hungry, you're hungry. Don't fight it."

"How's the shoulder?"

"It's a dull throb right now. Completely tolerable."

"I don't think I've said this yet, but... thank you. Thank you for coming after me."

"At this point in our rela—At this point I hope you know I'll always come for you, Barnaby."

He smiled broadly but tried to hide it behind his hoagie. Then he sobered and asked, "Why?"

"Huh?"

"Why come for me?"

Charleston squinted at him in confusion. "I thought I'd made that clear."

"No, you haven't." He read the hesitation in Charleston's eyes. "Look, I'm not asking for a profession of undying love here, but what do you want from me? Dinner and a movie, a quick fuck, what?"

Charleston frowned, Barnaby's coarse language obviously striking home. "Well...."

"Yes?"

Charleston sighed but didn't say anything more. Barnaby watched him struggle, and for a moment felt guilty for pushing him, but not guilty enough to let him off the hook. He turned to gaze out his window and did some struggling of his own. On top of his joy and excitement at having

Charleston sitting right next to him—no longer only in his memories, dreams, or on canvas—there sat a load of doubt and resentment in his heart, and Barnaby wasn't sure how to deal with that.

Charleston cleared his throat. "Barnaby, so far all we've had is your past and our present. I'd like us to try to build a future." Barnaby looked at him, startled by his simple honesty. Charleston grinned back when he saw the surprise on his face, and he shrugged. "I don't want to waste any more time, so I thought I'd cut through all the bullshit."

He searched Charleston's earnest expression. "Ask me anything," Barnaby said.

Charleston nodded, watching the road. "Rossom."

"We've been seeing each other for a year or so, but we recently ended it." He sighed deeply and stared at the road. "In fact, we were going to tell Coral and India at dinner tonight, but we decided to wait until after the show… didn't want to spoil the celebratory mood."

"If you don't mind my asking, why end it? He seems…."

"Gorgeous?"

"Somewhat appealing."

Barnaby snorted and smirked when he saw a grimace dance across Charleston's face. "There are a bunch of reasons for the breakup: it was time; I'm a homebody; he's a jet setter; he can be a bit shallow…." He stared at Charleston, examined the angles and lines of his face and the blond hair he wanted to bury his fingers in. He wished he could also see the blue of his eyes in the shadowed front seat. "But ultimately… he just wasn't you," he finished softly.

Charleston nodded, and Barnaby could see a satisfied grin fighting to emerge.

"My turn," he added brightly.

"Huh?"

"What's it like to travel through time, Chuck?"

Charleston frowned briefly. "Oh, uh… well… the first time is disorienting—"

"I bet."

"Newbies go with veterans on assignment, and while the vets complete the restore, the newbies wait at the retrieval point, usually vomiting, until they return. It's a bit like practicing antigrav before being sent to the space station. Your body needs an idea of what it's like, and it changes your brain, sort of the way learning to ride a bike does."

"And after that first time?"

"It's like stepping into another room."

Barnaby nodded, then sat quietly for a moment, thinking. "Do you notice the difference... the differences?" He turned in his seat and leaned closer to him. "I mean, can you immediately see how the present is affected when you... I don't know... pop back in from wherever, whenever you were?"

"We return to the Portal room, and no, not usually. The assignments—there were twenty-three total—usually aren't too closely related to our agents or the facility, so when the team is retrieved, any changes are so minute, we'd not be aware." Barnaby opened his mouth to say something, but Charleston cut him off. "Plus, before each step, our extrapolators have worked out, as best they can, what the ripple effects will most likely be. I mean—" Charleston chuckled. "—we wouldn't want to erase a president or something, right?" He continued to chuckle to himself, but there was more unease than any real mirth in it.

"But are your memories the same? Could a restore alter an agent's memories?"

"I'm not sure. I've never heard of it happening, but if it does happen, I doubt the agent would be aware of it... maybe at first he or she would, but that would fade over time. I guess it depends on how closely related they are to the target and the outcome. Honestly, I'm not sure what it would be like." Charleston glanced at him. "You're really into this stuff, aren't you?"

"It's time travel, Chuck!" Barnaby sobered, glanced down at his shirt, and smoothed a wrinkle. "And besides, I've been known to enjoy the odd sci-fi movie now and then."

"Fair enough. You're a nerd. Good to know."

"I'm not a nerd—"

"We never did a restore around a historic event. The ripples that would cause were impossible to determine." Charleston stared at the road in silence for a few moments. "My father wanted to make the world a better place by making tiny changes. One person, one *good* person at a time."

"And then there's me."

Charleston looked at him sharply. "You're a good person."

"I'd like to think so, but I'm a person who should have died several times."

Charleston opened his mouth, obviously to disagree, but a loud bang, followed by the SUV pitching violently to the left and throwing Barnaby hard against his door, ended that conversation.

"Fuck!" Charleston shouted as he tried to regain control. "Buckle up!"

"We blew a tire?" Barnaby asked as he struggled to locate and lock his seat belt.

"No!" Charleston gripped the steering wheel tightly and glanced in the rearview mirror.

Barnaby peered into his side mirror and saw another SUV coming up on them fast. As he braced himself, his gaze darted to either side of the road and into the distance, looking for an exit ramp to a town, any town or place where people gathered. He saw nothing. They were alone—alone, terrified, and unarmed. Hit from behind again, their vehicle gave another violent jerk, and Barnaby felt his stomach swim sickeningly as the car nearly tipped on its side, but Charleston kept it upright.

"Hold on!"

Through his window, Barnaby could see their pursuers rushing forward to slam them again, their headlights filling and reflecting off the side mirror. He shut his eyes and braced himself, but no jarring impact came. However, tires screeched, and there was another sickening tummy spin, coupled with the sensation of his head feeling heavy, being forced backward against the headrest by inertia—like he'd felt in carnival rides as a child. He wanted to scream but couldn't find his voice as fear seemed to trap the air inside his lungs.

As their vehicle stopped abruptly and rocked on its tires a couple of times before settling, he heard an engine rev and then the sound of an impact and tortured metal. He opened his eyes and saw Katch and Kaan's car flip once... twice... a third time—lacking the momentum for number four—before it came to rest in a rut by the road, two of its tires spinning silently.

He and Charleston watched the other vehicle for any other sign of movement. Barnaby turned to glance at his hero. Then he looked up and down the stretch of road, but no other cars were in sight. The crickets, birds, and other wild creatures had gone silent. The only sound was the purr of their own engine.

"Should we—"

A bullet pinged off the edge of Barnaby's door, narrowly missing the window.

"We should not!" Charleston gunned the engine and drove away. In the side mirror, Barnaby saw Kaan staggering out of the wreck and firing at them relentlessly, her hair tangled and whipped by the wind, her eyes wild and reflecting red—like a photo from a cheap camera. She looked like a monster—a bruised, bloodied, furious Medusa.

The best kind, Barnaby thought miserably.

CHAPTER 11

AFTER MAKING sure Barnaby was unharmed, Charleston didn't speak until they'd driven thirty miles. His mind raced, trying to understand how Katch and Kaan had found them. A tracer on the bullet didn't matter because it'd gone through him and likely would have only led them to the wall of the gallery's neighboring building. The call he'd had with his father could have been monitored, but only from his father's end. The call Barnaby had made to Coral might have been traced too, but.... *Shit.* He glanced at Barnaby, who sat curled into a quiet, frightened ball against his door.

"Barnaby?'

"I told you I'm okay," he snapped.

Clearly not. "Yes, but I need to ask, how long did Kaan have you before I showed up?"

Barnaby peered at him, at first annoyed, but then his face relaxed as he considered the question. "Less than ten minutes, I guess."

"Did she touch you?"

"Uh...."

"I mean did she grab you? Guide you? Shove you?"

"Yeah, all of the above. Why?"

Charleston yanked the wheel to the right, aiming for the shoulder. He threw the car in park directly below a roadway light, grabbed a flashlight from the glove box, and jumped out. Barnaby stared at him like he was a madman as he ran around the vehicle and yanked open the passenger door. "Give me your clothes," Charleston demanded.

"Say what now?"

"Your clothes! You've been tagged. They put a tracer on you somewhere."

Barnaby's eyes widened in understanding, and he unbuckled his seat belt and leapt onto the shoulder next to him. "I'm not giving you my clothes, Chuck. Just look me over."

Charleston sighed, turned on the light, and began to slowly run it over Barnaby's body. "She didn't inject you with anything, right?" he asked, dragging the light down Barnaby's front.

"No."

Charleston continued his perusal, turning Barnaby to examine his back. He began at Barnaby's feet and rose slowly with the light, examining his legs and the seat of his pants. "The easiest thing would be to strip you and toss your clothes in the bushes, but—" The light hit a small dead spot near the collar of Barnaby's tux, a tiny, dark gray square that didn't reflect the light. "Got it." He reached out and tried to pluck it from the fabric. It didn't want to let go, but he worked it loose.

Barnaby turned to see as Charleston held it in his palm. "That's it?"

Charleston nodded, picked up two palm-size rocks, and ground the device between them. Then he tossed everything into the bushes by the road. He smiled at Barnaby as he slapped the dirt from his hands. "Ready to go?"

Barnaby stared at him for a moment, then grabbed the front of Charleston's borrowed sweatshirt, spun him slowly, and softly said, "That was some good driving, Chuck."

"Uh... th-thank you?" Charleston's back thumped into the side of the SUV, and with Barnaby pressed against him, he could feel the artist's arousal next to his own, their cocks seeming to fill in unison. Gazing down into that beautiful, familiar face, he matched Barnaby's lopsided grin and gently combed his fingers through Barnaby's hair, stroking it out of his heated eyes so he could look into them.

"I'm ready for you, Chuck," Barnaby whispered.

Charleston's scrutiny dropped to Barnaby's mouth, and he took it with his own, gripping the younger man's face and holding him firmly in place, tasting him, trying to improve on their kiss at the Mitchners'. He tangled his fingers tightly in his curls, and when Barnaby winced and gasped, Charleston's hardening cock jerked excitedly. Then he deepened the kiss and slid his hands down Barnaby's body. He gripped his ass, lifted him with his uninjured arm, and turned him to press against the car door— the better to grind against him. Barnaby moaned hungrily and wrapped his legs tightly around Charleston's waist.

"Now…," Charleston panted as he nibbled and kissed and licked at Barnaby's lips, neck, and face, "now can I have your clothes?"

They chuckled against each other's mouths and each struggled to get his hands on the bare, hot skin of the other. That is, until Charleston glanced to the right of Barnaby's head and froze. He saw a dented chip in the paint of the passenger door where the bullet had hit. Had that bullet struck an inch to the right, Barnaby would not be warm and writhing in his arms right now. An iciness settled over him, and his eager hands stilled.

"Wha-what is it?" Barnaby asked breathlessly, confused, his fingers caressing Charleston's face. "Why'd you stop? What… what are you looking—" Barnaby turned his head and saw the scar in the paint as well. He sobered too as he watched Charleston caress the damage with his thumb, lost in thought as he stared at it. Without another word, Charleston lowered Barnaby to the ground and opened the passenger door. After straightening his clothes, Barnaby climbed in and buckled his seat belt.

Light-headed, sweating, and painfully hard, Charleston walked around the back of the car and paused to fix his clothing and catch his breath, to settle his pounding heart, to will his arousal away. When he eventually reached his door, he felt Barnaby's gaze tracking him, but neither of them spoke.

BARNABY STRAIGHTENED in his seat and looked around as they took the Coburg Rd. exit into Eugene. For the past hour or so, after his aborted clinch with Charleston by the side of the road, he'd had very little to say. Seeing that mark on the car, so close to his head, had definitely killed the mood. And there was a family to rescue, after all.

"So what's our plan?"

"Hmm?"

"This family we're supposed to save…."

"Not you."

"Huh?"

"I'm meeting up with the team, and we're going in to pull them out. You'll wait in the hotel."

"No."

"You can watch from the car."

"No."

Charleston looked at him, surprise clear on his face. "I can't... can't have you getting hurt."

"Ditto, Chuck." When Charleston grinned, the knot in Barnaby's gut relaxed. "You said, and I quote, 'He stays with me.'"

Charleston sighed deeply and glanced at him. "You have to stick close to me. I want you on my six the whole time, got that? You have to do what I say. No questions."

"Got it," Barnaby said with a curt nod. He had a vague idea of what "on my six" meant.

Moments later, they pulled in to the parking lot of a twenty-four-hour restaurant on Franklin Boulevard. "We're meeting your team here?"

"Yep, though I'm not sure who it'll be." Charleston hopped out of the car, and Barnaby followed slowly, eyeing the L-shaped building with doubt. It was mostly windows, but at this hour, the back portions of the dining area were in shadow, apparently closed off for the night.

They entered and were eventually greeted by a very tired-looking young woman, who radiated apathy. "Just the two?" she asked.

"Actually, we're meeting—"

"Meeks!"

Barnaby flinched at the booming voice and turned to see a large man rushing toward them, waving a small black case in one hand. He tossed the case to Charleston, who caught it deftly before the newcomer virtually swallowed Charleston in a hug, lifting him off the floor for a moment.

"Oh, man, it's been a while. How you enjoying retirement?"

"Handal? What the fuck are you doing here?"

"I'm Team Leader on this one, bud." The man laughed and slapped Charleston hard on the back, causing him to stagger a bit, and then he glanced down at Barnaby. "Who's the little guy?"

Barnaby bristled, but Charleston quickly interrupted. "This is Barnaby Rosenthal. Barnaby, this is Handal, a former colleague."

"Good to meet ya, kid." Handal held out his massive paw, and Barnaby reluctantly shook it as he used his eyes to try to communicate his annoyance at being referred to as "little guy" and "kid." But the behemoth before him, whose twinkling black eyes, graying, buzzed hair, and smile looked more like that of a hungry predator than a warm old friend, was oblivious and hardly quaking in his big-ass boots.

"Hello," Barnaby began, but his voice squeaked a bit, so he cleared his throat, deepened his voice, and said, "Good to meet you." Out of the corner of his eye, he could see Charleston grinning at him, clearly amused.

"Come on back," Handal said. "Breakfast arrived about five minutes ago."

"Is there time?"

"Sure. I've got Vislou watching the place."

They stopped at a booth by the front windows. Charleston slid in after Barnaby, and Handal sat facing them across the table. Two plates of scrambled eggs, bacon, and toast awaited them, but Handal shoved his over to Barnaby. "Looks like you could use this more than me, little man."

He wanted to argue, but he was hungry again, so Barnaby said thank you, piled some eggs on toast, and dug in. Maybe his increased appetite was due to his excitement over Charleston being so near. Whatever the reason, Ross was sure to have some pudgy comments ready for him. The model could always somehow tell when he'd put on a couple of pounds. He paused and glanced at Charleston. Would he even be seeing Ross again?

He ate in silence as Handal and Charleston began talking about old assignments: a hit and run, a drive-by shooting, a convenience store robbery, a car accident, a drowning. There was quite a variety of incidents where one different choice or action could make all the difference and save someone's life, or change their fate. Barnaby was soon fascinated, and hearing about their exploits got his imagination going.

"If I could go back, I know what I'd change," he said suddenly, drawing their attention as he gazed wistfully out the restaurant window at the night traffic.

"Yeah? What?" Charleston asked before taking a sip of his coffee.

"Newtown School Shooting."

Charleston coughed and sputtered violently, prompting their server, who was approaching to top off their coffee, to pause and pound on his back, something a server bot wouldn't be able to do.

"You okay, hon?"

"Just… went down… wrong w-way," he gasped before thanking her and waving her off. Then he looked at Barnaby in shock as Handal grinned and watched, his face filled with expectation.

"What?" Barnaby asked, glancing between them.

"You couldn't do that."

Barnaby laughed. "Why the hell not?"

"A couple reasons. First, more than twenty people died in that shooting—"

"What? There's a limit to the number—"

"No, there's not a certain cutoff number," Handal said. "It's a matter of extrapolation. Stopping that shooting, restoring everyone…." He shook his head. "I can't even wrap my head around the number of people that would affect—families, the entire community…."

Barnaby felt a bit ganged up on when Charleston nodded, agreeing with his former colleague, and said gently, "Look, it's natural to want to undo a nightmare like that, but some events leave too deep a mark on our existence. Bad or good, if the scar runs deep, reaches too far, or affects too many, then odds are that undoing it will undo us, everything around us. Understand?"

He nodded slowly. "It never should have happened," Barnaby muttered.

"There are a lot of things that shouldn't have happened, little man," Handal said. "Like that Martin kid—"

"Oh shit! That too," Barnaby said excitedly. "I'd change that too. He was one teenager." He held up one finger, a challenge in his eyes. "Couldn't I just appear next to George's car and ask him the time or something? Stop him from following the kid."

"Barnaby, the only reason you even know what happened to Trayvon is because it was such a massive story, on a national—hell, a worldwide scale." Charleston glanced at Handal, who nodded, and then continued, "Just like Sandy Hook. It's not so much just the number restored. It's more about whether it seeps into the national and world consciousness.

"Think for a moment about what came after the acquittal. Think about how it prompted people to get involved with their local elections, to change the face of their communities and law enforcement. And it was just the latest in a string of events putting a spotlight on racial profiling and disenfranchisement in this country. Remember those voter ID laws that swept through the states back then?"

Oh yeah, he remembered. Barnaby had helped register voters in his area and walk them through securing their identification. Last year he'd even bullied Rossom into helping drive people to pick up their IDs.

"All those things had a profound effect on the outcome of the 2016 election, among other things. Now imagine plucking that one event from the timeline. I'm not saying things would be drastically different, but they could be different enough to... well, I don't even want to think about it."

Handal jumped in. "More bigoted loons like Collard could be empowered."

"We don't need that," Barnaby said. "Racism, homophobia, and misogyny have deep roots and are tough to dig out as it is."

Handal chuckled. "Let's not add fertilizer."

Barnaby nodded. "Yeah, they produce enough of that themselves," he admitted. He glanced at the remainder of his eggs, which had grown cold during their impassioned conversation.

"Plus, RPP regulations wouldn't have allowed it," Charleston added. "We weren't *usually* allowed to go back and undo something just because we didn't like what happened."

"You've got more self-control than me, Chuck, I'll tell you that." Barnaby spread jam on his toast and took a bite.

Charleston looked a bit sheepish and avoided Barnaby's gaze until he admitted, "I said usually. There was this one time I went back to stop a man I cared for from ruining his life."

They smiled at each other, and Barnaby slid a hand onto Charleston's thigh and squeezed. "A life you helped make possible."

Handal sighed and stood. "Okay, if you're sufficiently full, I'd like to get going before the two of you begin making out." He looked at his watch. "Vislou didn't check in at the arranged time, and I'm getting worried."

As they headed for the exit, Handal waved his sausage-like fingers at the hostess. "Hey, honey? Thanks for the grub."

She nodded in their general direction and continued to sulkily wipe down the hostess stand. The restaurant had been deserted except for them, and now they were bailing on her, so when Handal handed her a fifty-dollar tip, it was like the sun coming out on her face.

CHAPTER 12

AS THEY piled into Charleston's car, Barnaby sat in the backseat because Handal needed more legroom than he did. Getting in, his heel kicked something beneath the seat—the tool kit that came with the rental—so he slid over to sit behind Handal.

"Remind me to thank Pop for the gun," Charleston said.

Gun? Barnaby leaned forward and watched Charleston crack the seal on the case and remove a sleek handgun. Charleston popped in a standard clip and chambered a round with practiced precision. After removing a thin green sheath from the trigger, he gripped the weapon as though he were firing it and winced minutely as a DNA sample was taken from the heel of his hand to activate the gun, making it his own. Then he holstered it and clipped it to his belt.

"The family lives in Hendricks Park, up the hill," Handal explained as Charleston started the car and drove. "It's kinda swanky. Vislou's had the mother and kids under surveillance all day. She even followed—Hey, turn right here—followed the wife to the airport to send Hubby on his way to San Diego on some business trip. Take a left here."

Barnaby noticed the homes on the quiet, early-morning streets were growing progressively more beautiful and elaborate. And the twists and turns they were making explained why they'd met at the restaurant.

"How will you get them out?" he asked suddenly, and Handal turned to look at him as if just remembering he was there. Barnaby narrowed his gaze. "Seriously, what are you going to say to get a mother at home alone with her children at three in the morning to open the door to you, let alone leave with you?" Both Handal and Charleston opened their mouths to speak, but Barnaby cut them off. "And, assuming you do get them out—"

"Oh, we'll get them out," Handal said.

"—where do they go? Where will they be safe?" Too late, Barnaby realized how much fear had come through in his tone, how much he worried for his own safety. He glanced nervously out the window at a particularly large home as they passed, trying to avoid their eyes. Charleston awkwardly reached over the seat, and Barnaby took his hand for a reassuring squeeze.

Handal glanced at their clasped hands and asked, "This is the restore you fell for? I was just kidding back at the restaurant. I'd heard rumors, but—"

Barnaby missed the warmth when Charleston quickly took his hand back and said, "Let's stay focused, shall we?"

"Here," Handal directed, "take Fairmount and we're looking for Parkside Lane."

"Barnaby, in answer to your questions, once they're out, we'll send them to a safe house, where they'll be met by the husband, who is probably being picked up as we speak. Whoever my father has assembled to handle that end will keep them safe and comfortable until this is put to rest. Any ideas about that, Handal?"

The big man shook his head. "He's calling in favors across the board, putting together a network, and trying to stay off the radar, because Collard is connected throughout the country." Handal reached into his front pocket and pulled out a cell phone and cash card. "Speaking of your father, you can reach him or Leaundra on this. The line's secure. And this is untraceable—for incidentals."

Charleston pocketed them. "Thanks."

Barnaby sighed. "Again, how are you going to get them to open the door, let alone go with you?"

Handal reached into his back pocket and produced a wallet. He flipped it open, and Barnaby had to admit the badge looked authentic. He pulled out a second one and tossed it to Charleston. "We're detectives with the Eugene Police Department, don't cha know?"

Barnaby smirked at the huge man but couldn't help thinking it wouldn't be that easy.

CHARLESTON SAW the faint, flickering light against the night sky and smelled the smoke before he heard the distant sirens. "Shit!" he shouted as he pulled over to the curb, threw the car in park, and jumped out, Barnaby and Handal right behind.

Though Vislou had been watching and following the family all day, it was a last-minute assignment, and there hadn't been anyone to watch the house as well. Anything could have been done to it while the family was busy elsewhere. The deaths of five restore subjects would look like accidents—just life being a bitch and snatching them from it.

"How old are the children?" Barnaby asked as they all ran toward the tri-level home. Flames flickered in many of the windows on the first floor, so the family was likely trapped on the second.

"Six, three, and one!" Handal shouted. "I've got the back." The big man disappeared along a path that led down a small hill and wrapped around the house.

"I've got the front!" But before running off, Charleston paused and looked at Barnaby, the concern clear on his face as he stood beneath a street light.

"Be careful!" Barnaby ordered. "I'll stay right here."

Charleston turned quickly and went directly to the front door. He kicked it in, flinched back from a momentary surge of flames, and entered a large room, heavily clouded with smoke and being consumed by fire. The heat was daunting as it licked out toward him, inviting him to join the party. He struggled briefly, trying to override his sense of self-preservation, but then he dashed through an opening and into a hazy, dark hallway. Most of the heat now at his back, he called out "Miranda!" over the crackling and popping fire. He rushed forward, checking the rooms on the first floor, but when he heard glass shattering below him, he ran down a set of stairs to the basement. It was finished and stylish, with a wall of floor-to-ceiling windows that looked onto a wooded hillside.

One of the windows had been broken out, and Handal was kneeling over the mother, who lay unconscious on a plush sofa, a wine bottle and glass on the end table nearby. Handal looked up at him, fear in his eyes. "She won't wake up, and it's not just the smoke."

Charleston felt himself go cold, but there wasn't time. "Get her outside. I'll collect the kids."

WHEN CHARLESTON disappeared through the front door, Barnaby looked around the tiny neighborhood. There were only five homes on the street, and he searched for any sign of other people: a light in a window, a curtain being pulled back, or a door opening to reveal a suspicious homeowner to interrogate him while they tried to tie their robe closed. Nothing.

The sirens were getting louder, and he considered going down the steep hill to flag them down, but movement on his left stopped him. The bushes across the street from the burning house were twitching, and at first Barnaby tensed, afraid of what was about to emerge from them. A tall, slender woman fell free of the foliage and staggered toward him. She was clutching her neck, trying to stem the blood streaming through her fingers. Barnaby caught her as she collapsed in his arms.

She managed to point with the hand not on her neck. "Ch-chil… dren—" she gurgled before passing out. Barnaby allowed her to slide to the ground as he turned the way she'd indicated and looked up. A security light shone onto a tall, narrow window on the third floor at the back of the house, and curled against the bottom of the window was a tiny bundle of blanket and a child's hand.

"Holy shit!" Barnaby took off, running as fast as he could to the car. He opened the driver-side door, reached over the seat, and grabbed the tool kit he'd kicked earlier. Once he had the bright orange, window-punch tool in hand, he ran back to the house. He couldn't seem to move fast enough, having never felt so lead-footed in his life. The flames were higher now and could be seen on the roof itself instead of simply licking at the windows from the inside.

As he scrambled up a gnarled tree to reach the window, the fire engines turned the corner. The sounds of sirens and screeching breaks rent the quiet of the neighborhood, and lights began coming on in windows along the street. But Barnaby kept his eyes focused on that tiny hand and blue blanket. *Three kids. One, three, and six. One, three, and six.*

"Hey, you!" someone shouted—at him, possibly, but he ignored it and, balancing carefully on a hardy branch, drew back with the tool, and broke the window. As smoke poured through the top part of the window, stinging his eyes and choking him, he quickly removed the larger, dangerous-looking shards remaining in the frame and tossed them to the ground below. He used the tool to clean away the smaller bits and then took hold of the small body within reach, just inside the window.

The little boy had obviously been trying to open it when he was choked unconscious by the smoke. Barnaby grabbed him, pulled him free of the window, and tried to get his arms around him, but as anyone who has ever had children knows, they're tough to handle when they go limp—tantrum tactic number two. For one breath-stealing moment, he feared he might lose his grip and drop the boy to the ground below.

He looked at the angelic, light brown face, at how lifeless his slight form was, and felt his own heart lurch and thud. *Please, please, please*, he thought as he rubbed the boy's arms vigorously. He couldn't perform CPR in his position, so he pinched the kid, and the little guy flinched, gasped, and started to whine. *Thank God*!

"Sissy," he croaked. "My sissy." He looked up into Barnaby's eyes, blinking away the smoke and tears and soot that streaked his face. "Sissy."

Barnaby peered through the window frame and, extending from the darkness, he saw a tiny foot at the end of a chubby leg wrapped in a pale green onesie. *Shit*.

"Give him to me," a woman's voice commanded from below him. Barnaby looked down through the branches and spotted a firefighter reaching up toward him and the boy. He passed the child to her, and she began carefully descending through the branches.

"Sis… sssy," the boy called out before coughing violently.

Barnaby said, "There's a baby—"

"Don't go in there," the firefighter ordered before disappearing.

He looked at the window and knew he couldn't fit through it, couldn't get in the room, but that little foot seemed so close. If he just stretched as best he could from the very end of the branch….

Suddenly Barnaby was doing it—sliding forward, lying down, and balancing his bottom half on the branch while straining, reaching his arm into the room, trying to snag those tiny toes and that one chubby leg. Then he saw the edge of the blanket was closer and grabbed it. Sissy was sort of wrapped up in it. Barnaby tugged gently and was thrilled when the baby's body moved closer, close enough for him to grab her foot, ankle, and leg. *Gotcha*!

"Out of the way, buddy," the firefighter shouted. "I'm coming up."

If he could barely reach in the room, he knew a firefighter with all that gear wasn't about to, but it didn't matter now. He had Sissy in his arms. He carefully sat up, cradling the girl against him. She was just as limp as the boy had been, but he couldn't bring himself to pinch her.

"I've got oxygen. Pass her over."

Barnaby did and watched the firefighter place a tiny mask over the baby's face and search for a pulse. He counted to thirty as he stared at the tiny person, watching for the rise and fall of her chest, feeling his throat tighten at the image of that small fist still clutching the satiny edge of her blanket. The rest of the night seemed to have gone silent around them.

"You did a good job, ya know," the firefighter said softly. "Regardless of what happens, you did good." Barnaby didn't say anything as they continued to wait. "My name's Sandra."

"Barnaby," he whispered.

Suddenly the baby's little body spasmed, and she began coughing, then crying. Her throat sounded rough, but she was breathing. Sandra whooped and smiled at Barnaby, but then they heard a thunderous racket as part of the house caved in. They looked at each other.

"Before I came back to you, a big guy with short white hair carried out an unconscious woman. Anyone else in there you know of?"

"My…." *The man I love.* "My friend and a three-year-old.

CHAPTER 13

As PART of the house collapsed, Charleston stumbled out the back, through the hole Handal had made previously, and promptly slid a few feet down the wooded embankment before he stopped himself. In his arms he held a struggling toddler who was having none of it, but who was so smoke-choked that he couldn't make much noise.

"Mah... M-Mama!" was all he could manage with his croaky little voice.

"I'm taking you to your mama, kid. Just let me get us back up this hill, okay?" The toddler whined and growled and clawed at Charleston's face. *Jesus*!

The house was much bigger than it appeared on the outside, not so much a TARDIS situation as a "multilevel, wrap around, and down the hill" situation. He'd found the kid at the back of a closet in the fourth room he'd searched on the top floor. Why did kids do that? Why hide in the closet when the house is on fire?

When he was a kid, he was terrified of his closet, convinced it was a portal for child-eating demons. But he suspected that when the outside world became more frightening than what you thought lurked in your closet, it probably seemed like a safe place to be. And snuggling back in there *had* kept most of the smoke out of the kid's lungs.

The toddler scratched him again and yanked his hair as Charleston tried to get a handhold on the crawling shrubbery littering the hillside and stop them from tumbling ass over noggin all the way down the hill to the road. *Fuck*! It was like trying to wrestle a pissed-off cat, a pissed-off cat with downy-soft, curly blond hair and a pudgy face.

"What's your name, kid?"

The boy looked up at him with suddenly questioning, wide green eyes, as if he were surprised Charleston spoke his language. "Pooper."

"My name is Charlest—Wait, are you calling me Pooper or is that your name?" *That can't be his name.*

"Jack says all I do is poop."

"Is Jack your big brother or baby brother?"

"Big *bruhver*," Pooper said, tears pooling in his eyes as he looked up the hillside at his ruined home. "I'm Sissy's big bruhver."

"Let's go find your big bro, okay?"

"And Sissy!"

"Yes. And Sissy."

Despite shuddering and gasping after his crying jag, the boy calmed for the most part and clung to Charleston, not giving him any more trouble as he fought their way back to flat, stable ground. When they rounded the house, the chaos that met Charleston nearly overwhelmed him. He quickly searched among the flashing lights, vehicles, and rescue personnel for Barnaby and Handal, but didn't immediately see them, so he carried Pooper toward an ambulance and the paramedic standing beside it.

"This kid was on the top floor in a closet," he said, handing the three-year-old over. "He needs checking out." The paramedic took the boy into the back of the ambulance to examine, and Charleston spotted an older boy in there wearing an oxygen mask. He was sitting on a gurney with his arm wrapped protectively around what Charleston guessed was his one-year-old sister, also wearing a mask.

He pulled out his phone and speed-dialed his father. "Pop?"

"It's Leaundra, Meeks. Your father is on the other line with your mother."

With the running engines, raised voices, and squawking radios surrounding him, Charleston plugged his ear with a finger and said, "Not much to tell at this point, other than we have the family out." He wandered among all the activity searching for Barnaby's face as Leaundra took over the conversation.

"Handal's already filled me in. Vislou is dead. Her throat was cut. The fire suppression system in the home was deactivated. Handal thinks the mother was drugged, but we'll have to wait on an analysis of the wine glass or bottle, if either survived the fire. We have a guard meeting Miranda at the hospital. I'm afraid she's still unconscious. Handal will accompany the kids. How are you and Rosenthal?"

The haze hanging in the air was sporadically cut by sunbeams from the slowly rising sun, and Charleston searched the faces around him. Many were darkened with soot or covered by a mask, but none resembled Barnaby.

"Uh… well, Bar—" *There*! Barnaby sat on the side steps of an engine, a portable oxygen mask in one hand and a cool towel in another. He wiped grime from his face, but Charleston could still see streaks along his cheeks, as if he'd been crying. He began to slowly make his way over there. "I see him."

"Good. Get some rest. Eat something. We'll talk tomorrow."

"What about the other subjects?"

"We've almost got the rest of them rounded up."

"Yes, ma'am." He ended the call and took one step toward Barnaby, but he thought he heard his name carried on the wind and turned to see Handal heading his way.

The man appeared hollowed out, exhausted, devastated. "Vislou's dead," he said.

"Leaundra told me. I'm sorry, man." Charleston laid a hand on his friend's shoulder as he watched him wrangle his emotions into submission.

Handal stared out above the treetops before lowering his gaze to Charleston's. "Thanks. She was a solid partner, always had my back." He cleared his throat and glanced beyond Charleston at Barnaby. "I guess you're headed that way?" Charleston thought he saw tears in his friend's eyes.

"Are you gonna be okay?"

"Yeah I will, eventually." He nodded in Barnaby's direction. "He didn't see you come out. Better go tell him you're all right, man."

"I will, thank you." Charleston patted Handal once more on the back and turned away.

"Meeks?"

He stopped and turned back.

"We'll get them, won't we?"

"Hell yeah."

He walked down the street, past the charred remains of the Lazarus home, and toward a man he planned to protect with his life. When

Barnaby's wounded, tired eyes met his, there was disbelief, shock, and a hesitant joy in them. Charleston smiled as he nodded at Barnaby and quickly found his arms filled with the artist. Barnaby clung to him, tried to climb him, and finally kissed him deeply in front of a crowd of people too busy to notice.

BARNABY EXAMINED the hotel room through exhausted eyes. After the night's events, he was ready to drop where he stood, but lingered by the door while Charleston carried in the doughnuts he'd stopped to buy and placed them on the small table in front of the curtained window. Every muscle in Barnaby's body ached, and he felt covered in crud.

"I have to take a shower," he whispered.

"Huh?" Charleston paused, half a glazed filling his mouth. He looked about as filthy as Barnaby felt, his hair hanging in his face, smoke smudges on his clothes, hands, and cheeks.

"I'm gonna…." Barnaby pointed to the bathroom.

"Oh, sure. Go ahead." Charleston glanced at the sweet in his hand, then back up at Barnaby. "I'll try to leave you some."

"I'm not really that hungry," Barnaby mumbled, shedding his clothing as he walked slowly to the bathroom and then shut the door. Once he was alone, he looked in the mirror, trying to read the night, all of it, in his own eyes: the sinister duo of Katch and Kaan trying to kidnap him, kill him, a woman dying at his feet, saving those sweet children, and then the relief of seeing Charleston standing there among the chaos.

All he saw was exhaustion.

He started the shower, and while the water rose to the right temperature, he slid off his glasses, socks, and briefs. He carefully stepped over the rim of the tub and beneath the spray, wincing briefly at the sting but quickly becoming accustomed to it. He sighed and grinned as the water flattened his hair to his head and face. He opened his mouth to rinse it of that smoky flavor, then watched the sooty water swirl down the drain, rinsing him clean, helping him be reborn.

When he closed his eyes, he saw the children, remembered how lifeless they'd felt in his arms. Barnaby shuddered. He needed to focus on the fact that Jackson, Louis, and Grace Lazarus were doing well—just like their mother, just like him—back from the dead.

He snorted. *Lazarus.*

On the way to the hotel, Charleston had told him the mother apparently had a nightly glass of wine before bed, and last night, once the children were tucked in, she had followed her routine. But this bottle, a gift from her husband, had been tampered with while she was away from the house. So when she took just two sips, she would have been out until morning. And by that time the house and everything in it would have been mostly ash. It would have looked like an accident, bad luck, poor timing, faulty wiring. A mother and her three children killed in a house fire while the husband was away.

Barnaby washed his hair, then his body, and then he did it all again, and again. He lost track of how long he'd been in the shower, and his thoughts began to swirl around the moment he thought he'd lost Charleston. When he heard part of the house collapse, it had been so thunderous and final.

In a daze he'd climbed out of that tree and put one foot in front of the other until he was standing in front of the wreckage. People didn't live through something like that, did they? He'd dropped to his knees on the grass and remained there until someone in a blue uniform had helped him to his feet and led him over to the fire engine.

They had looked him over, given him oxygen, but it hadn't felt like enough. He couldn't get his breath. Charleston was gone, and he'd only had him for less than a day. Did his friends meet him? Would they remember him? And if no one else did—like his stepfather—would he ever have existed?

He had begun to cry softly.

Then Charleston was there, on the other side of the shower curtain, pulling it back and gazing at him, worry etched on his features. Charleston was shutting off the now cool water and wrapping him in a towel and lifting him out of the tub. Then he was using another towel to dry Barnaby—his hair, chest, arms, legs, feet. Then suddenly in the bedroom, Charleston was kneeling in front of him, and Barnaby reached out to touch his still grimy face.

"You're here," he whispered.

Charleston frowned and covered Barnaby's hand with his own, holding it against his face. "I'm here, babe. I'm right here, and we're all okay."

Barnaby smiled. "I missed you so much."

Charleston sat next to him on the bed and wrapped his arms around him. "I know, but I'm here now."

Barnaby closed his eyes and relished the warmth of Charleston's lips against his forehead. In a move that belied his exhausted state, Barnaby suddenly captured Charleston's lips with his own, danced his tongue off Charleston's, and gripped either side of his head to hold him still until Barnaby had tasted his fill. He could taste the smoke. When they parted, Charleston looked drunk. "Stay with me," Barnaby whispered.

"I will, but you need to rest, and I need a shower."

"No. Stay," he insisted as the covers were drawn back and Barnaby slid beneath them. Charleston stretched out on top of the covers and wrapped his arms around Barnaby. "I don't want to sleep."

"Why?"

He clutched Charleston's sweatshirt in his fist and whispered, "If this is a dream, you'll be gone when I wake up. I'll lose you again." He could feel himself going, knew he was powerless to stop it.

Before he slipped away, Barnaby thought he heard Charleston whisper, "You won't lose me. I won't leave you again. I promise."

CHAPTER 14

CHARLESTON LAY there for an hour, watching Barnaby sleep: his lips were parted, small puffs of air escaped in a steady, soothing rhythm, and his dark curls were a chaotic mess and obscured part of his face. Charleston pressed his nose into Barnaby's hair. It smelled like vanilla from the hotel shampoo, and his skin smelled just as good, but both still held hints of fire and destruction. Charleston sniffed himself and found the stench of the fire hung horribly heavy on him, nearly making him cough, but he caught himself before he woke Barnaby.

When a shower was first mentioned, Charleston's mind went instantly to "naked Barnaby," and "naked, soapy Barnaby, standing under a spray of steaming hot water." Then he'd watched, pulse quickening, mouth going dry, as Barnaby began to strip on his way to the bathroom. But he was in there a long time, long enough for Charleston to eat his fill of sugary, fried dough… long enough for him to sit, waiting and painfully hard, while he periodically stared out the one-way window at the darkened parking lot in search of suspicious activity. And when Barnaby didn't return, he'd gone to check on him.

There was nothing sexy about the man he found in the shower, and his arousal had wilted beneath his concern. He chastised himself for not picking up on the signs of shock much earlier. Barnaby was overwhelmed, and considering all he'd been through, all he'd seen that night, it wasn't surprising. The cooling water hadn't helped the situation, so he'd known it was important to quickly get Barnaby dry and warm. But when Barnaby had unexpectedly kissed him, his desire came roaring back. However, he knew—his brain knew, anyway—that comfort and security were needed, not hot, sweaty sex.

Now, with Barnaby in his arms, Charleston thought he could lie like this forever. Unfortunately, there was work to be done, arrangements to be made, logistics to work out. He needed Barnaby safe and well, while he and any other random RPP personnel his father and Leaundra could cobble together went after the people behind the few deletions they knew about. Stopping and catching Senator Collard was on the tip-top of Charleston's list.

Therefore, when he was certain Barnaby was sound asleep, he began trying to work his shirt free from his fingers. But Barnaby had a good grip, even in his sleep, so Charleston eventually just slid out of the Marine sweatshirt, leaving the arm firmly in Barnaby's grasp, and went to take his shower. The water was boiling hot again, and he relished it, allowed it to beat the ache from his shoulders. When he lathered his hair, he was assaulted with the same faint, sweet fragrance that clung to Barnaby's hair and skin. He grew hard again.

Jesus!

Despite all the other things on his mind, he knew until he took care of his traitorous, selfish dick, his mind would be no good to him. He took himself in hand and began to stroke. He needed to take his time for it to be fully satisfying, needed to stroke slowly, squeeze at just the right moment, brush his thumb over the tip the way he hoped Barnaby someday would.

Barnaby. Yeah. Barnaby on his knees in front of me. His hair spilling through my fingers. His mouth—

When his head cleared, and he'd caught his breath, Charleston opened his eyes and waited for them to focus on the tiny pattern of the tile in front of him. *Okay, so much for taking my time*. He finished bathing, brushed his teeth with the implements the hotel stocked, and then put his and Barnaby's clothes (newly liberated sweatshirt included) in the washer-dryer combo in the alcove just outside the bathroom. Next, he set the room coffeemaker for 11:30 a.m. Their shirts, pants, socks, and briefs would be clean, dry, and horribly wrinkled in about an hour, and there would be fresh-brewed coffee waiting for them when they woke.

As he towel-dried his hair and body, he strolled back into the room and, after checking the voice-activated security lock on the door was secure, he plopped down on the other bed. With the corner of his bath towel, he carefully cleaned Barnaby's glasses, which had been left on the bathroom sink, and gently placed them on the nightstand. Then Charleston watched him sleep for a few moments, grinning at how badly Barnaby had twisted in bed and kicked off most of his covers.

The sun would be high in the sky soon, but he needed his sleep too. He placed his gun on the nightstand, within easy reach. With the room secured, and coffee and clean clothes on the way, Charleston crossed to the other bed, lifted back whatever covers were left, and slid up close and personal against Barnaby's warm body, their bare skin touching from top to toes.

Barnaby moaned in his sleep and turned into Charleston's arms, curling against him. Though his dick gave an interested lurch, Charleston talked it down and welcomed Barnaby, who fit perfectly against his chest, just under his chin.

He was smiling when he drifted off to sleep wrapped in a dream come true.

BARNABY WOKE too warm. He moved to throw the blanket off, but found it wasn't a blanket but an arm, a torso, a thigh, and *more*. The soft breath against his neck kept him from any panicked struggling... well, that and the hardness pressing against his hip. That had the opposite effect.

Charleston.

In his sleep, Charleston snuggled closer, tightening his arms around Barnaby and kissing the pulse point of his neck. Barnaby grinned and worried his bottom lip as he enjoyed the sensations Charleston sparked in him. He felt safe, warm, wanted and... horny, terribly horny and hard. His desperation wasn't the only thing growing.

"Chuck?" he said softly. "You wanna wake up... sweetie?"

"Mmhfm."

Barnaby shivered as Charleston began unconsciously nibbling his earlobe. He tried to lift a leg, but the man was too heavy. Pinned and unable to create any friction, unable to bring himself any closer to release, Barnaby growled in frustration, not because he wasn't enjoying Charleston's attention, but because he wanted him fully awake and aware if they continued with the morning's—he glanced at the sunshine pouring through the sheer curtains—afternoon's activities.

Barnaby closed his eyes as Charleston's scent filled his nose, as the heat from his body made him sweat. Charleston began to slowly grind against Barnaby's hip, and his hand slipped down to Barnaby's crotch.

Oh, yes! Right there. Barnaby lifted his hips as far as he could, eager to feel Charleston take hold of him.

Charleston's hand froze, his body stiffened, and his eyes shot open. "Barnaby?" Charleston jerked away from him and moved to the other side of the bed, nearly rolling off the side, and stared in shock. "I... I'm sorry... I d-didn't mean to...."

"*I* mean to," Barnaby said, immediately sliding over to Charleston and straddling him. He grabbed Charleston's shoulders and kissed him. It was his turn to be pinned, and Barnaby would do his best and take what he wanted, even though he knew the big man could probably toss him onto the other bed from where he was.

Barnaby explored Charleston's mouth with his tongue, ground against him, mangled his hair, and made his eager desperation crystal clear. There was so much skin and muscle to touch and lick and taste, Barnaby felt like he was going to fly apart. That is, until Charleston took hold of his arms and stilled him, staring up into his lust-drunk gaze. Barnaby tried to lean down and capture Charleston's mouth again, his puckered lips opening and closing like a fish, but he was suspended at arm's length as Charleston continued to look up at him.

"What?" Barnaby whined, trying to wiggle free and get closer.

"Are you certain?"

"Positive."

"You haven't seen me in seven years."

He blinked at Charleston, his mind struggling to make sense of what he was feeling and keep any vulnerability and exposure at bay.

"I've lov—*wanted* you for those seven years."

Suddenly he was on his back, and Charleston was above him with a hunger in his eyes that made Barnaby shiver partly from desire, partly in fear. He opened his arms to him, embraced him, accepted his kisses, his tongue, his grin against his lips. He welcomed Charleston's moaning, his eager, big hands, and imagined the bruises he'd find later on his body.

Dizzy with delight, Barnaby heard his name being whispered repeatedly as Charleston slowly worked his way down his body, as if he were a recently discovered treasure. His nipples hardened and rose to attention under Charleston's busy mouth. A nibble on the bottom of his ribcage, a kiss to his belly, a bite at his hipbone—Barnaby gasped and shuddered after each. Then those deep blue eyes looked into his as Charleston slid his mouth over the head of Barnaby's cock, teasing the slit with his tongue.

Barnaby jerked beneath him, the wet heat of Charleston's mouth, the suction, and his busy tongue driving him beyond coherence. But they continued watching each other as Charleston slowly swallowed more of Barnaby with each bob of his head. Barnaby thrust upward. His thighs quivered and flexed, and it was all he could do to keep his eyes open—to not lose sight of what Charleston was doing to him. He smiled, reached out, and gently stroked Charleston's hair, but when the man swallowed him completely and fingered his balls, Barnaby's eyes slammed shut, he yanked Charleston's blond mane, and came up off the bed, shooting down the man's throat.

Grinning, light-headed, and limp-limbed, Barnaby heard the side table drawer open and close, and then he felt Charleston's presence hovering over him and the gentle touch of a finger brushing the hair out of his eyes.

"Babe, you okay?" Charleston kissed his forehead.

He opened his eyes and smiled weakly up at him. "I'm fabulous," Barnaby drawled. His gaze flicked down to the lube in Charleston's hand (*this hotel really does provide everything*) and to his rigid cock. "You got something else for me?" He almost laughed out loud at the color rising to Charleston's face. "Give it to me, Chuck," he urged as he reached out and brushed his fingers down the man's abs. "Give it to me good."

CHAPTER 15

CHARLESTON GRINNED at Barnaby's eager encouragement and leaned in to kiss him gently. "Patience, baby." He opened the lube and drizzled some on his fingers and Barnaby's entrance.

"C-condoms?" Barnaby asked.

Charleston nodded toward the side table drawer. "We have them," he said as he worked the lube around Barnaby's hole, pressing in with his thumb. He smiled crookedly at Barnaby's gasp and at the tension filling the man's body and gripping his digit. "Haven't had the vaccine, but... haven't had a lover in more than a year, and a routine RPP test six months ago came back clean."

He said all this without looking Barnaby in the eye. He was mesmerized and clocking the quivering reactions taking place throughout Barnaby's body, just from this small bit of contact. Perhaps he was still sensitive after his orgasm only moments before. He watched as Barnaby's muscles jerked and jumped beneath his pale skin, watched as his mouth fell open and his eyes closed, watched as his chest rose and fell rapidly, and watched as he worked his bottom lip, frowning and then smiling through the ecstatic tension Charleston was building in him.

"I... I'd like to use a c-condom," Barnaby said, disrupting the flow of his lusty show by opening his eyes and meeting Charleston's soberly. "Just to be safe. I haven't had the vaccine either, and Ross is... he's a good guy, but he's...."

"Vain, shallow, self-absorbed—"

Barnaby grimaced and looked away briefly. "More so than not, yes, and he does like to party."

"Thank you for not mentioning how gorgeous he is."

"You're welcome. So... the condom?"

"Understood," Charleston said, leaning forward and delving deeply between Barnaby's lips with his tongue for a few moments. Then he removed a strip of condoms from the drawer, tore one free, and ripped the foil packet open with his teeth.

"Here," Barnaby said, "let me help you get dressed." He snatched the condom from Charleston's fingers, then gripped the hardness throbbing between his legs to roll it on. "There ya go." He patted the weeping cock, making it jerk. "Lovely."

Charleston laughed. "Are you done?"

"If you are."

Charleston grabbed Barnaby's legs and lifted them over his shoulders. "Not even close," he growled as he nearly bent him in half to enter him. Barnaby seemed relaxed enough, needy enough at this point, that thrusting into him as he did, Charleston suspected he wasn't hurting him. Despite that knowledge, however, when Barnaby tensed and winced, he froze, suddenly uncertain. But Barnaby's "What the fuck? Get going, Chuck!" snapped him back into action.

"Don't call me Chuck!" he said driving into him repeatedly until Barnaby keened, until a sheen of sweat appeared on both of them and reflected the muted sunshine spilling through the curtains. As he neared his finish, Charleston slowed, and Barnaby opened his eyes, glaring at him. *Bossy, boy.* But he didn't relent. Charleston slowly slid in and out of Barnaby, feeling each and every quiver and contraction of his body as it gripped him and tried to keep him inside.

"I've w-wanted this," Charleston ground out, "ever since that d-day in the b-bank." Barnaby couldn't speak, so he continued. "I wanted to kiss you that day."

Reaching out and clawing down Charleston's chest, Barnaby gasped, "Yes," before arching off the bed and spilling what cum he had left within him over his stomach. With the scent of Barnaby's spend filling his nose once again, Charleston came hard, his body and mind locking up, refusing to release him for several seconds.

Afterward, as they lay together panting, the sweat and cum cooling on their bodies, Barnaby asked, "Why didn't you?"

"Why didn't I what?"

"Kiss me."

He looked askance at Barnaby. "You were a kid, eighteen, nineteen years old."

"So? I was legal, and you wanted me." He held up Charleston's hand to examine, rubbing his thumb over the man's knuckles. "We wanted each other…. You should have taken me."

Laughing, Charleston stared up at the ceiling and let Barnaby continue his exploration of his hands, his fingers, his arm, his chest. He sighed. "I didn't know the depth of what I was feeling then, and even if I had known, it's not like I had a lot of time to get my point across."

Barnaby snorted and kissed his shoulder. "True. You vanished on me again."

"It varied, but each time step had a set amount of time built into it, because the longer we stayed, the more we risked affecting something we shouldn't. So we tried to allot just enough time to get the job done and no more."

"Yeah," Barnaby said, absently toying with one of Charleston's nipples, "it would be a bummer to return and find the world ruled by elephants, huh?"

Charleston's laughter filled the room. "Why elephants? Shouldn't it be apes?"

Barnaby shook his head and yawned as he tucked Charleston's hand between his and stared at them. Barnaby didn't seem to want to let go, to stop touching him. "No. I've always been partial to Babar. The elephants dress better, they never forget, and they live in matriarchal societies." Charleston smirked and turned in bed to watch Barnaby's mouth as he talked. "So you had time to save my life but not kiss me and promise me you'd be back?"

"I couldn't make that promise. And my reasons for eventually returning were shaky at best… actually forbidden by my father."

"You disobeyed your father because of me? I can see he and I will get along great."

"You will. He's helping me help you and the others Collard is after. He knows what you mean to me."

"What's he like?"

Charleston thought on that for a moment. "He's brilliant, stern, not the most demonstrative with his affection and… there's a bit of arrogance there, I guess."

"Lovely."

"Well, he imagined and built a time machine, Barnaby. I think he's earned a little 'how ya like me now' time."

Barnaby chuckled, and Charleston welcomed the tiny vibrations wracking the smaller man's body. He took hold of Barnaby's chin and tilted his head up to face him. "I disobeyed him because I just couldn't accept I'd saved you for a loveless marriage. I suppose that's when I realized I loved you."

THE NEXT time Barnaby woke, he was alone, not pinned to the bed or covered by a hulking mass of muscle. He heard Charleston talking nearby but couldn't quite make out the words. His voice was pitched low and urgent, almost a whisper. He rolled over, the chill of the room bringing goose bumps to his bare skin, and saw Charleston's shadow moving near the bathroom entrance. He was talking on the phone while gathering their clothing in the laundry alcove.

As Barnaby stretched, he heard and felt a number of joints popping, and he practically willed away a charley horse developing in his calf. Then he felt the ache deep within him from Charleston's earlier attentions. He smiled at the memory. *He loves me.* He closed his eyes and ran one hand down his bare front, while he tangled the other in his hair and scratched his scalp. When he opened his eyes, he discovered Charleston had disappeared into the bathroom. Then he heard the shower turn on.

He sat up on the bed and considered joining him, but before he could head that way, the room's phone beeped. He pressed the intercom button. "Yes?"

"Sorry to disturb you, sir, but we have a call for a Barnaby Rosenthal."

He glanced at the bathroom door, puzzled, and said, "Put it through, please."

"Yes, sir."

The phone beeped again. "Mr. Rosenthal." The voice oozing out of the speaker was female and deeply southern, with a grating edge to it.

"Yes. Who is this?"

"Sorry to bother you this afternoon, especially after your harrowing experiences last night."

"Again, who is this?"

"My name isn't important. What's important is I know where you are."

"A lot of people do. I'm not impressed."

The laughter from the speaker chilled Barnaby, and he glanced at the bathroom again.

"Really? Well, how many people, at this moment, know that your mother is preparing three hundred cupcakes for her church bake sale tomorrow? Or that your stepfather is getting ready for his home health care therapist to visit. Shame about his stroke, but I understand he's making quite the comeback."

Barnaby's heart skipped and then sped up. He began to sweat, and he once again looked to the bathroom, willing the door to open and Charleston to appear.

"He can't help you, Mr. Rosenthal."

Barnaby whipped back around to stare at the phone. "What?"

"Meeks. He can't help you."

He slid on his glasses, rose, and quickly crossed to the window where he pulled the curtain back slightly. No one could see through the one-way window, at least he didn't think anyone could. "How—"

"What happens next needs to be your decision, Barnaby. May I call you Barnaby?"

He turned and stared at the phone for a moment, then said, "If I may call you Penny."

The silence that followed brought a smile to Barnaby's face. *Didn't expect that, did ya?*

"I see Meeks has been speaking out of turn."

Barnaby walked back to the bed and dropped down on it. "Hardly. He wants me fully informed. Now… what decision do I need to make?"

"We'd like you to lose Mr. Meeks and meet my people in the Rose Garden in Hendricks Park."

"Not on your life, sistah."

"Listen to me, you fucking fa—"

"*Ah-ah.* It's 2020. There's no room for such offensive language in today's world, young lady. You should know better."

"I *do* know better. You weren't meant to be here. You are an abomination twice over, and God's plan doesn't involve—"

"You don't know shit about God's plan, you toxic bimbo, any better than I do." All Barnaby heard coming through the speaker now was sputtering, and his smile broadened. "And, as far as abominations go, you, ma'am, tried to kill a mother and her children last night! I think you should slap that label on yourself."

The sputtering stopped. Silence once again filled the room, and in that silence Barnaby heard the shower shut off.

"We'll speak again, Mr. Rosenthal."

The call ended just as Charleston reentered the room and stood at the foot of the bed, toweling his hair and gazing at Barnaby's naked form as rivulets of moisture slid down his own. "Hey," he said, with a wicked grin.

"Hey, yourself," Barnaby said before knee-walking toward him, kissing him, and then moving around him and off the bed. "My turn." He grabbed his clothes and rushed into the bathroom, saying over his shoulder, "I just got a call from the senator."

CHAPTER 16

BUSY CHECKING the rearview mirror for some pursuing, anonymous SUV, Charleston didn't speak to a sulking Barnaby until they took the exit for the airport. "Am I gonna get the silent treatment all the way to Kansas?" he asked.

Barnaby turned and fixed him with a withering glance. "You could have let me shower."

"No. You had just gotten a call from a senator who's trying to have you killed. She's a powerful woman, Barnaby. You didn't have time for a shower."

"Chuck, she knew where we were and she seemed even to know when you had left the room. If her people wanted to come in and get me, they would have."

"Don't call me Chuck."

Barnaby snorted as Charleston pulled in to the unloading zone where two airport security officers stood waiting. "It's still running," he shouted to one of them. "Turn it in for me, will ya?"

"Yes, sir." One officer got behind the wheel, while the other escorted them into the building, through security, and onto the plane.

"You have an hour layover in Los Angeles; then it's a straight shot to Wichita," the officer said as Charleston and Barnaby secured their seat belts in first class. "Have a good flight, sir."

"Thanks."

"Now that's customer service," Barnaby quipped.

"Pop's calling in a lot of favors. I'm sort of afraid of how few he has left."

"It was him you were talking to earlier, right?"

Charleston nodded and glanced around the first-class cabin, checking for any familiar or threatening faces.

"Well, what did he have to say?"

Charleston finally turned to look at Barnaby and recognized the concern in his eyes. "After we land in Wichita, we'll drive to Salina."

"To your facility?"

"Nope. I can't go there anymore. My time's up."

"Don't say that." Barnaby turned and looked out the window again. "It's not funny."

Charleston sighed, feeling guilty… for a lot of things. Once again Barnaby's life had been turned upside down, and he was busy trying to right it. The last thing he wanted to do was drag a struggling, naked, wet Barnaby out of the shower—he would have preferred to drag him back to bed—but the most important thing on the agenda was keeping the man alive. That had to happen. Charleston wouldn't accept anything less. *All I wanted to do was ask the guy out, take him to dinner… woo him, but once again we're tied up with life and death.*

"I'm sorry. Bad joke." He paused, waiting for Barnaby to show some sign of acquiescence, but it didn't happen. "My parents have a ranch there."

Barnaby appeared to absorb this as he worried his bottom lip, then said, "You know, I've tried to stay calm about all this, be at ease, especially when talking to that Collard bitch on the phone, but I think I'm out of energy and can't pretend anymore." Charleston waited, watching Barnaby alternate between gripping his armrest and tugging on his dark curls. "What about my parents? That freak made a point to let me know she knew where to get her hands on them."

"Since Collard seems to be focused on you, we have people ready to step in if something starts to go down with your folks." Barnaby shifted in his seat, and Charleston watched him warily. "What are your parents like?"

"Don't you know? Don't you have loads of background on me?"

He blushed and admitted, "Well, your mother's name is Rowena Gilbert, formerly Rosenthal, and she looks remarkably like a young Anne Bancroft."

"Huh?"

"Trust me on that," Charleston said, fixing him with a stare. "Your father, Albert, was killed in Afghanistan when you were ten or so.

Sometime later, your mother met and married Donald Gilbert. They had a baby boy and named him Nelson. Am I right so far?"

Barnaby nodded, not saying anything.

"So, what was your father like?"

"What I remember of him—he was great. Probably more huggy than your dad, but he could be stern too. I loved and respected him more than I feared him."

"I get that."

"Donald was great too. I lucked out. He loved me like his own and worked to help me be a good man. He never really understood my interest in art, but he knew I thrived on it, so he supported me with it."

"What about...."

"The gay?"

Charleston laughed and nodded.

"He and Mom figured it out and suspected long before I did that I wouldn't be settling down with a nice girl and having a bushel of Ohio Valley babies." Barnaby grew quiet, frowning. "I sometimes think I broke my mama's heart when I called off the wedding." He sighed. "She got closer to that moment with me than she had thought possible, so to have it snatched away sort of stung. She got it into her head that if I just *tried* a tiny bit harder...."

"Sorry."

"No worries. She loves me, but... it's strained between us right now."

"Once this is over, maybe you can spend some quality time with her, mend some fences."

"Yeah." Barnaby didn't sound convinced.

"Are *we* good?"

Barnaby sighed and rolled his eyes. "For the moment... yeah, we're good, Chuck."

Charleston snickered and tried to relax as the announcements came over the intercom and the plane began to back away from the gate and roll into takeoff position. "We should try to sleep while we can," he said as he covered Barnaby's hand with his and closed his eyes. Barnaby didn't pull free, and Charleston was relieved. Maybe they *were* good.

Sen. Penelope Delnoit Collard activated her secure link, and as she waited for the call to connect, she gently drummed her manicured fuchsia fingernails on her desk.

"Kaan here."

"Where are you?" she demanded.

"On our way to the airport... as instructed."

"I detect a note of disapproval in your voice, Ms. Kaan. Do you think attempting to grab Rosenthal from his hotel room in broad daylight would have been the smarter choice?"

"No, ma'am, but what did you say to him?"

"Why do you ask?"

"The big guy carried Rosenthal out over his shoulder, and they tore out of there like their asses were on fire."

"I'm sure their asses were, the heathens."

She heard a sickly chuckle from Kaan's partner, Katch, over the open line.

"As for our conversation, I told him it would be better for everyone he holds dear if he were to make himself available to me." It was a currently empty threat, she knew, but if it became necessary, she had a number of people to choose from who would get Rosenthal's attention by grabbing a loved one. *Maybe that little brother of his. He should be simple enough to lay hands on.*

"And?"

Collard considered her response, then said, "He's oddly flippant about the situation." She grimaced at her understatement and didn't share with them just how easily and quickly the artist had angered her. However, she was back in control now. Fully.

"I've noticed," Kaan said.

Katch snorted, covering it too late.

"Is something amusing, Mr. Katch?" Collard asked.

"No, ma'am. Sorry, ma'am."

She allowed the silence to stretch as she fingered the edge of a silver picture frame on her desk. The picture was of her son Terry at age fifteen.

"Ma'am?" Kaan prodded. "You still there?"

"According to my information, they're on a commercial flight out of Eugene to Wichita," the senator explained. "Your chartered flight will get you there ahead of them, and a car will be waiting for you when you land."

"We'll take him in the airport. You still want him alive?" Kaan asked. "We could easily—"

"Even Ramirez failed to erase the Lazarus woman and her spawn, and *he's* a psychopath. Easily? Nothing is turning out *easy* about this."

"It is normally less complicated to kill than to capture."

"I want him alive and… not too badly harmed. I want to look in his eyes before he dies. Explain why it's necessary." No one spoke for several seconds, and then Collard said, "Understood?"

"Yes, ma'am. What about his 'hero'?"

Collard didn't say anything as she pondered the fate of Dr. Meeks's son.

"You know who he is, don't you?" Kaan asked.

"If he gets in the way, kill him." She ended the call and slowly spun in her chair, her gaze examining the plush beauty of her study. She continued to turn until she faced the study window and looked out over her expansive backyard.

She gazed at the abundant greenery of her property in Austin, Texas. Her apartment in DC was also rather plush, but she didn't have this much space. This had been left to her by her father, Palmer T. Delnoit, a veteran of two wars, an evangelical preacher, and a senator in his own right. But what most people didn't know about the man was that, for a time, he had also been a covert operative and privy to a network of shady characters and security personnel from all over the world who would do whatever job was asked of them for the right price.

Penny had learned at his knee how to protect herself and how to work any system to that end. That's how she'd found Katch and Kaan, who had been very useful in the past. But this assignment, this collecting of Barnaby Rosenthal, was proving to be more difficult than she'd expected. Before Meeks had entered the picture, the erasing of previously restored subjects had been a breeze compared to this one boy, this boy who shouldn't exist. *But I'm not just asking them to erase him.* She briefly considered calling them back and telling them not to worry about bringing Rosenthal in and just to kill him. Then she dismissed that idea.

She turned back to examine the photo of her son. She picked it up and held it to her chest for a moment before looking into his bright green eyes, his smiling dimpled face, so full of life and energy and joy. She had tried to do her best by him, had tried to make him the man he was meant to be, a man his grandfather would have been proud of.

Identifying his wasted, broken body at the morgue so long ago had practically sucked the life from her chest, but then she reminded herself that this was God's will, part of His plan for her... no matter how much it hurt.

Then, years later, when she'd heard of the Restore Point Program, heard that some crazed scientist was mucking about with that plan by restoring people to their lives after God had removed them? Oh no. She couldn't have that. Her broken heart had quickly swelled with rage. If her boy was meant to return home to his heavenly father, then surely, so were those people.

And the worst insult? This Rosenthal, this filthy sodomite, was restored a number of times! She hadn't been able to block Dr. Meeks's little experiment at the time. She had come to be on the panel too late, and the other committee members had outvoted her. They were curious, just as Meeks had been. The fools! Now, after a number of years, she had enough dirt on each of them to swing any vote she wanted. The Restore Point Program was done, and soon all the restorations they'd accomplished would be erased too.

Collard replaced her son's photo on the desk, positioning it just right. The more modestly framed photo next to it was of Stanley, her late husband of thirty years, his insipid, chinless face staring out at her dimly. Equally heartbroken after their son's death, Stanley had fallen into depressive episodes. After the last episode, he'd had questions about some of her activities, expressing curiosity about the people she met with and the mysterious phone calls she took late at night.

Arranging his car accident last year had been the right decision and, as it happened, an excellent test run for Katch and Kaan.

She activated the slideshow function on Terry's frame, and a number of images of the boy were projected before her in holographic form. They dissolved from one image to the next: Terry playing basketball, headed to his first dance, an usher at Grace Will Baptist. As the images faded in and out, a recording of Terry's voice repeated, "I love you, Mama."

"It's all right, darling. Mama will put everything to rights."

CHAPTER 17

BARNABY GAZED at Charleston's face in slumber as his chest rose and fell gently, noting the faint lines around his eyes had vanished altogether. He marveled at his rumpled good looks and that he didn't toss and turn in his sleep, not even on a plane hurtling through the sky. He turned to look out the window at the clouds and wondered what awaited him in Kansas. How long had he hoped Charleston would reappear?

Well, ta-da! Barnaby's life had descended into chaos. Was that an improvement over the years, months, weeks, days, and hours of less than? Wasn't his current situation better than killing time with Ross and the others preceding him or drinking himself into a stupor? He turned back to Charleston and smiled. *Here he is*. He covered Charleston's hand with his own again, remembering how strong it had felt gripping him as they rolled around in bed together. Barnaby grinned sweetly, lost to those memories.

"May I get you something to drink?" a flight attendant asked softly.

"Uh… no. Thank you. But could I have a blanket for him?"

"Of course. Just a moment."

"Thank you." After the attendant had delivered the blanket and he had spread it over Charleston, Barnaby leaned forward, removed the phone handset from the wall in front of his seat, and quickly dialed. It rang nearly five times before his mother picked up.

"Hey, Mama."

"Barnaby? Is everything all right?"

He smiled weakly because that was "mom-speak" for "why haven't you called sooner" or "you only call when something's wrong," which, in this case was true, but he wasn't about to tell her that. "Everything's fine, Mama. Just missing you guys."

He could hear she was busy with something… *cupcakes*? "Well, we're all still living in the same place. Haven't moved into a new house or anything."

"Mama—"

"Here, talk to your brother. I have to get this next batch out of the oven before they burn."

The phone was passed, and Barnaby smiled when Nelson said, "Hello?"

"Hey, little man. It's Barnaby."

"B!" The delight in Nelson's voice warmed him to the core, though he suspected his mother was nearby wishing Nelson had asked, *Barnaby who?* "Where are you?" Nelson continued. He wasn't one of those sullen, jaded teenagers. He was still open and eager to experience and learn. Barnaby hoped that positive energy would last, hoped it wouldn't be oppressed out of him.

"I'm on a plane, but I wanted to let you know I'll be coming to see you all soon. You, Mom, and Dad."

"When?"

"I'm not sure because I have something I have to take care of first, but I'm definitely coming for a visit."

"Are you bringing someone with you?" his mother asked, cutting in on another line.

"Did you get your cupcakes out of the oven?" Barnaby said with snark.

"How did you know I was making cupcakes?"

He faltered but quickly added, "You said you had to get the batch out of the oven. What else could it be?" That seemed to satisfy her. It wasn't like he could say, *a homicidal senator told me you were baking them during a threatening phone call.* "And I may be bringing someone, yes."

"Is it that Ross person?" He smirked at the chill in her voice. *Don't hide your feelings, Mama.*

"No, Mama. It's… someone new." *And change the subject.* "How's Donald?"

"He's doing really well," she said, her voice brightening. "Working hard, building his strength. He's even lost some weight." She sighed. "He's almost back to the man who caught my eye all those years ago."

"Mama, that's great to hear. Give him a hug for me, and I'll see you soon."

"I'd like to hear more about this new… um…."

"Man, Mama. It's a man."

"Yes, well…."

He laughed. "Nelson? You still there?"

"Uh-huh."

"Love you, buddy."

"Love you, B. Bye."

"Be careful on your trip, dear. Love you."

"I will. Love you, Mama."

Barnaby took several deep breaths before he dialed Ross's cell, thinking he was probably in the middle of his L.A. photo shoot. He'd been nervous calling his mother, but he knew Ross was more dramatic than passive-aggressive, so he prepared himself.

"Rossom."

"It's me," Barnaby said firmly, steeling himself for the conversation.

"Where the fuck are you!"

"Ross, calm down, please."

"Calm down? Are you out of your fucking mind! Someone kidnaps you at gunpoint, and that phantom from your paintings shows up? And I'm supposed to calm down?"

"I called Coral—"

"And told her jack shit!"

Barnaby didn't contradict that, and they were both silent for several moments. Finally, Barnaby asked, "What do you want to know?"

"Are you with *him*?"

"Yes."

"Barnaby—"

"He saved my life, Ross… again."

"Please don't start that—"

"I wasn't hallucinating. I never lied. What I told you was true, all those times I'd seen him, but I stopped mentioning it because it clearly made everyone uncomfortable." He took a deep breath, lowered his voice, and rushed on. "But now you know he's real. He always was, and I'm with him."

"Are you *staying* with him?"

Barnaby didn't answer right away but instead stared at Charleston's peaceful face. "There are some things we need to work on together, but... I'm staying with him for as long as he'll have me."

"Barnaby, where—"

"Please tell Coral and India I'm fine. I'm safe, but I don't know when I'll be in touch again."

"What if your parents call? Have you talked to them?"

"I just spoke with Mama. And *do not* call her, Ross. You're not her favorite person."

"Don't be ridiculous. I'm everyone's favorite person."

Barnaby snorted. "Take care of yourself."

"Barn—"

He hung up, replaced the handset, and relaxed into his seat. After that abbreviated chat, he could imagine the explosion that was Rossom Bailey unleashing itself upon the unsuspecting minions at the photo shoot. If Ross had hoped they could work things out, that phone call had ended those ideas.

"How is he?" Charleston asked, startling him.

"Hey, sleepyhead."

Charleston stretched and yawned. "Hey, yourself. How's Ross?"

"Probably destroying camera equipment right now, but for the most part, he's pissed at me. Maybe...."

"Maybe what?"

"Maybe a little jealous?" Barnaby suggested, lifting an eyebrow.

"I know the feeling."

"When have you had time to be jealous of anyone?"

"When my friend Jeri filled me in on you and Ross. I can't say I was very confident you'd bother with me when I *did* manage to catch up to you."

"Charleston, I've been waiting and wishing for you longer than I can remember."

That seemed to silence Charleston and give him pause. "Ross still wants you."

"Of course, he does," Barnaby said with a smirk. "Look at me." They laughed together, and then Charleston surprised him with a kiss. "But honestly, even though he agreed to the breakup, a lover walking away is a new experience for him. It'll take Ross a while to acclimate."

Charleston's blue gaze searched Barnaby's face. "Did you get any sleep?"

"Couldn't." Barnaby leaned in for another kiss. "How about joining me in the restroom?"

Charleston glanced at the tiny bathroom door. "I doubt there's enough room in there for what I'd like to do to you. How about, when we get to Salina, I help you finish that shower you started at the hotel?"

"Deal," Barnaby said, grinning wickedly as he rested his hand on Charleston's thigh. "I still smell like sex."

"Mmm… yum," Charleston said before kissing Barnaby's neck, making him squirm and giggle.

The plane landed sometime later, and the two of them disembarked and threaded their way through the crowd toward the car rental kiosk. As Charleston and their agent worked to fill out the registration on a kiosk tablet, Barnaby leaned back against the counter, his elbows propped on it, hands dangling, the picture of ease.

On his left, another rental agent finished up with a man and woman, who were also trying to wrangle their luggage and three overstimulated children. The family left just as Charleston neared the end of his transaction.

"Thank you, sir. Please place your print on the touchscreen." Charleston did, and after a faint beep, the agent asked, "Is there anyone else you'd like to have access to the vehicle?" She glanced at the back of Barnaby's head as he watched the comings and goings of the travelers flowing by them. "There's only a small fee, and he would also be able to unlock and start the car."

"Give me your hand," Charleston said, turning to Barnaby.

"In marriage?"

The agent giggled quietly and blushed, but Barnaby turned and pressed his thumb against the screen as well.

"Very well. I now pronounce you cooperators of a 2021 Ford/Beemer Lux. Enjoy," the agent announced cheerily. "We only had the two available, and you've snagged the other." She transferred the documentation to Charleston's phone and said, "Slot 12C, sirs. Just take the hallway on your left to the parking lot behind the building. Have a nice day, and thank you for renting with Lisnoble."

They headed down a hallway, the noise around them dropping in volume dramatically as they walked farther from the crowds. One of the children from the vacationing family tried to dash past them back toward the airport, but his father caught him and carried him screaming to the parking lot. He gave them an apologetic smile as he went.

"Lux," Barnaby mused as he trailed after Charleston, his gaze riveted on his ass. He smiled to himself. "Sounds chichi."

Charleston didn't turn but kept walking out the parking lot door. "It's got pickup and maneuverability. That's what we need right now."

"How do you plan to shut down Collard?"

"We need to establish a link between her and her goons. It'll probably be a money trail from her right-wing organization to some shady mercs-for-hire website, but we'll work all that out once we reach—Ungh!"

Barnaby watched in horror as Charleston crumpled to the ground in front of him. Katch followed his initial kidney punch with a swift kick to Charleston's middle, stealing the man's breath. As he went in for another strike, Barnaby broke the hold fear had on him and delivered his own kick to Katch's middle, knocking him backward into a metal awning support. Katch's head bounced off it, and he appeared dazed for a moment.

Barnaby knelt to help Charleston to his feet. "Come on, Chuck. Let's go. Now!" he shouted, tugging on Charleston's arm.

"You go! Get in the car and drive, babe!" Charleston stood and staggered a bit.

"I'm not losing sight of you again!"

"Aww, aren't you two the sweetest thing?" Katch teased as he drew his gun, but Charleston launched a kick that disarmed him neatly, depositing the gun at Barnaby's feet. He picked it up because even though he couldn't fire it, he didn't want Katch getting hold of it again.

Charleston pulled his weapon, but before he could take aim, Katch growled and charged him, wrapping his arms around Charleston's middle, lifting him off his feet, and slamming him into the wall behind them. After catching his breath, Charleston kneed Katch in the balls, and once he'd doubled over, he grabbed the back of Katch's neck.

"Hope the senator offers dental," he said, ramming his knee into Katch's mouth and then letting the man drop to the ground like a crash dummy.

A bullet pinged off the metal support beam on Barnaby's right, and he and Charleston turned to see Kaan jumping from the only other 2021 Ford/Beemer Lux the rental agency had and running toward them, her gun raised. *That's oddly familiar*, Barnaby thought as he dropped to the ground, wrapped Katch's hand around his gun, and returned fire along with Charleston. Kaan dove for cover, while Barnaby marveled that the two hours they'd spent on quick thinking in crisis situations during his self-defense course had actually produced results.

"Go! Get the car!" Charleston shouted, and Barnaby went, shouting *12C, 12C, 12C* in his head. He raced through the rows of cars blindly at first but quickly calmed and began paying attention to his location. C was the next row on his right. He stayed low and skirted along the backs of the vehicles until he came to slot 12.

Across the row and down several slots was the family. The kids and husband were secure in a family van, but the mother was hunched down talking urgently on her cell phone. Barnaby gave her a thumbs-up as the shooting continued. He pressed his thumb to the hatchback lock. It opened with a hiss, and he scrambled in and shut it behind him before climbing over the seats to get behind the wheel.

He adjusted the seat forward—the mirrors adjusted automatically— started the car and threw it in reverse. *Lux, indeed*, he thought. "Navigation."

The GPS activated with a gentle *ding* as he tore down a row of cars, heading back to Charleston. "*State destination, please*," a woman's voice intoned calmly, completely at odds with his racing heart and the sound of approaching sirens.

"Salina, Kansas."

"*Mapping*."

The wheels of the car squealed as he took a corner a bit too sharply and came to a rocking stop right in front of the door he and Charleston had exited moments before, the doorway where Charleston sat huddled. Barnaby unlocked and shoved open the passenger door as Charleston jumped up, stood tall, and fired in Kaan's direction.

Charleston scrambled through the door and closed it as Barnaby hit reverse again at full speed. "Buckle up, Chuck," he ordered. He could see

Kaan crouching next to a groggy Katch and urging him to get to his feet. When Barnaby reached the end of the building, he whipped the wheel to the right, threw it into drive, and headed for the lot exit.

"Continue forward two hundred yards, then head north on South Tyler Road."

Barnaby glanced at Charleston and saw he was frantically trying to secure his seat belt. "That was quick thinking with Katch's gun," Charleston said.

"Thanks, Chuck."

"Listen—"

"I know. I know. Don't call you Chuck."

Charleston was silent until Barnaby looked at him with a question in his eyes. "Oh, *you* can call me anything you like, baby." He smiled and gave Barnaby a quick peck on the lips.

"Turn right onto West Kellogg Drive."

"Our other GPS sounded better," Barnaby said as he tried to refocus on the road ahead. "See if you can find Sexy, Deep-Voice Guy on that thing, will you?"

"I'm on it."

CHAPTER 18

CHARLESTON COULDN'T stop himself from glancing in the rearview mirror and over his shoulder. He expected Katch and Kaan to be hot on their asses. He grabbed his phone and speed-dialed his father.

"Meeks."

"Same here."

"Junior. Where are you? Do you have Rosenthal?"

"Yeah, Pop." Charleston could hear his mother in the background, agitated and throwing questions at his father. "Tell Mom I'm fine and so is Barnaby."

"Hello, Dr. Meeks," Barnaby shouted without taking his eyes from the road.

"Listen, don't put me on speaker, Pop." Charleston heard the background noise decrease as if his father had moved into a smaller room to be alone.

"Where are you, son?"

"We're on I-235 North, headed your way, but…." He noticed Barnaby frowning at the rearview mirror and looked over his shoulder again. In the distance, beyond the other traffic, he saw a dark vehicle much like their own approaching. "We might have company coming up fast. We were ambushed at the car rental lot."

"I'll get Leaundra and her team on their way to you."

"Thanks, Pop." He looked at the overview map in the console. "We'll be on I-135 North in a few minutes and then near Newton thirty or so minutes after that." He ended the call and looked at Barnaby. "Trade seats with me."

"Are you out of your mind? I'm not pulling over now!"

"Don't pull over, just trade." Their seat belts popped open with one command, and despite his dubious expression, Barnaby adjusted his seat back, ordered the car in cruise, and lifted himself so Charleston could slide beneath him, all while keeping his hands on the wheel. Charleston gripped Barnaby's hips and dropped into the seat with him in his lap. "Mmm, I'd love to keep you right where you are, but we're likely to get pulled over or crash."

Barnaby laughed as he slid over to the passenger seat and immediately secured his seat belt. Charleston locked his in place too, shut off the cruise, and gunned it. He rode one guy's bumper until he saw his pissy brake lights one too many times. *Prick!* He whipped around the guy, continued on, and took stock of the traffic. It wasn't exactly rush hour, but there were a few vehicles in sight. He spotted a semi far behind them but coming up fast in the passing lane and wondered if he could use it to shake their pursuers.

"Did they find us because of my phone calls from the plane or us renting this thing?"

"No," Charleston explained. "They were there ahead of us, waiting on us. We've got a mole somewhere."

"There are other cars out here. They wouldn't try anything with witnesses, would they?" Barnaby asked as he peered over the back of his seat again.

"Take exit 16B. Merge onto I-135 North. Continue north for 86.5 miles," Sexy, Deep-Voice Guy intoned calmly.

"At this point there's no telling. It might not even be them." He glanced at Barnaby and grinned. "I might have shot out one of their tires. But if it is them, they're probably a bit frustrated with us—"

"Ya think?"

"—sort of the way cops feel when they finally catch a guy after a high-speed chase."

"Ouch."

"Right. I'd rather they simply not catch us."

Barnaby nodded. "Agreed."

"Leaundra's on her way to us with some backup, but she's a while away."

Barnaby checked the back window again. "They don't seem to be gaining at the moment." He turned back around. "So that's something."

Yeah... something.

They rode in silence for several miles, but Charleston's constant checking of the mirrors seemed to annoy Barnaby enough to make him speak up. "What? You look like you're up to—"

"No good?"

Barnaby smiled. "Possibly. Why don't you let me in on it, and I'll decide?"

"See that semi back there?"

Barnaby glanced out the back window. "Yep. What of it?"

"It's been steadily gaining on us, and when it passes, I'm going to pull right in behind it."

"When you say 'right in behind it' you mean what, exactly?"

"Just that."

"Drafting?"

"Yeah, we'll make better time."

"That's a myth. Saw it on an old episode of *Mythbusters*."

Charleston frowned. "That was about gas mileage. This is speed, and it works for racecars."

"You're going to follow *that* closely?"

Charleston did a double take. "You've watched racing?"

Barnaby shrugged. "You meet a wider variety of people than you'd think in the art world. The wife of some racing champion bought one of my bio-generated pieces a year or two ago and suggested me and my boyfriend at the time might enjoy a day at the track."

"Did you?"

"Blake did—that was his name, Blake. He's a librarian and a bit sheltered, so all those sweaty men and racing engines were a bit overwhelming for him. I caught him in the staging area locking lips with a member of said champion's pit crew."

"Ouch."

"Meh."

"What's that supposed to mean?"

Charleston glanced in the rearview and saw the semi was almost on them, and Barnaby copied him with a look over his shoulder.

"It wasn't love, Chuck. The best part about the day, though, was when one of the lady racers took me for a spin. *That* was mind-blowing."

"Wait... a 'spin'?"

Barnaby snorted. "Around the track, you jackass."

Charleston felt his face heat but quickly checked the mirror again. "How fast did you go?"

"I think we topped out at one hundred and fifty."

"We won't be going quite that fast, I'm afraid." As the semi came abreast of them, Charleston glanced in the rearview to see they were alone on the road save for the tractor-trailer and their possible pursuers on the horizon. "Here we go, babe."

Barnaby squeezed his thigh and said, "I love it when you call me b—"

The semi's horn sounded, and the cab slammed into their SUV before Charleston could register what was happening. They careened sharply to the right and off the road as he fought to regain control of the car. While Charleston's breath froze in his chest, Barnaby let loose with a string of profanity to set his hair on fire, but he was silenced when the car took to the air and flipped and rolled... and kept rolling.

Charleston smelled the smoke before he saw it. The car had landed upside down, and he was hanging, suspended from his seat. His first thought was of Barnaby. He turned, trying to orient himself, and saw Barnaby suspended similarly next to him, but he was unconscious, his brown locks hanging to the SUV's roof, where his broken glasses rested.

"Barn.... B-Barnaby," he croaked, then coughed in the thickening smoke. He reached out for him and snagged his wrist, praying there would be a pulse. He closed his eyes, blew the air from his lungs, and concentrated on finding it. *There! There it is. Okay. Just knocked out.* He found himself breathing easier despite the acrid cloud in the car.

Next Charleston tried to work himself free of his seat belt, but as he located the release, he heard footsteps approaching slowly—definitely not the sound of someone rushing to their aid. He quit his fumbling with the belt and went immediately for his sidearm, but the safety belt prevented him from sliding it free. He peered out the window and noticed the semi parked on the side of the road just as a pair of butt-ugly snakeskin boots appeared by his shattered window.

"Uh... a little help here?" Charleston said weakly.

The owner of the boots squatted and looked in the window. "Sorry 'bout gettin' a bit rough back there, but you have somethin' my boss wants," the man drawled as he gazed in at him. The guy was big, really big, at least six three or more. His buzz cut was white as snow, and his heavily tanned face looked about ready to crack if it saw even another moment of sun. "Name's Ramirez," the man said, slowly looking him up and down with calculating, ice blue eyes.

"Nice to meet you?" Charleston managed.

"Not usually." Ramirez stood and strolled around the front of the car to the passenger side. "Got some gas leakin' out here. Hope it don't explode."

Ramirez wrenched the door open, giving it a couple of solid kicks to widen the opening. The onboard system hissed and crackled, the screen blinking to life.

Collision de… contacting emer… personnel, Sexy Deep-Voice Guy said between blasts of hissing static. The screen went dark and flashed to life again. *Plea… try… ay calm… re… where you are.*

Meanwhile, Ramirez produced a Bowie knife so impressive, the sight of it made Charleston's testicles try to climb inside his body. He began to struggle anew with his seat belt.

"Don't touch him!" he shouted.

"Now, now, little buddy," Ramirez said, pointing the shiny knife tip at him, "I'm not gonna hurt the boy. Just givin' him a lift to the boss." The man leaned in and paused before taking his knife to Barnaby's seat belt. "Why, he's right pretty, ain't he?" Charleston's gut clenched with nausea as Ramirez gently ran the knife tip along Barnaby's cheek. "Though this bruise on the side of his head looks worrisome." He sliced through the belt like it was butter, and Barnaby crumpled to the roof of the car. "Come on, sugar," Ramirez said as he dragged his unconscious, limp form free of the wreckage.

Not a single car had passed by the scene in the past ten minutes, even though it felt more like he'd been hanging upside down like this for an hour. The smoke was choking him, making him see spots, but he could see well enough to watch Ramirez pause to light a cigarette before hefting Barnaby over his shoulder.

He tracked the man's boots as he walked back by the spider-webbed front window, sweet as you please, not a care in the world. Charleston tried to memorize everything he could about the semi. The extended cab was bright blue, the trailer a nondescript silver, the tires expensive. No other identifying markings. *Fuck!* His head was beginning to pound as the blood pooled in his skull, and he was afraid he'd black out. He had to stay awake, get free, save Barnaby. How often had he focused on that thought? *Save Barnaby*. Charleston felt himself slipping away, but then he noticed Ramirez had paused again by his side of the car. The man was far enough away that Charleston could read his face. Ramirez was smiling as he took a long, slow draw from his cigarette.

"So long, sonny," he said and flicked the cancer stick at the SUV.

"WHAT DOES she mean head back?" Katch mumbled, his mouth once again bleeding.

At this point, Kaan figured her partner should just get a completely new set of teeth. There was no saving what he had left. "She said Rosenthal was secured by Ramirez, and we're to stand down."

"So we're just giving up?" Katch asked through his latest cold pack.

Kaan sighed.

"Fuck that!" Katch spat. "I want that fucker dead!"

"Agreed."

"How did Ramirez get to them before us?"

Kaan thought about that. That lunatic had to have been put on the job before they boarded their flight. Katch opened his ruined mouth to speak again, but an explosion in the distance suddenly marred the horizon. Kaan could see it was off the road and about ten miles ahead of them.

After spending precious time avoiding the authorities at the airport, the two of them had waited in ambush for the right target to stroll their way. Katch was a bloody mess, so he remained out of sight as Kaan approached a harried-looking businessman at the side of his newly secured SUV. Kaan was a handsome woman—if her voice hadn't been so deep and damaged, she might have attempted a seduction.

But as it was, she simply walked up, pressed her silenced gun into his side, and said, "I'm going to need this car." He was startled, incredulous, even amused for a moment, but she clarified by producing a switchblade. "Start her up for me or lose a thumb." He quickly started the car.

Katch skulked over and slid into the passenger seat. "He's seen us," he mumbled.

Kaan had fixed her eyes on their target and pouted apologetically. "He's right, you know." She shot the man through the heart and deposited his body beneath a neighboring vehicle, where she then removed his thumb and wrapped it in a handkerchief. "Just in case," she told Katch, patting her jacket pocket before pulling out of the parking space to give chase. But judging by the call from the senator and that explosion up ahead, they were definitely too late to the party.

"What do you suppose that was?" Katch asked.

Ramirez, Kaan thought, and her gut tightened with something she would never admit was fear.

AS THE helicopter made a beeline for the site of the black smoke rising into the sky, the rotors were deafening, and Leaundra found herself shouting into her mic as she briefed Dr. Meeks on the situation. She didn't sugarcoat her suspicions about what they were looking at.

"Oh dear," Dr. Meeks fretted, sounding nothing like the pompous ass he normally was.

"We're on our way, sir," she shouted. "Five minutes, tops."

"My son is the priority, Leaundra. I do hope Rosenthal is okay, but Junior is our main concern."

"Understood, sir." She ended the call, told the pilot to pick it up, and tried to keep her own concerns about Charleston at bay. *I knew this was a bad idea, kid.*

CHAPTER 19

CHARLESTON OPENED his eyes and saw puffy white clouds floating across a blue sky above him. He was on his back in a field of tall grass and, until he detected the odor of destruction on the breeze, he thought he might be in heaven. Then a pinched, weak-chinned face entered his vision.

"You all right there, fella?"

All he could do was cough in response. His head hurt, his chest, shoulder, neck, skin... hell, everything hurt, but he guessed that's what rolling a car would do to a man. *Barnaby*! He tried to sit up but was held down by his Samaritan.

The guy glanced over his shoulder at the smoldering wreckage, then back at Charleston. "I was afraid something like this would happen with the way you were riding my bumper earlier."

Charleston tried to reconstruct events in his mind. He remembered the semi and Ramirez. The big, ugly motherfucker had taken Barnaby, and as he was walking away, he'd tossed a—"Shit!" He struggled to get up again and was held down again. He didn't seem to have the strength to fight his rescuer off.

"Take it easy, fella. Help's on the way. I think your car, or what's left of it, called for help."

Charleston remembered a whooshing sound as the fuel caught fire, followed by intense heat. He knew he was dead and that Barnaby was lost to him. He'd started to struggle for all he was worth, to shout in fury and bang the dash with his fist.... Then the computer had flickered to life again, hissing and crackling. Charleston shouted, "Release safety belt!" and it did, dropping him to the roof where he scrambled out Barnaby's door seconds before the car blew. He'd felt the impact, then woke to a beautiful sky and toxic smoke in the air, with Pissy-Brake-Light Guy leaning over him.

Speaking of which… he watched the guy's eyes go wide and then narrow against a sudden strong wind, his hand lifting to shield his face. "Wow, that's some onboard service you got there, mister."

Charleston heard the unmistakable *thump thump thump* of rotors, and the grass around them flattened in the wind, looking almost like water as it undulated beneath the onslaught. He wished he could sit up and see what was happening, but he was too weak, achy, and sleepy. Then Leaundra's beautiful, yet stern face was hovering over him. As he was lifted and moved to a stretcher, he managed to grab her uniform sleeve and jerk her to him. He groaned Barnaby's name above the whine of the powered-down helicopter. "Blue semi. Ramirez. Sick fuck." Her eyes locked on his. She nodded, and Charleston passed out.

KATCH AND Kaan studied as much of the scene as they could while driving slowly by the wreckage. A cop ahead of them directed traffic around emergency crews in the right-hand lane.

"That SUV is toast," Katch said after they'd passed the scene. "Survivors?"

"Maybe. An EMT climbed into the copter before it took off."

"Medical examiner was there."

Kaan shrugged.

"I bet it's Hero Boy," Katch said, turning to Kaan. "It has to be him, right? If Rosenthal is secure and on his way like Collard said, then"—he glanced in his side mirror with longing as the crash scene grew more distant—"it has to be Hero Boy who's dead or dying." He smiled wickedly, and Kaan shook her head. She was more interested in why the senator hadn't told them to expect Hero Boy, hadn't explained who the guy was or how much trouble he could be. Collard knew. She was sure of that, and Kaan resented being kept in the dark about a detail that big.

The senator had obviously called in Ramirez, because, lunatic though he may be, he wouldn't go against orders… at least Kaan didn't think he would. If he'd taken it upon himself to butt in and snatch their target from under their noses without orders, then he was further gone than anyone suspected, and it was unlikely Rosenthal would even reach Balmorhea intact.

Whatever difficulties she and Katch had on this job could be laid at Collard's feet for not briefing them properly. So ultimately, their misfires were all the senator's fault, not theirs. Katch and Kaan's record should remain unblemished. She gripped the steering wheel a lot harder than necessary, imagining Collard's neck between her fingers.

She took the first exit they came to.

"What are you doing?" Katch asked.

"We're going after Ramirez. If Collard wants Rosenthal, she'll have to deal with us, not him. And we're gonna need another car."

Katch nodded, then repulsed his partner with his now ghastly grin.

BARNABY WOKE to the stink of vomit. He recoiled but found he couldn't move very far, certainly not far enough away from the sick. His head began to throb as if brains were leaking from his ears, and then his stomach dropped when he brought his fingers to his face and discovered he couldn't see them. Not only that, but his glasses were gone. He started to pant as he frantically felt around himself, mapping his surroundings. He remembered the car going airborne, the fear.... At first he thought he was in the wreckage, perhaps pinned, but he was stretched out flat, not crumpled up in twisted metal.

Wherever he was, it seemed slightly smaller than a twin bed, but it was a... a *box*? His mind went immediately to coffin; then his heart skipped and started rabbiting.

"Chuck! Charleston!" he shouted, banging on the sides and top of the box. He kicked, shouted, slapped, pounded... then he just started screaming, screaming at the top of his lungs. Headache be damned! He screamed so loud and for so long that he didn't hear a latch opening and was startled by the light suddenly washing over him. He squinted, cringed, and went silent, raising his hands and curling up defensively as if the light were painful or might bite him.

"What are ya? Claustrophobic?" a deep, rasping voice asked. The man standing over him was huge. It was like lying at the base of a big, blurry Redwood and trying to see the top, but he attributed that to his concussion.

"I *wasn't*," Barnaby answered acidly.

A big hand latched on to his arm and hauled him to his feet. "Come on, runt!" the guy commanded. Once free of the box, Barnaby swayed for a moment, his head swimming, but he steadied himself on the guy's arm. He could feel the muscles there, rock hard. He looked around the elaborate sleeper compartment of a tractor-trailer and knew this was the guy who had run them off the road. "You puke again, you'll be cleaning that up too, got it?"

"I'm not cleaning up shit! You don't want a guy puking in your goddamned storage box, you don't lock a guy with a head injury in it!"

The man stared at him for several seconds, seemingly stunned speechless by his attitude, but then a slow smile spread across his face, and Barnaby felt his blood run cold.

"Yer quite the little spitfire, ain't cha?" He held up a couple of fast food bags and wiggled them at Barnaby. "Ya hungry? Probably are since you yacked up whatever ya had in yer tummy. We got about eight hours to go, and I ain't plannin' on stoppin' again, so ya better eat while ya can."

Barnaby's gaze traveled from the stupid cowboy hat on the man's head to his snakeskin boots and back again. "Who the fuck are you?" he asked, eyeing the food bag cautiously.

"Name's Ramirez, runt."

"Ramirez Runt. Hmm… that's an odd name."

The man snorted, but no real mirth warmed his eyes. Barnaby tried to peer around Ramirez to see through the windows. They were parked outside some massive truck stop. "Where… are we?"

"Wichita Falls, Texas… for the moment." Ramirez raised an eyebrow and grinned crookedly. "Why?"

Barnaby shrugged. "No reason."

He could see a few people walking near the truck, people within shouting distance, and beyond them, at the truck stop, the foot traffic was much heavier. He reached out for the food, and Ramirez narrowed his gaze as he handed over one of the bags. Barnaby opened the bag, took a whiff, and grimaced. There was a lot of beef and grease in there. He took a step toward the passenger seat but paused, seeking the go-ahead from Ramirez.

"I don't suppose you happened to grab my glasses when you kidnapped me?"

"Nope. Not important for you to see where you're goin'," Ramirez said, leering at him, his gaze slowly traveling up and down Barnaby's body. He gave a curt nod, inviting him to have a seat. Barnaby stepped forward, but the man didn't move an inch, so he ended up having to squeeze by him. He sat in the passenger seat and pretended to dig out his meal, but in reality, he was glancing sideways at a group of young men walking by the semi. They appeared to be college age, healthy, strong. If they worked together, they might be able to overpower Ramirez.

He placed a hand on the door handle, tightened his grip, but then Ramirez was directly behind him. Barnaby could feel his presence, his body heat. He turned slightly and found the man's crotch at eye level, blurry but massive.

"D-don't you want to sit and eat?" he asked, blinking up at him. Barnaby turned away quickly because the man's eyes were windows to nowhere.

"Naw, not yet. I'm waitin' to see if you have the balls to try to open that there door and get them boys' attention." Ramirez leaned over to whisper in Barnaby's ear. "They're pretty, ain't they? Wouldn't mind havin' one a them keepin' me company on this haul, but I guess you'll hafta do. Good thing you didn't come to before the toll roads. How would I explain the ruckus you was makin'?"

Barnaby threw open the door, but before he could shout, Ramirez grabbed a handful of his hair and twisted it tight in his fist. He winced, breath stalling in his chest, and tears springing to his eyes from the pain and the possibility of having his hair and part of his scalp ripped off.

Ramirez held a struggling Barnaby in place while he reached across him to shut and lock the door before dragging him backward over the seat. Barnaby continued to shout and nearly kicked out the passenger window, but if the ruckus caught the college kids' attention, it didn't hold it for long, because no one came pounding on the cab door. No one came to his rescue.

Ramirez stood him up against the cabin wall, pinning him there, and pressed a knee into Barnaby's crotch, causing him to gasp in pain. Then Ramirez closed a hand around his throat and began to squeeze. He couldn't move, and now he couldn't breathe. He fought, he clawed, he tried to kick, but none of it had any effect.

Leaning in and resting his lips against Barnaby's ear, Ramirez drawled, "Stop. Shhh." Barnaby slowly stopped struggling, and Ramirez loosened his grip. "There ya go, runt," he said softly, while he remained pressed up against Barnaby, rubbing his thigh between his legs. Barnaby's eyes fluttered closed, but he felt bile rising in his throat. "Ya know, yer awful pretty for a Jew."

"Wh-where… where's Ch-Charleston?" Barnaby rasped.

"Yer friend from the SUV? Sorry, kid, he died in the crash. Now—" He grabbed a stunned Barnaby by the arm and threw him to the floor by the lockbox. "—before ya get to eat, I suggest you get to cleanin', or I'll make you lick it up."

He died? Barnaby threw up in the box again.

Chapter 20

Charleston moaned as he reached out for Barnaby. He slid his hands up his thighs to his waist. *Mmm….* Barnaby tried to squirm away, but Charleston tightened his grip and held fast, probably bruising his flesh. Suddenly Charleston flipped him, pinning Barnaby to the bed with his weight and kissing him. His sweet, hot, beautiful man tasted so… so much… like… *cherries*!

He jerked up and away from the body beneath him. "Light!" Charleston called out. The bedside lamp came on, and he grimaced at finding Jeri Sato lying beneath him instead of Barnaby.

She frowned right back and wiped her mouth with the back of her hand. "Hey, I'm not thrilled about what just happened either, Chuck." She sat up in bed next to him. "You're not exactly my type, ya know, with all that—" She gestured in the direction of his nether region. "—penis going on."

"Where the fuck—"

"Shush! I'd rather the rest of the house not come running just yet. I've got intel for you." She narrowed her dark eyes at him. "How *are* you feeling anyway?"

"Angry, desperate, confused, headachy, stiff—"

"No shit," she said, grimacing again. "You've got a concussion, and I've got news."

"Do we know where Ramirez is headed with Barnaby?"

"Later… listen—"

"No," he said firmly, brushing his hair out of his eyes. "Not later. We need to get to him now. The guy who has him is one sick—"

"I can help with that, but you need to let me—"

"How long have I been out?"

She sighed and rolled her eyes. "A couple hours, but you have to know—"

He tried to throw the covers back, as if to get out of bed, but Jeri jumped on top of him, straddling him. His bruised ribs complained, but he let her, too stunned to toss the tiny woman across the room, which he easily could have done. She hovered above him staring intently into his eyes. "I. Know. Who. Our. Mole. Is."

"Our what now?"

"The fuck who's been leaking info to that critter bitch of a senator."

Charleston shook his head and instantly regretted it. "Yeah, I remember now…," he began, "They knew about our flight, got there before us, knew where we were headed. Who is it?"

"Dr. Hiram Lancaster."

"But… no, he helped me stop Barnaby—"

"From getting married. Yeah. I was there."

"So why would he…?"

It had turned out Lancaster, too, was gay and resentful of Charleston living out and honestly. Blackmail? No, he'd only recently come out to his wife… and daughter.

His daughter.

Charleston had seen numerous pictures of the girl in Lancaster's office nearly two months ago when he'd sought his help with the unauthorized step. She clearly meant the world to him and was worth all the years of playing it straight.

Charleston stared into Jeri's eyes. "They took his daughter," he whispered.

"Yup." Jeri hopped off him, sat on the bed, and began tapping her tablet, bringing up a load of data she'd collected since being brought on by his father. "She hasn't been in school for several days. They believe she's in Europe with her mother, but I can't find any flight records showing them having left the States."

"Jesus. Who snatches a little girl?"

"Probably the same people who would kill a mother and her three kids?"

Charleston frowned, thinking of Barnaby in Ramirez's hands. He stared at the bottom of the bedroom door where the light from the rest of the house leaked in. He couldn't hear any voices beyond the door or see any shadows passing. "Who's out there?"

Jeri glanced at the door as well. "Everyone your father trusts—Leaundra, her team, Dr. Plumb… and Lancaster. Even though the RPP is being mothballed, your poppa thought it best to do our planning out here, away from the bulk of the personnel packing up the equipment." She shrugged. "It was a good idea, but…."

"Why Plumb?"

"You're hurt, and she's a medical doctor he trusts and doesn't have to explain anything to, not to mention she knows your physiology better than anyone on the planet. Lancaster… sort of *tagged* along."

"Did Leaundra put you on to Lancaster?"

Jeri nodded. "She's got a good mind for rooting out the backstabbers. I tell ya, if she weren't straight and married—"

"And you were single—"

"Anyway," Jeri said with a smirk, "it was clear Collard had info she shouldn't have access to, and someone in the know had to be feeding it to her."

Since the moment he met her, Jeri Sato had been his ally. He gazed at her closely, really looked. She was tiny, almost doll-like, and had full lips, flawless skin, long lashes, and eyes darker than Barnaby's—eyes shining with a fierce, rapid-fire intelligence he suspected could one day rule the world. He grinned. "Where's your lollipop?"

Jeri pouted. "I ran out, and we haven't been allowed to leave for a couple days. My girlfriend is going apeshit wanting to know where I am. I expect an all-expense-paid vacation for the two of us after we wrap this up, Chuck."

"You got it."

He slowly slid out of bed, found himself naked, but did not stop to wonder about who'd stripped him. His chest was badly bruised where the seat belt had held him, and he rubbed the area unconsciously, working stiffness out of his left shoulder, the bullet wound in his right forgotten.

There were small bandages here and there for minor scrapes, and one larger one on the back of his head, covering an injury probably sustained from the explosion. The activity made his head throb as he hunted around for something to wear. He discovered some older clothes of his tucked away in a dresser drawer. He was grateful but had no idea why his mother had hung on to them. *Maybe just in case I'm nearly killed near the family ranch while running for my life?*

Charleston didn't want to think about what might be happening to Barnaby right now, but if he had to beat the shit out of Lancaster to find him, he'd do it. He slipped on his jeans and paused as another concern popped into his head. "How old's the girl?"

"Twelve."

"Why hasn't her mother raised holy hell?"

"I'm pretty sure she's as terrified as Lancaster and hasn't called the authorities." Jeri brushed her jet-black bangs out of her eyes and bit her bottom lip in thought. "It's a sticky sitch."

Charleston couldn't argue with that. He finished dressing, only stumbling twice from dizziness and traumatized muscles as he pulled on a T-shirt. Socks and shoes would have to wait. He left the bedroom with Jeri on his heels, clutching her tablet to her chest.

"They're in the study hammering out tactics," Jeri said.

The hardwood floor was chilly against his bare feet as the two of them walked through the house toward his father's study. Through the windows he caught glimpses of Leaundra's operatives walking the front and back porches. He hardly expected the senator to launch an all-out assault on the place—she had other fish to fry, namely *Barnaby*—but they appeared on alert.

When the two of them entered the study, his father's commentary petered out, and everyone turned to stare at them. His mother stood abruptly. "Charleston! You should be resting," she said, giving Jeri a stern stare.

"We don't have time to rest." He walked deeper into the room and looked over the faces of the people gathered there. From behind his large desk, his father watched him closely. Sitting on a leather bench, Dr. Plumb looked him over for any sign of pain, though the short, round woman smiled warmly while doing it, her keen eyes taking everything in. Standing at the window and behind Dr. Lancaster's chair was Leaundra, her gaze riveted on the back of Lancaster's skull, as if contemplating how best to crack it open. Charleston noticed Lancaster wouldn't meet his eye. "Where are we with locating Barnaby?" he asked calmly.

"Before we get into that," Dr. Plumb said, "how are you feeling, Charleston?" He saw his mother nodding silently in the affirmative. *Great. Gang up on me, ladies.*

"I feel—"

Dr. Plumb held up a finger. "Be honest."

"I had some dizziness as I got dressed, and some muscle aches. My head is killing me."

The doctor nodded. "I gave you a painkiller and a muscle-healing accelerant, so that stiffness should fade soon. It won't help much with bruised ribs, I'm afraid, but the anticoncussives should help clear your head. Any queasiness?" He slowly shook his head "no." Satisfied, Dr. Plumb folded her hands in her lap as if to say "carry on."

"May I continue?" his father asked. He looked into his son's eyes, almost apologetically, and said, "Unfortunately, we've lost track of Collard. She slipped our surveillance team in DC, but we suspect she's on her way to Texas. And since the only thing we're certain of is this Ramirez person is planning to deliver Rosenthal to her, we'll set up—"

"Hold on, Pop. I don't think you want to lay this all out in front of Lancaster."

Seeking confirmation, Leaundra glanced at Jeri, who gave her a curt nod, and then the former team leader stepped forward to stand at Lancaster's side as he leapt to his feet, his voice dripping with indignation as he demanded, "I beg your pardon?"

Charleston also saw the terror in the man's eyes and despite his own desperation and anger, despite his willingness to tear Barnaby's location out of Lancaster's hide, he took a different approach. "We know about your daughter," he said softly.

The doctor's prominent Adam's apple bobbed a couple of times as his gaze darted from suspicious face to suspicious face, and then he crumpled back into his seat and began to shake violently as he rubbed his short curly hair. "You don't understand," he wailed. "They'll kill her... my Tonya. They said they just wanted information as it came to me. Information about your movements, or...." His voice dropped to a disbelieving whisper. "Or they would kill my girl...."

Charleston allowed Lancaster a few moments of meltdown, then said, "We'll get her back... just like we'll get Barnaby back." He walked over to Lancaster and placed a comforting hand on his quivering shoulder. "But you need to help us. Tell us everything you shared with Collard."

Lancaster looked into Charleston's face, seeking reassurance, seeking certainty that his daughter would be returned to him. "Not much. Really." He glanced frantically around the room at everyone who watched him, imploring them to believe him. "I told her about your flight and your likely route to the ranch, but—"

"What about the restore subjects?" Dr. Meeks demanded.

Lancaster shook his head violently. "No... no! She already had that. She pulled the data from the RPP reports the oversight panel received." No one said anything for several seconds, just exchanged glances, silently asking each other if they bought his story. "And they're all accounted for now, right?" Lancaster rushed on, nodding rapidly as if that made everything okay. "They're protected, so Collard's people can't get to them any longer."

"Her people *have* gotten to Barnaby," Charleston said, leaning close to get in the doctor's face and tightening his grip on the man's shoulder, causing him to wince. His recent calm had evaporated, and he again wanted to wrap his hands around Lancaster's neck and squeeze until his hair stood on end, but he knew that wouldn't bring them any closer to the man he loved.

"Anyone want to know why I think that macadamia Collard is doing all this?" Jeri interrupted.

Startled, they all stared at her, and then Dr. Meeks grinned. "Ms. Sato, please enlighten us."

CHAPTER 21

FOR A bit more than two hours, Barnaby simply sat in silence, watching the highway stretch out before him. Ramirez alternated between talkative and contemplative, but Barnaby just kept thinking of the last time he'd seen Charleston, their last conversation. He'd been saying, *I love it when you call me babe.* He did love it, had grown to love it over the hours they'd spent together. His gut clenched at the thought of never hearing it again.

"Yer awful quiet over there, kid," Ramirez said. Barnaby didn't respond, because when he wasn't thinking about the last thing he'd said to Charleston, he was thinking about how best to kill Ramirez, how painfully to kill him, how slowly…. "Isn't it more comfortable up front with me than in that box? I told ya if you behaved, you could ride up here the whole way, though I figured you'd be better company than this."

Barnaby slowly turned to look at him through tired, swollen, tear-reddened eyes. He tried and failed to keep his temper in check. "Why the fuck would you think that? Why would you think I'd be better company than I am? You've got me shackled to this damn seat!" He lifted his left foot and rattled the ankle cuff at Ramirez. "And you murdered him!" His voice broke. "You ran us off the road, and he died."

"I had a job to—"

"You're a lunatic! Do you have any idea how long I've waited for that man?"

Ramirez peered out at the road. "Yeah, well, that's life, runt. I'd say ya'd find someone else, but I don't 'spect ya to be long fer this world after my boss is done talkin' to ya."

"Fuck your boss."

Ramirez laughed loud and long, so long that Barnaby grew even more uncomfortable, thinking he was cracking up right in front of him. But then it dawned on him as he watched Ramirez holding his sides in hilarity, his mind had probably shattered years ago.

When the laughter wound down to wheezing, Ramirez turned to him and sneered, "Senator's not my type, little man." He winked, and Barnaby's flesh crawled. "You're much more ta mah likin'."

"Are you trying to make me throw up again, you fucking asshat?" *Holy shit! What am I doing?*

Ramirez chuckled. "Ooowee! You got a mouth on ya, but I can be real nice if'n yer nice to me."

Barnaby looked Ramirez directly in the eyes and smiled. "Before I suck it, I'll bite it off and spit it down the shitter, you inbred piece of garbage."

My mouth, my mouth, I can't control my mouth.

The mildly pleasant expression that had been on Ramirez's face vanished, and his eyes grew hard.

Oh fuck.

It wasn't like Barnaby could take any of it back. He sat there on pins and needles, but it looked like Ramirez was done talking.

"BECAUSE HER son died?" Dr. Meeks asked, glancing at his son.

"What? RPP didn't select him for restore?" Charleston asked. "She's pissed because we didn't bring him back?"

This time his mother spoke up. "Dear," she said softly, "a mother's grief can manifest in odd ways."

"Well, I'd say turning into a homicidal maniac is odd, Mom."

"Watch your tone, Junior," Dr. Meeks warned.

"According to news coverage there was some accident at her home, and she found his body," Jeri said.

"I can't imagine what that must have done to her," Charleston's mother said, not looking at him.

Lancaster finally spoke up, albeit meekly. "Judging from our few brief conversations, she seems fixated on what she calls 'God's will.' That may be the only way she can accept her son's death, and she's someone who believes RPP flies in the face of that... of uh, 'God's will,'" he said, his voice barely audible in the now silent room. "It wasn't so much that her son wasn't selected for restore. It was that we didn't have the right to restore anyone... at least in her eyes."

"That's what has that critter bitch up in arms?" Charleston asked, ignoring his mother's shock. However, Jeri was clearly delighted at the use of her phrasing, and he shrugged at her slightly, acknowledging the term's accuracy in this case.

Dr. Meeks sighed. "It would seem so, Junior."

"Her reasons are irrelevant," Charleston snapped. "I need hard data to find Barnaby." He whirled away from them, raking his fingers through his hair and tugging at it as he talked to himself. "I should have tagged him. We'd know where he is if I had. Why didn't I tag him?"

Activating her tablet, Jeri came forward and tapped him on the shoulder. "Hard data? I got that. According to my research, Collard has property all over Texas." She touched her screen repeatedly, sliding from listing to listing. "A residence in Austin, commercial properties in Lubbock, rentals in Dallas and Fort Worth, an office building in Houston that houses her group, Conservative Path, and a vacation bungalow in Corpus Christi—"

"We don't have enough personnel to cover—"

"*But…*," Jeri continued, holding up one finger, "I also found—after plowing through several layers of shell companies and phony identities—a property called TDC in a tiny town called Balmorhea. Some sort of warehouse for obsolete office equipment." One of her eyebrows disappeared into her jet-black bangs, but they all just stared at her, waiting. She sighed and said, "Her son's name was Terrence Delnoit Collard."

Charleston grinned and began rushing about the room gathering his things: wallet, gun, jacket. Shoes… he needed shoes… shoes and socks. Collard wouldn't want anything unseemly to tarnish her conservative organization or her home or the businesses she owned or rented to, so their best bet was that obscure warehouse in Balmorhea.

"Charleston," Leaundra said, "you're not rushing in there armed with just a gun, determination, and your *love*, got it? You need a team. We need a plan. Eyes on the ground."

She was right. He stopped moving and tried to calm his racing thoughts because he'd be of little help to Barnaby in his current state. "Leaundra and Jeri, with me," he commanded, but the only thing his former team leader moved was an eyebrow—raised. "I mean, if you will, ma'am," he said much more softly.

"Wait!" Lancaster shouted, leaping to his feet again, but Leaundra immediately shoved him back into the chair. "My daughter," he said plaintively.

"We'll get her back," Charleston said. "I promise."

"You can't promise that," Lancaster said, shaking his head. "Now that she has Rosenthal, the senator doesn't need my help anymore. She'll kill her, won't she?" His face appeared overworked with worry, as if he'd aged during the past hour, his eyes tired, resigned.

"I can promise that the sooner we get started, the sooner we'll have them back with us," Charleston said.

"How can I help?" Lancaster asked, worrying the tablecloth between his fingers. "There must be something I can do."

Charleston glanced at Dr. Plumb, who simply nodded. A sedative would do Lancaster good right now. "Have some tea, and when we work out our plans, we'll come back and brief everyone, okay? Then we'll see how you can best help."

"Wait," Leaundra said. "A safe word."

"Huh?" Charleston asked, confused.

"My grandchildren use code words to let them know who it's safe to go with in case my daughter or son-in-law can't pick them up."

Lancaster considered for a moment. "Her mother told me once, but…."

"Think, man!" Leaundra ordered. "She's a preteen. Bella? Katniss? What is it?"

"No," Lancaster said, shaking his head as he tried to squeeze the answer from his panicked thoughts. "Tonya's in love with those Potter books…. Bilius! Her safe word is Bilius."

"What is that, some kinda spell?" Charleston asked.

"No, it's the ginger kid's middle name," Dr. Plumb supplied, much to everyone's astonishment. She stuck out her plump chin and drew herself up. "What? I have grandchildren too."

"Good to know, Lancaster," Leaundra said. "Thank you." She squeezed his shoulder before joining Charleston and Jeri. The three of them almost made it out the study door, but Charleston stopped and turned back abruptly, jarring both his colleagues.

"Someone—Jeri, see if you can get hold of Barnaby's eye doc." The tiny woman looked up at him as if his knock to the head was more severe than first thought. "He... Barnaby doesn't have his glasses." Embarrassed, Charleston glanced around the room at everyone. "He needs his glasses," he whispered before turning and walking through the door.

WRAPPING UP her third and last meeting of the day, Sen. Penny Collard broke protocol and bought a round of drinks for the table. Though they often courted her approval, she was now an old hand at schmoozing Conservative Path board members. She liked to trust that they were true believers, but one could never tell. Before leaving Austin she'd taken a tour of the new offices there. Her next stop had been Houston, where the organization was going strong. And now, finally, leaving San Antonio, she was confident the newest staff members for the area would prove a powerful force for conservative values. Her vision was taking shape nicely.

All she wanted now was to sleep all the way to Balmorhea, where she'd truly wrap things up once Rosenthal was delivered by Ramirez in the morning. She hoped the young man wasn't too badly hurt. She saw no need for cruelty in doing the Lord's work. If—no, when—everything went as planned, Collard could be back in DC by Monday, or Tuesday at the latest, and once again doing the government's business for her constituents.

Despite RPP personnel putting the remaining restored subjects in protective custody, Penny was confident she'd find them someday and end them. It was just a matter of time. She was in the right, after all, and trusted God to see that all would go as it should. It was a shame others didn't realize that. The arrogance of Dr. Meeks and his team to think they knew better than God himself—it turned her stomach. Rosenthal's death would be a major accomplishment, more so than the subjects before him, because he'd been restored several times... each an affront to the Almighty.

Her car waited outside the hotel, door open and driver standing by. After she was in, the driver rushed to slide behind the wheel. "Are you certain you wouldn't rather fly to Balmorhea, ma'am?"

"I'm certain, Cooper. My business can't be concluded until the morning, and I have no desire to stand around waiting at the warehouse longer than necessary." She also didn't want to take a room in town, preferring to keep a low profile in light of her plans.

Cooper gave a curt nod. "We should arrive in five or six hours."

"Good enough."

She sighed and kicked off her shoes, already feeling a yawn coming on. She stretched her aching feet, loosened her graying blonde updo, and peeled off her bright red suit jacket, then hung it on the hook above the door. Tomorrow she would be that much closer to making this stinking world a little more right.

Katch and Kaan should be arriving around the same time as Ramirez and Rosenthal, and she would have those two buffoons dispose of the girl. Surely they could handle a preteen. A twinge of regret hit her. Tonya Lancaster was only a few years younger than her own Terry had been when the Lord had called him home, but her father had been part of the Restore Point Program, and he might as well suffer for his involvement.

Her eyes grew heavy, but she startled awake, fear gripping her heart.

"Are you all right, ma'am?" Cooper asked.

"Yes. I'm fine, just... just forgot where I was for a moment." She smiled weakly and tried to remind herself there was nothing to fear anymore. The nightmares had grown less frequent—a development that told her she was on the right path. No longer was she kept awake each night with visions of her son's emaciated body on that hard slab in that cold, cold room. He hadn't even looked like himself. His once thick and lustrous sand-colored hair was dry and brittle. His lips were thin and cracked, drawn back over his teeth in a grimace.

Collard shuddered, but a few minutes later she was sleeping the sleep of the righteous.

CHAPTER 22

APPARENTLY HIS anger at Barnaby's harsh words had passed, because Ramirez did it again—gave him another lingering look. Barnaby shuddered at the thought of what might be running through the nutbar's filthy mind, but he had considered playing into it, flirting, whatever, just to get Ramirez relaxed enough to let his guard down. Assuming for a moment Barnaby had the fortitude to accomplish that, to not flinch or gag at the man's touch, would he have the strength to incapacitate him? Cut his throat? Bash in his skull? Or would he end up simply making the big ox angry, or worse yet, find himself at the mercy of a sexually worked-up lunatic?

"If yer tired, you could have a lie down in my bunk for a while," Ramirez suggested out of nowhere. "O'course I'll hafta pull over to uncuff ya."

Barnaby nearly laughed out loud. *Not on your life, buddy*. The last thing he wanted to do was prostrate himself in the man's vicinity.

"I'm thinkin' I'ma need ta pull over anyway. Gotta drain the snake, ya know. I'm guessin' you hafta do the same, don't cha?"

Barnaby did have to piss. "You've got a bathroom on this thing," Barnaby snapped.

"Yup. You want I should give you the wheel while I take a piss?" Ramirez laughed heartily at that. "'Sides, I'd like ta stretch mah legs too." He grinned wickedly before signaling to pull off at a small truckers' rest stop up ahead. Barnaby tried not to fidget in his eagerness to get his ankle cuff removed. How many others had been shackled in the truck's passenger seat? How many had woken up in that coffin beneath Ramirez's bunk? How many other men had kept the fiend "company" while he was on the road? Barnaby shuddered and stared out the window. It was dark out now as they slowed to turn into the parklike area, and he could see very little of the surrounding terrain. There were three other semis parked there, their windows curtained or shuttered in some other way. Ramirez shut off the truck and hopped out.

Barnaby tried to remain calm and get his bearings, squinting into the darkness while he waited for Ramirez to come around to his side of the truck. All he could make out beyond the rest stop and its lights were shadowed hills bathed in moonlight. It took Ramirez a while to make his way around, and Barnaby didn't hear him coming, so he jumped a bit when the door swung open.

"Yer awful wound up, little man." He laughed. "I done mah business, now it's your turn."

Ramirez climbed up beside him and leaned across to unlock the ankle cuff keeping him in place. He could smell the masculine, musky scent coming off him. If it had been coming from anyone else, Barnaby probably wouldn't have recoiled. He wondered what Ramirez smelled from him: sweat, Charleston, dried cum, vomit, fear? Very little of that could be appealing—he hoped.

Once he was free, Barnaby immediately lifted his foot into the seat and began massaging his ankle, but instead of hopping down, Ramirez paused and stared into his eyes. "Now odds are, if'n you were to shout out, none a these fellas would come runnin', but just in case they did… I'd kill 'em. You got that?"

Barnaby nodded slowly, his eyes wide. Ramirez grabbed him by the arm, practically dragged him from the truck, and quick-walked him into some bushes just beyond the rest stop lights.

"Do your business!" Ramirez barked. He shoved Barnaby forward and then folded his big arms over his massive chest to watch. Barnaby stumbled a bit in the dark but kept moving, glancing over his shoulder, until Ramirez told him, "That's enough leg stretchin'."

The world felt deserted as he relieved himself. Despite the cricket song, the occasional rustle of a nearby shrub, and the distant traffic noise, it was just him and the lunatic under the dark, star-filled, Texas sky. He looked up at how vast the heavens were and thought of Charleston, his heart aching for his hero, lost to him forever.

He thought of his mother, Donald, and his little brother Nelson. Oddly, he even thought of Connie and their aborted wedding. He'd broken his mother's heart that day—the ceremony she'd dreamed of only a tease, some cruel trick. Barnaby regretted growing apart from them over the years and wished he'd spent more time with Nelson. At thirteen, the little guy was about to enter some of the most difficult years of his life. Barnaby remembered. He could tell him. He was suddenly glad he'd taken the time to call them during the flight, but he lamented not being able to keep his promise to see them soon.

Coral, India, and Ross came to mind too, and all the people he cared for and who cared for him. How many days ago had he been surrounded by pretty people in pretty clothes gushing about his talent while they sipped champagne, nibbled hors d'oeuvre, and ignored inoffensive music?

But tonight he—

"Ya done yet?" Ramirez growled, standing right behind him, his breath on Barnaby's neck. He rushed to tuck himself away, but Ramirez stayed his hand and yanked him around to face him. "No need to put that away just yet."

Barnaby pulled free and made a point of tucking himself away, as if to say, "Off-limits." Ramirez's face was in shadow from the rest stop lights behind him, so Barnaby couldn't see his expression, but it couldn't have been pleasant, because Ramirez grabbed him by the back of the neck and bent him over to face his crotch.

Barnaby tried not to panic as he fought to free himself, but the man was too strong. "I got somethin' you can gag on, runt!" Ramirez fumbled with the front of his jeans, but he froze when a pair of headlights swept the rest stop as a car pulled in. Momentarily distracted, his grip loosened, and Barnaby wiggled free and kneed Ramirez in the nuts as hard as he could. The man sucked in a breath but didn't scream, then fell to his knees.

Now Barnaby *had* to get away, because when Ramirez recovered, he was likely to pull off Barnaby's arms, legs, and dick before he stomped him into the ground. He ran—ran off into the blurry darkness and anemic shrubbery, ran hoping to circle back around to the road and people and civilization. He almost chuckled at that, but Texas *was* more civilized these days and steadily working its way back from the dark ages of the Perry administration. He flinched when he heard what sounded like—*Was that a gun*? He hadn't seen a gun on Ramirez.

Barnaby paused to listen and heard raised voices and sounds of a scuffle. He took off again, searching for lights from the highway.

"I see you, Rosenthal," a gravelly voice said ahead of him. Barnaby froze. *What*? "I see you standing there, out of breath, lost in the dark, in the middle of nowhere, with a psychopath on your ass. Need a ride?"

"Uh... who's th-there?" *Fuck!* He couldn't stop his voice from shaking.

"Your old pal Kaan," the voice whispered in his ear.

Before Barnaby could react, he felt a pinch at his neck, and the world went all wobbly. Kaan took him by the arm and steered him a few more feet to a service road, where an SUV waited. He stumbled and weaved as they advanced toward the vehicle. The tilting of the earth beneath his feet became worse, nearly throwing him to the ground. Finally, Barnaby was able to lean against the car in relief while the world continued its lackadaisical spinning. Kaan opened the back door and shoved him onto the backseat.

"Have a nap, kid. When you wake up... well, if you wake up, maybe you could give me the number of that pretty boyfriend of yours, or does he only like dick?" She slammed the door. "If he does, I'll be happy to strap one on for him," she said as she slid behind the wheel. "Katch and I should be able to drop you off, collect our payment, and be outta there before your buddy Ramirez shows up. I bet he's boiling mad." Kaan chuckled to herself as she stared through the windshield.

Barnaby tried to sit up all the way, tried to speak, but whatever Kaan had injected him with was making that practically impossible. He didn't know how much time had passed, even thought for a moment that he'd slept a bit, but suddenly Kaan was speaking again.

"He should be here by now." Her damaged voice was a bit thicker with concern. From his position, his head propped up on the arm of the car door, he could see her hair was tamed now and pulled back into a loose ponytail. Barnaby took note that she looked much more put together than she had the last time he saw her, though a bruise extended beneath her dark hair. *There's probably a goose egg under there*, he thought and laughed softly.

Just then, a bloody hand slapped against the backseat window, and Barnaby cried out, pointing and struggling into a seated position, where he rested his dizzy head against the window and watched the hand leave a bloody smear across the glass.

"Shit!" Kaan leaned over and opened the door for her partner, and Katch struggled into the passenger seat. "What the fuck hap—"

"Go! Just go!" he shouted, an odd gurgling accompanying his words. He held a hand against his neck, but blood spilled through his fingers.

Kaan started the car and peeled out. "I got… his tires. Didn't see him…. Jumped me. Big-ass knife."

"Jesus! Jesus!" Kaan shouted as she glanced back and forth between the road and her partner. "Rico, man… that's bad. That's *real* bad."

Katch coughed violently, spewing blood onto the dashboard and windshield. "Finish… the job. Finish…."

Kaan must have floored it because Barnaby felt himself pushed back into the seat as the SUV bumped and flew and bounced, heading for the highway. In what seemed like a very short time, the garbled conversation from the front seat stopped, and Barnaby fell over, drifting into an impenetrable sleep.

AFTER AN hour of driving in silence through the night, Kaan finally pulled off the road, reached across the now cold body of her partner, opened the passenger door, and kicked Katch out. He flopped out heavily, as dead weight will. Before leaving the car herself, she glanced over the seat at Barnaby to make sure he was still unconscious. Then she marched over to Katch, took hold of his arms, and dragged him about a hundred yards into the bushes, far enough off the road for the coyotes to get to him before the authorities.

She paused to look down at him and wondered at the odd ache in her chest. Katch had been aggravating more often than not, annoying, talkative, and frequently more dense than Kaan would have liked. *The man needs looking after*. But after all those years of working side by side at stakeouts, breaking into compounds, cutting throats… well, a person got used to, comfortable with, another person.

While watching the life drain out of Katch, Kaan had felt a chill pass through her, as if her own body were cooling right along with… *her friend's*? She hadn't cried. She didn't do that anymore, but this ache and weight inside her was unsettling. She stared at Katch's pale skin, milky eyes, and ruined mouth and wondered—just for a second—how many people over the years the two of them had caused to feel the way she felt right now.

"I promise I'll finish the job. I'll finish it and take care of anyone who gets in my way." She knelt by the body and placed a hand on its chest. "And I swear, when I see Ramirez again, I'll make him hurt. I'll kill him, Rico."

She took Katch's gun, removed the ammo clip and pocketed it, cleared the chamber, and then dropped the empty weapon on his belly before walking back to the car. Barnaby stirred a bit when she slammed the door but didn't wake. She sat there for several moments, staring out at the night before buckling up and driving away.

CHAPTER 23

FOR THE second time in less than a day, Charleston boarded an airplane, but this time he had Leaundra, Jeri, and a small team of operatives with him. The flight between Salina and Pecos' airport was just under two hours, and after that, a thirty-seven-mile drive lay between him and Barnaby… at least if they'd guessed correctly.

"Charleston," Leaundra said, ending a phone call. "Handal is on site. Says there's not much activity at the moment. When he arrived, he witnessed an SUV pulling in, but no one has exited since."

"No sign of a blue semi?" He frowned when she shook her head.

"Our transportation is waiting for us at the airport."

"Got it. Thanks."

For some time after takeoff, Charleston struggled to get comfortable in the cramped quarters. The legroom in the charter clearly did not take full-grown men into account. Once again, he tried to cleanse his mind of fears about what Barnaby might be going through. He couldn't believe the two of them had come this far, across time and space, to lose each other now. He closed his eyes and tried to find some semblance of calm by remembering their time together in the hotel, how Barnaby had moved and moaned and gazed at him, like….

I was his hero. His eyes popped open; he was unsettled again.

"Hey," Jeri said quietly as she approached, "can I join you? I've got news." He nodded, and she dropped into the seat across the aisle. "About five hours ago, Senator Collard paid a bar tab at a hotel restaurant in San Antonio."

"Already in Texas, huh?"

Jeri smiled weakly. "We lost her in DC days ago, so yeah."

He closed his eyes again and breathed deeply before asking, "Jeri, what's RPP's status?"

"It's defunded. There's no—"

"I mean the equipment. Is it disassembled, crated, sold for parts… what?"

"Sold for parts?" she asked, smiling crookedly. "What would anyone do with a ten-foot-diameter titanium Portal?"

He shrugged. "Wall hanging?"

They broke up laughing, and Leaundra glared at them. "Sorry," Charleston mouthed. "So, what's the status?"

"Major Operations was disassembled and crated last week. I suspect they took the rumors to heart and began taking that Portal apart a while before that. We've been holding off in Temporal Research and Development, hoping for some miracle, but it's likely to be crated by mid-November." Charleston simply nodded, and Jeri narrowed her gaze. "Why do you want to know—Oh! Uh-uh! That's not happening."

"Keep your voice down."

"You can't step again. You'll come apart… literally." She sat back in her seat and stared into space. "I mean, I've never seen it happen, thank goodness, but Plumb once gave a pretty graphic description of what it would be like." She placed her tiny hand on his much bigger one. "You have to believe he'll be okay, Chuck."

He grinned sadly. "He calls me that too."

"Huh?"

"Chuck. He calls me Chuck, even though he knows I hate it."

They were quiet for a moment. Then Jeri said, "You can't go into this expecting disaster, and undoing whatever happens is not a contingency plan, Charleston."

She'd never called him Charleston before. He smiled at her. "Thanks, Jeri." He gripped the armrest. *Believe, believe, believe*, he thought.

Barnaby was no slouch. Charleston had seen him take Kaan out, but there was a difference between self-defense and lethal action. Self-defense was designed to give you a chance at escape, and the artist had those skills. But did he have what it took to take a life? He thought of Ramirez and knew Barnaby was surrounded by people like him. To men like that, killing was like breathing or blinking.

Charleston suspected everyone had the capacity to kill given the right circumstances. For instance, a few days ago, he never would have considered snapping the neck of a woman, someone his mother's age, let alone a United States senator, but now, depending on Barnaby's condition when he caught up to him, he could see it happening. He could see it happening without hesitation.

"MISTER? HEY, mister?"

Barnaby slowly came to, urged on by the soft voice near his ear. His eyes felt dry and rough like sandpaper as he opened them, and he blinked rapidly to moisten them. His tongue felt thick, and his head was pounding. He didn't remember getting drunk, so all of this was a rather unpleasant surprise. As he rolled onto his back, he thought he heard someone scamper away. He stared up at a ceiling with graying paint chipping off it.

Along the top of the wall ran three old, crank-type windows, and through them he could see a lightening sky. In fact he was bathed in what little light there was, a rectangle of it crisscrossing him with shadows cast by the window panes. The rest of the room was dark and smelled old and metallic or like chemicals.

The whisper came again. "Mister?"

He started and sat up too quickly, then feared for a moment his stomach might rebel as his head throbbed even harder. "Who's... who's there?" he croaked.

Out of the shadows at the other end of the room, a young girl emerged. She wore flowered jeans, a pale blue blouse, and sneakers that had once been pink. She had light brown skin, short curly hair, and the face of an angel. She didn't fit their surroundings at all. Barnaby thought for a moment he might have lost his mind... or was dead. But then he saw how dirty her face and outfit were and realized she'd been here for a while.

"I'm Barnaby."

"I'm Tonya."

He nodded and looked around some more, but there wasn't anything new to see. Maybe when the sun rose higher the room would be more interesting. "Where is here, Tonya?"

She came a bit closer. "We're in Texas. Not sure where exactly, but this is a warehouse. Probably old office supplies. I can smell the toner."

So that's what that is.

She held her arms around herself to keep from shaking, and Barnaby removed his suit jacket, filthy as it was, to give to her. An October early morning in Texas could be chilly. "Where are your parents?"

She shook her head and tears filled her eyes. Barnaby wrapped his arms around her and made soothing sounds. He didn't know how long she'd been in the room, trying to stay strong on her own, but now that she wasn't alone, she seemed to feel it was safe to break down. And it was.

"It's gonna be okay."

"They… they came into my room and took me. I couldn't yell for Daddy or Uncle Lee. They left a note… I saw… on my bed. A note for Daddy."

"How many of them were there?"

"Three."

"Big?"

She nodded, and Barnaby grinned. Of course they were big. All men are big to a little girl. "How old are you, Tonya?"

"Twelve. How old are you?"

Barnaby chuckled softly. *Good, the kid has spunk.* "I'm twenty-eight."

She stepped away from him, now seemingly under control, and clutched the jacket around herself. She was small for twelve, and the jacket nearly swallowed her, legs and all. He stood, and with the sun now a bit higher in the sky, he could see a cot against the far wall. She went to it and retrieved a bottle of water that she gave to Barnaby.

"Thank you. How long have you been here?" he asked between gulps. He hoped the water would help ease the queasiness in his stomach and clear his head.

"Four days, I think."

"Have you heard anyone talking, maybe discussing stuff like you weren't in the room?" He crossed his fingers.

"Grown-ups never notice I'm around," she said, nodding. Then she narrowed her eyes in concentration. "Something's happening today. I thought it was you when you showed up, but I think it's something else. After you were dumped in here, I heard them say something about expecting someone else, someone important." Her eyes widened. "Not that you're not important."

He laughed. "Don't worry about it, Tonya. We're all important to somebody." *Or at least I was.* Pain washed through him at the thought of Charleston, but he shook it off and tried to concentrate on staying alive. After all, that's what Charleston had worked so hard for all those times.

"You okay, Mr. Barnaby?"

"I'm good. Just thinking about somebody I miss."

"I miss my Daddy, Uncle Lee, and Mom."

"I'm sure they miss you too, so we'll have to get you back to them, huh?"

"You think they're looking for me."

"Are you kidding? I *know* they are." That seemed to make her happy, and she smiled and went to sit on the cot.

Barnaby stared at the locked door. *It has to be locked, right?* He walked over and gripped the knob.

"No!" Tonya whispered harshly. "They'll come in."

They were coming in anyway, sooner or later. "Guns, right?"

She got to her feet and nodded, eyes wide.

He stared up at the window, then at the cot. Rushing over to it, he tried to lift it and found the metal frame made it heavy, but it was doable. Tonya got to her feet as Barnaby explained, "We're going to move this beneath the window, stand it on end, and use it to climb up and try to open that window, okay?"

She smiled and nodded eagerly as she bounced on the balls of her feet. He removed the thin mattress and placed it beneath the bottom feet of the cot, then lifted the other end and dragged it over to the window without too much ruckus. Tipping it on end, however, proved difficult to do quietly, as the metal feet started to make a horrendous screech on the concrete wall.

Tonya's eyes lit up, and she ran to the corner and grabbed a threadbare blanket they'd given her.

"Excellent idea, my dear."

Through some careful wiggling and adjusting, they slid the cot into place, and shielded the top two feet with the blanket and Barnaby's jacket so it wouldn't scrape loudly against the wall.

"Up you go. I'll hold it steady."

Tonya scrambled up the makeshift ladder and peered through the window.

"It's mostly desert. I don't see any other buildings or people, just bushes and dirt and hills in the distance." Her voice broke on a sob.

"It's okay," he said, trying to calm her. He knew his idea of the cot had given her renewed hope, and he wasn't ready to take that away. "Take a look at the latch. See if you can work it loose and crank it open."

"Okay." She went to work on it with her small hands. "It's rusty, and hard to—Ow!"

"Come down and let me have a look at you."

Tonya prepared to climb down but stopped to gaze out the window.

"What is it?"

"I think... I think I see someone out there," she gasped. "A man staring at the building." She looked down at Barnaby with excitement in her eyes. "I think he has binoculars. That's good, right? That's a good thing."

He smiled up at her. "You bet. Come down and let me work on that latch. Hurry!"

Chapter 24

"We're almost there," Charleston explained to his father. "Fifteen minutes, tops."

"Be careful, Junior. We almost lost you once today. Your mother couldn't survive it again... neither of us could."

"I'll be careful, Pop."

"Handal's got contact!" Leaundra announced to the group packed into the SUV. Jeri was sitting on the lap of a rather handsome female special ops officer and appeared to be in heaven, while Charleston was smashed between two other team members.

"Gotta go, Pop!" He ended the call, cutting off whatever his father was trying to add, and focused on Leaundra.

"He's seen the Lancaster girl and Rosenthal in a high window of the warehouse." She listened to Handal on her comm link for a few moments. "Rosenthal has worked the window open, and Handal's going in."

"Can we go any faster?" Charleston asked. *It's the year 2020 for goodness sake. Aren't we supposed to have flying cars by now? We can go back in time. Why the fuck don't we have teleportation, beaming technology, something?* Charleston made a note to speak to his father about that once this mess was settled. Then the driver sped up dangerously as everyone waited for another update from Leaundra.

Barnaby could see the man running toward them from his hiding place in the brush. Though he kept low, his strides kicked up dust, and the closer he got the more familiar he looked. *Handal!* He smiled, glad to see someone else who would be missing Charleston. "Come on, Tonya. Time to go."

As she climbed, Barnaby turned to look out the window again, but Handal was gone. "Handal?" he called.

"Bilius!" came a harsh whisper from right below the window.

"Bilius?" Barnaby frowned. "What the fuck does—"

"Ooh! That's my word, my safe word," Tonya said, coming flush with him and beaming like it was Christmas.

"Hurry," Handal called up. "There's a vehicle coming up the road, and I don't think it's Leaundra's team. Not yet."

Tonya scrambled past Barnaby and wriggled through the window, then lowered herself to hang on the outside. He heard Handal urge her to let go, that he'd catch her.

"It's okay, honey," Barnaby said.

"C-come with m-me," she begged.

"I will, but you need to let go first, okay?"

She shook her head just as he heard someone outside the door. His heart rabbited as he glanced between that door and Tonya's little hands clinging to the window ledge. They needed time—time to hide themselves in the desert. At least that was preferable to the three of them being chased and shot at.

"Hold your breath!" Barnaby said to her.

"Why—"

He pried her tiny fingers free of the ledge, and all she managed was a faint squeak before Handal, he hoped, had her in his arms.

"Go!" he shouted before quickly cranking the creaky window shut, tipping the cot over, and riding it down to the floor.

"What was that?" a man asked from the other side of the door.

"Get it open. Now!" a woman ordered.

The door swung open so hard it slammed into the wall behind it. Senator Collard walked in, two thugs he'd never seen before following. Barnaby lay on the cot, wishing he'd known the senator had the nerve to enter the room ahead of her hired muscle. If he had, he would have knocked her on her ass when she stormed in all badass in her red power suit.

"Where's the girl?" she demanded, looking around the room.

"I'm gay, hon, but I'm no girl," Barnaby quipped. Obviously he'd never met the woman. He'd seen her in articles and on Fox News mouthing off about one thing or another, but the narrowed gaze she leveled at him gave him a chill. Penelope was not amused.

"Bring him!" She turned on her heel and pushed past her men, one of whom Barnaby recognized, the one who wasn't a man. Kaan stood there, sadness heavy in her eyes, as two other goons advanced on him and pulled Barnaby out to the main room of the warehouse. "She won't get far alone in the desert," Collard said. "It'll save us the trouble. You'll look for her body once I'm done with this young man."

Barnaby glanced around as he was dragged through the warehouse, not bothering to use his feet. He thought of how excited he used to get as a child when it was time to purchase school supplies. All those notebooks, pencils, Crayons, erasers, rulers, and pens seemed to always fill him with an exciting sense of possibility, of potential. But this, this office supply graveyard—haphazardly stacked shelves of old toner cartridges, broken printers and copy machines, dusty packages of colorful paper clips, half-used reams of paper—was where possibility came to die, where he had likely come to die. All potential for anything more… ever, was fading fast.

"You did a good job, Kaan," the senator said.

"We would have done a better job if you'd been upfront with us in the beginning about Rosenthal's protector."

"Charleston Meeks was immaterial."

"He was not!" Kaan barked, anger flaring in her eyes. "He was trained and gave us more trouble because you failed to make that known."

Collard appeared unconcerned, turning her gaze on Barnaby and looking him up and down. "He's dead now, so it hardly matters."

"Rico's dead too because you—"

"Rico? Who's Rico?"

"My partner! Rico Katch. He died because you called in Ramirez instead of trusting us."

"Trusting you?" she said, whirling on Kaan. "You failed repeatedly! You—"

"Because we didn't know Meeks had skills!"

"You knew after your first meeting, did you not? And still that knowledge had little effect on neutralizing him." Kaan fell silent, glaring at her. "That's what I thought."

Barnaby, who had patiently watched the exchange, finally spoke up. "Do I really need to be here for this?" he asked, grinning crookedly. "I could just walk to the road, maybe hitch a ride back to Oregon." He smiled innocently at the two giants holding him between them. When Collard turned her gaze on him, he realized he should have kept his mouth shut.

"You shouldn't be anywhere, Mr. Rosenthal, and I think you know that." She walked over to him. "You should have died when your mother lost control of your stroller. You should have been killed by that pedophile. You should have ended your own pathetic existence in that icy river." Her voice rose, and her eyes grew even wilder as Barnaby watched. "You should have died in that bank robbery. Yet here you are, an affront to Our Lord's Great Plan."

Barnaby grinned.

"What do you have to smile about, boy?"

"Seems to me God's made it pretty clear he wants me to stick around. I'm obviously here because he saw fit that I should be. I wouldn't think your all-powerful daddy in the sky could be thwarted by any creation of man. Would you?"

Her face reddened, and she backhanded him, hard. Barnaby immediately stomped on the foot of the thug at his right, causing the man to cry out and release his arm, and then he punched Penny Collard in the face. She staggered backward, and Kaan caught her out of reflex, keeping her from landing on her ass. She then shoved the senator away from her and into the arms of her driver as if Collard were something filthy.

Collard righted herself and kept her eyes on Barnaby as she wiped the blood from her lip. Shaking with rage, she said, "You… disgusting… sodomite! How dare you touch me!"

"Somebody had to. It looks like it's been a while for you, sister." He wasn't sure, but Barnaby thought he saw a weak smile grace Kaan's lips. Anyone who had been smiling stopped when Collard pulled a gun from her suit pocket and chambered a round.

"If my boy had to die, you should have stayed dead, Mr. Rosenthal." She pointed the gun at his chest. "Now that the RPP has been taken apart, no one will be bringing you back this time."

"Assuming you acquired that legally, they'll trace my death back to you," Barnaby said, proud he kept the quiver out of his voice.

"If they could trace the bullets? Yes, that's true." She smiled. "But these bullets release a toxin as they dissolve in human tissue. You'll be dead, for good, and there won't be anything left to match to my gun." The two thugs holding him each took one step away from Barnaby, uncertain of her aim.

"No need to worry, gentlemen. My daddy taught me to shoot when I was eight years old. I don't miss."

"THIS IS Tonya," Handal said in introduction. "Tonya, this is my friend Charleston."

"Hi."

"Hey there, kid."

"I'm not a kid!"

"Whoa, sorry. Got it. You're a young lady. Well, I'd like you to go with this other young lady. Her name's Jeri."

Jeri stepped forward and took Tonya's hand. "Let's go find somewhere to hide, and we'll give your father a call, okay?"

Tonya nodded but froze where she stood and looked up at Charleston. "Are you gonna save Barnaby?"

"Oh yes." He narrowed his eyes and grinned. "That's exactly what I'm gonna do."

She smiled and walked away with Jeri.

Charleston crouched down beside Leaundra and Handal as they watched the warehouse. "Is the senator inside?"

"Yeah," Handal said. "She showed up just as I ran in to grab Tonya."

"What about local law enforcement?" he asked Leaundra, keeping his eyes on the building.

"They're standing by, out of sight. They won't move until—hang on." She listened to her comm link for several seconds. "We've got company, unauthorized company," Leaundra said, standing to her full height. Handal did the same, as did Charleston. In the distance they saw a trail of dust rising behind a semi as it raced toward the warehouse.

Shit! "It's Ramirez! Everybody, move!" Charleston shouted. "Go! Go! Go!" *So much for stealth*, he thought, as everyone ran for the warehouse.

EXPECTING TO hear a gunshot, Barnaby was surprised by the sound of a truck horn blaring at them across the Texas desert and growing louder as it approached. He opened his eyes, eyes he hadn't realized he'd closed, and saw Kaan grin at him, turn, and walk away to disappear behind some shelves. Collard and her men turned toward the sound and peered in confusion at the entrance of the warehouse, then collectively shrieked as Ramirez's blue semi tore through the front wall and sent them scattering.

Nobody thought to hang on to Barnaby, so he went his own way and found shelter behind a row of copy machines along one side of the room. He eyed the door to his previous prison and thought he might be able to avoid the ensuing melee by climbing out Tonya's window. *Better late than never.* But then, above the automatic gunfire, he heard "Barnaby!" in a voice he never thought he'd hear again. "Barnaby Rosenthal!"

He closed his eyes and remained crouched there, trying to breathe calmly, trying to clear his head of the shocked emotional fog that had crept into it. As his heart hammered, he slowly rose to his feet and searched for the owner of that precious voice in the chaos filling the room. He saw Ramirez nestled behind the right front wheel well of his truck, spraying the room with an Uzi, as what looked like SWAT team members—with aim about as good as any Imperial Stormtrooper—fired back and missed him completely. He saw the senator's thugs shooting at Ramirez *and* the SWAT team. He didn't see the senator or Kaan any longer, but he did see.... *Charleston?*

Chapter 25

"Chuck!"

Charleston turned toward that voice and saw Barnaby vault over the remains of a copy machine (that had apparently caught fire at some point during its life) and run toward him, oblivious of the gunfire blowing past. Barnaby slammed into him and knocked him to the floor where he kissed him to within an inch of his life. He saw fresh bruises in his future but decided to enjoy the weight and heat of Barnaby in his arms instead of worrying about that.

"He… he told me you were dead," Barnaby said through his tears. "Ramirez told me you died in the crash."

"No… uh, n-no," Charleston managed between kisses. "He tried, but I was just banged up a bit. Mild concussion, I think." He noticed the mark on Barnaby's face and saw red. "Who hit you?"

"Collard, but don't worry. I tagged her."

"You hit a woman?"

"Are you kidding? Of course I punched the bitch."

Charleston laughed, forgetting he'd been prepared to snap her neck. "Are you okay?"

Staring into Charleston's eyes, Barnaby said, "I am now."

Charleston kissed him. "As much as I'm enjoying this reunion, we need to find cover." He took Barnaby's hand and tugged him to a darkened corner of the room, where they crouched together while Charleston checked his magazine. "You're gonna stay behind me until we reach that truck, and then you're gonna take off outside through that handy hole Ramirez made. Jeri, Tonya, and an officer are in an SUV two hundred yards to the west."

"No fucking way I'm leaving here without you, Chuck."

"Barn—" He looked into Barnaby's dark eyes and knew the argument was over. "Fine," he sighed. "I have to round up the senator."

"She went left, and she's armed."

Charleston nodded and eyed that side of the warehouse, searching for any movement. "Stay behind me."

They moved as one along the wall, Charleston watching the firefight on their right and holding his gun at the ready. Ramirez was still pinned down on the passenger side of his truck as the assault team worked its way closer. Charleston saw Collard's two thugs drop—one stopped moving, and the other lay screaming in pain—taken out by SWAT or Ramirez, he didn't know or care.

Over the remaining gunfire and shouting, Charleston heard Ramirez demanding his money, complaining about his cargo being stolen, and demanding Kaan be brought to him. Apparently the mercenary had pissed off the psychopath. Well, they could have each other.

"There, behind that rack of paper," Barnaby suddenly whispered in his ear. "She's wearing red. You can't miss her."

He left Barnaby by a pile of office furniture—desks and chairs and bookshelves—and advanced on Collard. Just as the shooting suddenly stopped and the rest of the room fell silent, Charleston shouted, "Come on out, Penny. You're done."

She stepped out from behind the shelves, eyes on Barnaby, hair coming undone, her suit a tad wrinkled, jacket open and revealing a lovely white silk blouse. "I'm a United States senator, boy! You don't speak to me in such familiar terms."

"Show me your hands... *Senator*."

Collard held out her hands, one sporting the gaudy diamond that had marked Barnaby's face, and walked slowly toward Charleston. Her gaze never left Barnaby as he stepped away from his hiding place and walked forward.

"You don't deserve to exist," she shrieked at him, "not when my Terry was taken from me!" Her eyes filled with tears and rage. And insanity, Charleston noted. "He was good and perfect and beautiful, but God called him home." She pointed at Barnaby. "He did the same to you, Rosenthal... but you defy him! You still live with your twisted desires, and I lost my Terry when I tried to turn him to the right path. It's wrong. It's of Satan!"

Charleston frowned in confusion. "He was 'good and perfect and beautiful.' What was wrong with the path he was on?" he asked calmly.

The senator's expression clouded. "I saw him… the way he watched other boys. I could see the sin growing in him, and I took action!"

"What action?" Barnaby asked gently. He sounded frightened, and Charleston didn't blame him. He wouldn't be surprised to see Collard's head spin on her neck at any second.

Collard's face relaxed, and she tried to smooth her hair back into place, to tame her upsweep, but it wasn't cooperating. "I found a place in Tennessee: Pastoral Healings in Love. They could fix my boy, rid him of his sinful—"

"A conversion camp," Charleston said flatly.

Collard fell silent and again tried to tame her chaotic hair.

"Your son died," Charleston explained calmly, "because you sent him to strangers to have him 'fixed' instead of accepting him as your God created him, Senator. You're the one who defied your Lord."

"No!" she moaned, her fury-filled expression cracking under her grief and guilt. She looked as if her stomach turned at the thought, as if she might be sick or faint.

"Sir, her men are down," a team member said as he rushed over to take possession of Collard. "One's dead, I think. Her driver is being held outside, and Ramirez is gone."

"Gone?" Charleston holstered his weapon. "What do you mean gone?"

"He stopped shooting, and by the time we reached his position…." The man shrugged. "He was just… gone."

"Track him! Get everybody on it!"

"We are, sir. All personnel are searching the area, as we speak." The operative began patting the sobbing Collard down and quickly discovered her gun. "We'll get the local authorities to help."

"Good. He can't have gotten—"

Collard shrieked, shoved the team member backward over a stack of dead laser printers, and snatched her gun from his flailing hand to point at Barnaby. Charleston moved without thinking, raising his own weapon as he did, but two bullets tore into his chest before his finger could squeeze the trigger.

He fell to the floor with Barnaby's "No!" echoing in his ears.

BARNABY RUSHED to Charleston's side just as Collard turned her gun on the team member she'd caught off guard and put a bullet through his skull. Charleston tried to speak but couldn't, his eyes deep blue and wild as they searched Barnaby's. *No no no no no no*, Barnaby repeated to himself, his focus only on Charleston, on trying to will him to stay. He stroked Charleston's hair out of his eyes and cupped his face between his hands. *Please... please don't go.*

He sobbed as he asked, "Why? Why did you do that, Chuck?" Blood darkened Charleston's shirt and spread through Barnaby's fingers when he pressed down on the wounds, trying to stop the flow. *No... no, please no. Not now.* "Not now," he whispered, tears dripping onto Charleston's chest as the man, his man, used the last of his strength to press his gun and the hand that held it into Barnaby's.

Charleston stopped moving, an almost-smile on his face, as a shadow hovered over them.

"My daddy was a great man! And what I did for my boy, I did to make him someone my daddy could be proud of," Collard rasped, choking on her fury, her insanity. "But you…. Today was your last sunrise. I hope you paid attention. Look at me, you filthy—"

Barnaby turned to look up into the muzzle of her gun as he lifted Charleston's gun hand and pulled the trigger Charleston no longer could, just as he'd done with Katch's weapon at the airport.

An expression of confusion came over the senator's face, and she staggered back a step, staring down at the growing stain on her white silk blouse. She touched her chest, then looked at her hand, trying to make sense of the dark red moisture her palm came away with.

"Wha…?" she gasped.

Barnaby pulled the trigger again and again and again, each time knocking Collard back another step. She stumbled, losing one red pump before dropping to her knees and falling on her face, dead.

He turned back to Charleston and held his face again, turning it to look in his eyes, but he knew those eyes didn't see him anymore.

"Chuck?" he asked, his voice breaking as he clutched at Charleston's shoulders and shook him. "Chuck?"

He was vaguely aware of people running into the room, muffled shouts, frantic energy building around him, but all he did was stare into Charleston's face, not wanting to believe he was gone. "Please look at me," he whispered, "the way you did that day in the hotel. Look at me like that. Please...."

There were people standing around them now, people with different uniforms than he'd seen earlier. They were speaking, but he didn't understand what they were saying. Then there were hands on him, under his arms, lifting him away from Charleston, people closing in around Charleston and blocking Barnaby's view. One of those people was a handsome older woman in uniform, with dark, flawless skin. She turned to look at Barnaby, and her flinty gaze softened.

He closed his eyes, heart aching, and lost time.

WHEN BARNABY became aware once again, he heard Coral and Ross chatting softly near him, discussing their work, his well-being, India's flight, some conversation Ross had had with Barnaby's mother, and various other things that didn't matter anymore. He didn't want to open his eyes because then they'd want to talk to him, worry over him, ask him how he felt—did he need anything, anything at all? The only thing he needed was Charleston, and that, they couldn't give him.

There was mention of him going back to Chillicothe, and he almost sat bolt upright in bed to protest but stopped himself. That wasn't happening. He'd fought to get out of there, to see the world and chase his artistic dreams. He'd made it. He was financially comfortable and for years had simply been waiting for Charleston to reappear so they could share their lives somehow.

Now, all those people who'd thought him insane when he talked about the mysterious man who came to his rescue throughout the years, those people who never believed in Charleston Meeks... they would be right. That man didn't exist anymore, and he wasn't coming back.

Barnaby tuned out Coral and Ross, and not once did he let on he was aware, because he didn't want to be, and eventually, he wasn't any longer.

THE NEXT time he woke, he opened his eyes before checking if he was alone and found an elderly man sitting by his bed. He had thick, graying blond hair and blue eyes—eyes like…. "Dr. Meeks?"

The man nodded. He looked much older than Barnaby had expected, but he could see the resemblance. "How are you feeling, my boy?"

"Tired."

"I'm sure you are." Dr. Meeks turned and looked out the window. It was a sunny day. Barnaby could see the blue sky from his bed. "I'm feeling rather exhausted myself." He reached over to the bedside table and picked up an eyeglass case. "Your… uh, friend Ross brought these by for you. Your spares."

"Oh… thank you." Barnaby opened the case and slipped on a pair of thick-framed, leopard-patterned glasses that Ross had bought him as a gag gift last year. The room came into sharper focus, as did the fatigue on Dr. Meeks's face. "Sir, I'm sorry for your loss."

The man turned back to Barnaby. "And I'm sorry for yours."

They regarded each other for several moments.

"He was very proud of you," Barnaby said.

Dr. Meeks raised an eyebrow. "Really?"

Barnaby nodded. "I could tell by the way he talked about your accomplishments, could hear it in his voice."

"Oh, well…." Dr. Meeks stared at the floor. "He was a good son. Always." He shook himself and treated Barnaby to a miserable smile. "I wish I had told him that more often." They sat in silence for five minutes, just breathing, thinking, remembering. Then Dr. Meeks jolted in his seat, realizing he'd come there for a reason. He said, "We're having the funeral in two days, and we'd very much like you to be there."

Barnaby's heart skipped before he asked, "Sir, isn't there something—"

But Charleston's father was already shaking his head. "The program is defunded. The equipment is being repurposed, the personnel reassigned, and we'd need time-line extrapolators and someone to make the step."

"I could—"

"No, Mr. Rosenthal. I don't know how much my son told you about temporal mechanics."

"Just that the first step makes you sick."

"Well, something else you need to understand is that you can't step into a room where you already are. And you were there in the room when—" Dr. Meeks's breath caught. "—when Junior died. You can't step through and run into yourself. It would be cataclysmic."

"I see," Barnaby muttered.

"I'm retiring next month, around the same time the program will be completely mothballed. I just don't have... I don't seem to have the energy or curiosity I once did. It's a young person's game these days, and I've never felt so old." He smiled weakly. "That Jeri girl has what it takes, I think." He began to stare out the window again.

Barnaby watched him, studied the profile that was so much like Charleston's. He fisted his blanket and closed his eyes against the ache in his chest. Who would have thought emptiness could be so painful?

CHAPTER 26

SITTING BY a window, sunshine bathing him, Barnaby picked at the finger food on his plate. It looked delicious and pricey, but he didn't have an appetite. Coral, India, and Ross sat close by, ready to shore him up if necessary. That was nice. He didn't really know anyone else at the Meeks's house, but some of the people at the postfuneral gathering seemed to know him.

Dr. Meeks had greeted him earlier but was now busy supporting his wife, who looked about ready to fall apart at any moment. Barnaby had spotted the officer he'd seen kneeling next to Charleston's body. Her name was Odette Leaundra, and according to Dr. Meeks, she had worked closely with his son for several years. He'd also been introduced to a Dr. Melody Plumb, a Jeri Sato, and a Hiram Lancaster, who turned out to be Tonya's father and who was effusively grateful for Barnaby's help in rescuing his daughter.

"She can't stop talking about you," he'd said.

All of them seemed to know Charleston well, and they clearly felt a kinship with Barnaby. There was an air about them that said they understood what he was feeling. His mother hadn't understood. She'd never known what Charleston had meant to him over the years, thinking the blond man from his paintings was simply a figment of her son's overactive imagination. And he couldn't explain everything that had happened over the phone. There was too much between him and Charleston to convey. He smiled. *Too much history.*

She and Donald and Nelson had urged Barnaby to return to Chillicothe, where he'd be surrounded by his family and "normal" people... not those "odd folks out West." He'd promised to visit soon and had asked Nelson what he could bring him. It was some violent video game, and Barnaby had vowed to sneak it to him regardless of their mother's objections.

Nelson had stayed on the line after their parents hung up and eagerly told Barnaby about his gay friend at school. Her name was Rebecca, and she was "super cool." Nelson had also proudly told him that when kids bullied her, he helped put a stop to it. He stood by her when she stood up to them.

"They back off if they're challenged in front of everyone," Nelson had said, "and all it takes is one person to call them on it and tell them bullying only shows what losers they are."

His thirteen-year-old brother's chutzpah had surprised a laugh out of him, what felt like the first one in forever, and the delight he'd felt seemed to crack something hard in his chest.

"Aren't you worried they'll think you're gay too?"

"They've already called me faggot—no offense, bro—but I told them my older brother's gay and an artist and totally awesome."

"I am? I'm totally awesome?" he'd asked, laughing.

"Well… that's what I tell them, doesn't mean I think you really are or anything."

"Fair enough." He'd told Nelson how proud he was of him for sticking up for his friends and said he'd be home to see him as soon as he could and that he'd like to meet this Rebecca.

Now Barnaby sat staring at a tiny plate filled with food he didn't want. How long did one stay at one of these things? The funeral had been well attended, just a lot more faces that Barnaby didn't recognize. He'd ridden to the cemetery with his friends in silence. He wanted to tell them all about Charleston, but he held back, afraid giving voice to his memories and impressions would somehow dilute them, erase them. It looked like he was back to keeping quiet about the man of his dreams—no, the man of his reality.

He glanced up and met eyes with Jeri Sato. They gave each other sad, crooked smiles, and then she did the strangest thing. She glanced around and then tilted her head to the side, directing him to join her in the next room.

He frowned as she slipped through the doorway and disappeared.

"What is it?" Coral asked, ever-watchful for any sign of distress.

"Uh… nothing," he said, setting his plate aside.

"You're not gonna eat that?" India asked, eyeing the food.

Barnaby shook his head and passed her his food, which she began to gobble down. "I'll be right back. Excuse me." As he crossed the room, he heard Ross warn India, "You're going to get fat."

Barnaby ducked through the same doorway Jeri had, then down a hallway that led to a huge kitchen. Sunlight spilled in through all the windows, and he had to squint until his eyes adjusted. Despite sitting at the window, the first room had seemed so much darker to him, what with all the sadness in it, muting any light that seeped in. Jeri stood by the back door, gazing out at the deck, her shiny black hair glowing in the sunshine. She reached in the pocket of her black suit jacket, removed a lollipop, unwrapped it, and popped it in her mouth.

"Hello?"

Jeri turned and smiled brightly around the sucker. "Join me on the deck?" She went outside, and he followed her. Once outside and seeing they were alone, Jeri invited Barnaby to have a seat on the steps. "How are you feeling?"

He frowned. "Well, I—"

"I mean after shooting a United States senator."

"Oh...." He thought about it for a moment, searched his conscience. "She'd just taken someone I love from me." He nodded. "It was surprisingly easy."

"And she was about to kill you."

"Yeah, there was that." Barnaby stared out over the massive yard that was only a small portion of the total ranch. Statements taken at the scene had cleared Barnaby of any wrongdoing, senator or not. Trackers had determined Ramirez hadn't left of his own free will but had been overcome and taken by someone—dragged, if the heel marks of his ugly-ass snakeskin boots could be trusted—to a waiting vehicle, which authorities had yet to identify.

"Sucker?" Jeri asked, holding out a cherry lollipop.

"Thanks." He took it, unwrapped it, and gave it a good suck.

"So you loved him."

"All my life." She nodded, apparently mulling something over. "You were a good friend of his?" he asked.

"Uh, well… the first time I met him, I almost knocked him over. I'd just transferred to TRD from the lab above."

"TRD?"

"Temporal Research and Development. It's where we did the experimental, minor steps—smaller teams, sometimes one man only." She squinted up at him, shielding her eyes from the sun. "It's where we did all the Rosenthal... uh, your steps."

He nodded slowly, trying to wrap his head around a team of people working together to save his life... repeatedly. "I guess it's all packed away now, huh?"

"Not TRD, just Major Operations."

"What do you mean 'major'? Chuck said big events couldn't be undone."

"Major only in the sense that more personnel were needed for coordination. They still only restored the one subject, but sometimes there was traffic to affect, people to distract... all sorts of things. And it all had to be choreographed like clockwork. I never worked on those jobs, although I would have been awesome at it."

A gentle but chill breeze blew through the yard, and they both watched it dance through the colorful leaves on the trees at their right. "What did you want to tell me?" Barnaby asked.

She grinned, and her eyes took on a mischievous glint. "Well, I have this... *idea.*" Barnaby blinked at her, and she focused on the trees again as the wind picked up. "Came to me a few nights ago."

"In a dream?"

"No, as I was nodding off following a rather athletic bout of lovemaking with my girlfriend."

"How nice for you. What's this idea got to do with me?"

"I have a couple other people to talk to, but I'd like us to meet up somewhere tonight and discuss things."

He stared into her dark eyes. "Why would—"

"Because you love him."

Barnaby closed his eyes against the sudden ache in his bones, the tightness in his chest, the lump in his throat, and the sting of tears. When he opened them again, he said, "My hotel room?"

"What about your friends?"

"We're supposed to fly out together tonight, but I'll say I'm meeting up with people who knew him best... say we're having drinks, toasting him or something."

"Good enough. See ya tonight. Now, I'd better go round up my woman." Jeri stood, but before leaving, she paused, removed the sucker from her mouth with an audible *pop*, and squeezed Barnaby's shoulder. "Don't worry. I'm scary brilliant." Then she and her sucker were gone.

He continued to sit alone for a while, contemplating all Jeri had said. As he worried his lollipop, his heart kept speeding up with excitement, with hope (or sugar), but he would breathe deeply and slow it back down. The branches of the trees were bending in the wind now, and he looked left and saw thunder clouds gathering.

"Hey, you," Coral said, coming up behind him. He hadn't even heard the door open. She sat next to him and took his arm, leaning into him and resting her copper-red head on his shoulder. "Dr. Meeks made his wife go lie down. Are you about ready to go? We still have to check out of the hotel, and I'd like to get to the airport early. You know how Ross and India are about security and all the crap they travel with. What do you say?"

He patted her hand on his arm and gave it a squeeze. "I'm not flying out with you, hon."

"What?" She sat up straight and stared at him, concern and suspicion all over her face. "Why not?"

He gave her his excuse.

"Is that what that girl was talking to you about just now? Sato? That's her name, right?"

He nodded. "She and her coworkers knew Charleston best. I'd like to… I don't know, commune with them for a night. Listen to stories about him."

Her expression softened. "I get that… I guess." She smiled weakly and kissed his cheek. "I wish I'd met him properly, gotten to know him."

"Yeah, me too."

She grinned. "You know you're sentencing me to India and Ross talking photo shoots, fatty foods, and fashion on the flight home, right?"

He kissed her alabaster cheek. "I know. Sorry. I'll make it up to you. I promise."

"You'd better," she said, peering at him through narrowed eyes. "Come home to us soon, okay?"

CHAPTER 27

BARNABY MADE himself stop fussing with the room service cart. He didn't have any idea how many people would be showing up, so he'd ordered a variety of appetizers and drinks. He'd called the hotel and made the order while driving back from the airport after saying a long good-bye to Coral, India, and Ross.

Now he sat on one of the beds in his room, staring at the bland art framed on the wall, listening to his breathing, counting the beats of his heart, and wondering what tonight would bring. A knock sounded at the door, startling him.

"Hey there, Barnaby," Jeri said when he let her in. She carried a bright purple data tablet. Following her into the room were Lancaster, Plumb, and Leaundra, who closed and locked the door behind them.

"Everyone, please have a seat," Barnaby said, plopping down on a bed and unconsciously grabbing a pillow and hugging it to his chest, "or help yourself to some food. I didn't know what or how much to order, but—"

"It's all good, Rosenthal," Leaundra said. "Why don't we just get down to business? Sato?"

Barnaby's grip tightened on the pillow, and he waited.

"I believe we can restore Charleston," Jeri said.

Barnaby closed his eyes and held his breath. *Please, please, please....*

"And we agree with Jeri's assessment," Lancaster added.

"Mr. Rosenthal?" Dr. Plumb said. "Are you all right?"

"Y-yes, I'm f-fine, but... but Dr. Meeks said—"

"He told you it wasn't possible," Lancaster finished.

Barnaby nodded. "Because you didn't have the personnel any longer." His four visitors glanced at each other. "What?"

"You could make the step," Jeri said, maintaining eye contact with him.

"Dr. Meeks said I couldn't step into a room where I already… was? Something like that."

"He's right," Lancaster said, "but that's not where we'd like to send you."

Shaking his head, Barnaby said, "Why? He was shot in the warehouse. Where else would I go to stop Chuck from being killed?" They all looked at each other again. "Stop it! Stop looking at each other like you're not sure you should continue! We're in this. I'm in this. Just spill it."

Jeri activated her tablet. "Working with what you said Collard told you at the warehouse, I did some semi-illegal digging and was able to uncover the actual circumstances surrounding Terry's death. You'll be sent back twenty-eight years to a small town in Tennessee, the site of a conversion camp for gays where Terry died after being starved and beaten for weeks. You need to save him, Barnaby, and by doing that, you'll restore Charleston."

"We think," Lancaster added.

"You think?" Barnaby's thoughts raced.

"Lancaster's the only one here who has experience with temporal extrapolation," Jeri said. "I've played with it some but never on an actual step."

"Chuck told me undoing something big, something in the national consciousness, would be bad."

"The boy's death was hushed up, records forged, people bribed or possibly threatened," Leaundra said. "There's no way the senator would have allowed the truth of what happened to come out, so it never became part of our national news beyond a tragic accident at his home." She nodded toward Jeri. "Luckily we have someone who can break through all the lies."

Barnaby nodded, deep in thought. "I see. It would have made a much bigger media splash if it had come out that the senator lost her son while trying to make him straight." He took a deep breath, his mind starting to accept what they were telling him, but he still had questions and fears. "Chuck said the first step makes you sick, and I'm guessing none of you have ever been?"

"I went on one years ago," Leaundra said. "I didn't feel right sending in my people without knowing what it was like firsthand."

"And?"

"It made me sick… a little dizzy and queasy for about twenty minutes."

"And you? You don't have anything to add?" he asked Dr. Plumb.

"I like to think of myself as a 'temporal physiologist,' Mr. Rosenthal. I've spent a few years studying the effects of time travel on the human body and mind. I'll give you a complete physical and try to explain what you might experience during and after the step."

"From the information Sato has provided," Leaundra explained, "I'll be going over tactical logistics with you: the layout of the facility, where the boy's body was found, data collected at the autopsy, and what you'll need to do to help him."

"Exactly how does this help Chuck?"

Lancaster stepped forward. "Collard's motivations, her fixation on the RPP and you, stems from the loss of her son and the guilt she couldn't face. If you save him, there should be nothing to launch her on a path to slaughtering restored subjects." He frowned. "In fact, I'm a little concerned about that." He began to pace. "You see, all the RPP subjects she had deleted would be restored."

"As would Vislou," Leaundra added.

"And the Lazarus family would never have been targeted?" Barnaby's mind buzzed. "Everybody lives," he whispered in awe.

"Excuse me?" Leaundra asked.

"Cult TV show reference," Jeri offered. "Don't worry, I know what he's talking about."

"Well, I'm Dr. Plumb, not Doctor Who. I hope we're all taking this seriously."

Jeri ignored her and plopped down on the bed beside Barnaby. She placed her hand on his thigh and looked into his eyes. "Yes, Barnaby," she said in earnest. "If we do this right, then just this once, everybody lives."

"Nerds," Leaundra muttered, shaking her head.

"Hey, who was it that knew about Bella and Katniss?" Jeri demanded, turning to face her.

Leaundra scowled and returned hotly, "Because of my grandkids, not because I—"

"Will I remember saving the Lazarus kids?" Barnaby asked suddenly.

"As time goes on," Dr. Plumb explained, "it will feel more like a dream or a story you might have read about online, instead of something you actually experienced." She smiled brightly. "I've learned the human mind can accommodate quite a bit, even realities that no longer exist."

"Is this really possible?" Barnaby asked as he examined each of their faces and tugged his fingers through his hair. "Can I do this?"

"We're going to find out," Jeri said, "if you're game."

He was game.

AFTER SETTING up shop at Dr. Plumb's practice in Goodland, the nearest to the RPP facility, they all got to work. Barnaby spent the next week learning the bare basics of time travel, emergency medical assistance, counseling, and self-defense. During that time he also fielded calls from his mother, who wanted him home in Ohio, Coral, who wanted him home in Oregon, and Ross, who just wanted him. But all Barnaby could focus on was bringing Charleston home.

"The first thing you'll want to do when you locate the boy is give him the Re-Anim, but do it slowly, a sip at a time," Dr. Plumb said as Jeri and Lancaster looked on, awaiting their turns at him. "Don't let him gulp it. And give it a good shake before you give it to him. It'll restore his electrolytes and stabilize his metabolism until help can arrive."

"Okay," Barnaby said, making a note. "Now what if he's not alone? I doubt the staff are going to let me help him if they're trying to pray and starve and beat the gay out of him."

"I suggest you ask Leaundra that. I'm a healer, not a fighter."

Barnaby chuckled. "Okay, Bones."

Lancaster and Jeri exchanged smiles.

"Excuse me?" Plumb squinted at him from behind her wire-frame glasses. Apparently, she, just like Barnaby, preferred the eyewear to surgically modifying her eyes. He recalled Kaan's comments about eyeglasses, then tried to think of other people in his life who wore them.

He frowned when he only came up with Donald, his stepfather, and Dr. Meeks. "Who's Bones?" Plumb asked.

"Uh… it's a character from the *Star Trek* universe," Lancaster said.

"And the title character from the crime show about a forensic anthropologist," Jeri added.

"Yes," Lancaster continued, "but I believe Mr. Rosenthal's reference was to the iconic *Star Trek* character."

"What's going on in here?" Leaundra asked, entering the room.

"Sorry, we're having a bit of a nerd moment, got a bit distracted," Barnaby explained.

"No time left for distractions, I'm afraid. You're stepping tomorrow."

"Tomorrow?" they all asked.

"They're breaking down TRD tomorrow night, so Rosenthal steps in the morning."

"It's not supposed to be disassembled until mid-November," Dr. Plumb said, looking concerned.

"They moved up the timeline… I think for the holidays or maybe because Ramirez's body has been identified. They found him in a gulley outside Midland, Texas. According to autopsy, he'd been skinned alive." She sighed. "Rather gruesome and apropos of Halloween, don't you think?" Barnaby felt bile rise in his throat as Leaundra turned to Jeri. "Sato, set up the floor plan for Pastoral Healings In Love. He should look it over one more time before we fire up the Portal." She turned to Barnaby. "Rosenthal, follow me. You have to look the part."

Barnaby gulped, his eyes wide. "I'm… I'm n-not ready."

"You'd better be. We're only getting one shot at this." The former team leader left the room, ignoring the stunned expressions on everyone's faces.

BARNABY TUGGED at the collar of his uniform. "How do you wear these things?"

"Stop fidgeting," Leaundra said as they drove up to the RPP facility in her pickup. The building was fairly nondescript. Barnaby had been expecting something a bit more modern-looking, more space-agey, not bricks and bland landscaping.

"I know it doesn't look like much," Leaundra said, reading his expression, "but it has state-of-the-art security with redundancies, though over the past week or so, they've been relying more on manpower than technology. That's good for us."

She parked, and as they exited the truck, Barnaby asked, "Are they really going to just let us stroll in and empty your office? Aren't there top secrets to keep?" Struggling to keep up, he shuffled the collapsible, transparent packing crates and slid them under his arm as they approached the entrance.

"Any high-priority files were removed last month," Leaundra explained. "We're here to collect... personal items or knickknacks, for lack of a better word." Watching her purposeful stride and rigid posture, Barnaby doubted any knickknacks existed in Leaundra's office.

His heart sped up, and his breathing became more shallow as they neared the building. *I can do this. I can do this for Chuck,* he thought as he willed his body not to sweat through his uniform. He went over everything in his head: make the step, vomit for twenty minutes or so, enter Pastoral Healings In Love (or PHIL) through the kitchen, and work his way to counseling room four. According to police reports Jeri had dug up, Terry's body had been found in that room on March 20, 1992. Barnaby shuddered at the thought of finding the boy in such bad shape, but if he saved him, it would all be worth it.

They paused at the entrance, and Barnaby opened the door for Leaundra like a good little soldier.

"Good morning, T.L. Leaundra," a guard at the front desk said.

"Huntington. How's it going?"

"Busy, ma'am."

"Really?" Leaundra asked, feigning surprise as the guard scanned her print. Every other member of their little team—Dr. Plumb, Jeri, and Lancaster—had already staggered their arrivals to RPP this morning, ten to fifteen minutes apart. Leaundra and Barnaby were the last two.

"Looks like everyone had the same idea."

"Ah, I see. Cleaning out the offices before tonight, huh?"

"First person in this morning was Dr. Meeks." Barnaby tensed, but Leaundra didn't react. "I don't want to speak out of turn, ma'am, but he seemed a bit.... Well, he appeared to have been drinking."

"That's understandable, considering the circumstances. I'll check his office."

"Yes, ma'am, but he said he wanted to look over some equipment in the basement. Not sure what's down there. My clearance doesn't allow it, but he told me to expect some power spikes."

"Thank you, Huntington," she said, through grinding teeth. "I appreciate your discretion."

Once they were on the elevator, Barnaby asked, "What does this mean?"

"It means we need to get downstairs now."

"You seemed angry with that guard."

"Angry doesn't begin to cover it." Leaundra turned to him. "What good is a guard who allows an obviously intoxicated and emotionally compromised scientist access to mysterious equipment that produces 'power spikes'?"

"Good point."

She huffed and turned to watch the digital numbers count down on the control panel. When they reached the basement, the doors opened onto a long, poorly lit corridor of reinforced concrete. *Cheery*, Barnaby thought. Leaundra rushed forward and passed through a set of double doors into a hallway that met Barnaby's previous space-agey expectations with its low lighting and seamless, polished-white surroundings. They hurriedly made several twists and turns until they came to a white door that hissed open.

Dr. Plumb waited inside. "Thank God. You'd better come quick." They followed her into the locker room, and Barnaby tried to examine his surroundings, but there wasn't time for sightseeing. "Jeri and Lancaster are trying to input the correct coordinates, but Dr. Meeks is being difficult. They're trying to calm him, keep him away from the panel, but...."

"Rosenthal," Leaundra said, pausing before another set of doors at the back of the room. "Get changed." She tossed him her briefcase. "Then follow us." She and Plumb disappeared through the door, and Barnaby began to quickly strip out of his uniform. He pulled the clothes he'd be wearing for the step from Leaundra's briefcase, and once he was changed, he followed them.

He found himself in yet another long hall and felt a vibration through the floor. He rushed through another hissing door. The room he walked into was cavernous, and Barnaby stood a moment, staring at the ceiling high above him. A commotion on the far left of the room brought his attention back down to ground level.

Barnaby's breath caught when he saw the Portal and the image taking shape within it. It was the warehouse where Charleston had died; the chaos of Ramirez's battle with the assault team played out as if it were on a giant television, but there was no sound.

Dr. Meeks struggled with Lancaster and Plumb, fighting to reach the controls. "My son! I have to save my son!" he shouted. "Let me go!"

Leaundra stepped forward and put the man in a half nelson. "That's what we're trying to do, you controlling nincompoop!"

"Should we power down?" Plumb asked.

"No!" Jeri said. "Rebooting for a power-up will take too long."

Dr. Meeks finally went limp in Leaundra's arms, and she let him drop to the floor like a sandbag. Lancaster moved to the monitors and typed like a madman for a moment before giving Leaundra a curt nod. She turned to Barnaby and shouted, "Go!"

He rushed forward, thinking a run at the Portal would be easier. "Here!" Plumb shouted, tossing him a sports bottle filled with an orange liquid. Barnaby caught it and stepped into 1992.

CHAPTER 28

Peabody, Tennessee - March 1992

I FELT *the soft forest floor beneath my sneakers as the world spun, and I fell over and retched. My vomiting drowned out the night sounds around me, and I tried to breathe deeply between bouts, taking the fresh, moist night air into my lungs. I kept my eyes closed. Hadn't they told me that would help? I couldn't see the world spinning, but I could feel it. I continued to dry heave, clawing at the damp earth, twigs, and moss.*

Sometime later—I don't know how long—the spinning slowed and stopped, and my awareness returned. I found myself surrounded by darkness and clutching a tree trunk. I wound my arms tightly around it as far as they could reach, like I was trying to hang on to something that was too big and strong to be flung off into space, something with deep roots. The chill in the air had seeped past my clothing, but I opened my eyes and looked around.

All I saw was more trees and darkness. I could see stars through the treetops, stars and moonlight. The Re-Anim! I got to my knees and began to sweep the area with my hands, trying to find the bottle Dr. Plumb had given me. I couldn't have screwed up already, could I? One hand slid through vomit—luckily I'd only had a giant soda and some crackers in my stomach—so I knew I was getting close. There! My hand closed around the bottle, and I took a moment to breathe a sigh of relief, clutching it to my chest.

I wiped my fouled hand in the grass and got to my feet. Through the trees I could see security lights lining the roof of a long, low building, and I began to make my way toward it. The entrance to the kitchen was in the back of the building, and that's where I ended up when I exited the forest.

I saw a guy exit the back door struggling with three garbage bags. He looked to be in his midtwenties and wore the same dark blue windbreaker, ball cap, and white shirt as I did, so I ran forward and grabbed one of the bags.

"Hey, need a hand?"

"Thanks... uh...."

"Barnaby," I said with my most trustworthy smile.

"I'm Keifer. Don't think we've met before."

"Yeah, it's kind of a big place."

"True," Keifer said, slamming the lid closed on the Dumpster and then leading me back inside the kitchen. "What's that?" he asked, pointing to the Re-Anim bottle.

"Just a sports drink." I unscrewed the top, put the bottle to my closed lips, and pretended to take a healthy sip. I knew all of it had to go to Terry once I located him.

"Well, thanks. I'm gonna grab something to eat. Have a good night."

"You too."

He began digging through the refrigerator, and I casually walked past him. I left the kitchen and walked through a deserted dining room. Just beyond that was a massive great room with a fireplace. At either end were stairs, leading to the second level and sleeping quarters. Definitely worth millions, it was basically an elaborate cabin and, according to Jeri's data, donated to PHIL by a conservative Christian with deep pockets but poor research skills. Collard had trusted her son to a fellow right-winger who had hooked up with this group of quacks because he needed to believe homosexuality was a condition that could be changed or cured.

There were ten or so young men spread around the room, reading, working on laptops, watching television, or surreptitiously giving each other the eye. Some were dressed like I was, clearly staff, but most wore gray T-shirts and sweatpants. I turned right, heading straight for the counseling rooms below the stairs. No one seemed suspicious or tried to stop me.

Walking like I knew where I was going, which I did, and what I was doing, which I didn't, I returned any smiles or waves they tossed my way. I glanced at the watch Leaundra had provided me: 8 p.m. The atmosphere seemed fairly relaxed, which made sense. It wasn't like it was eight in the morning. The day was winding down.

I passed counseling rooms one through three. They were soundproof, so there was no way to tell if there were teens in there right now undergoing some bogus "bonding" with a father figure to reorder their sexual preferences. When I reached room four, I hesitated, braced myself, and slowly turned the knob.

The door was jerked open, out of my grip, and a tall, muscular man in a white orderly uniform loomed over me.

"What?"

I tried not to show the terror I was feeling, steeling myself... for Charleston's sake, for Terry's sake. I shook my bottle at him. "I've got something for Terry Collard."

"He's not allowed anything," the man said, smirking and turning his back to me. "He's got two more days of punishment for his stubborn attitude." He strode to a bed in the corner, where a painfully thin young man lay. The orderly feigned a punch to Terry's gut, causing the boy to recoil and whimper. "You want to eat, Terry? You want something to drink? Then you start working harder, praying harder to give up those unnatural desires. That's why your mama sent you here, boy. Get with the program!"

"Please stop...," Terry whined, covering his head with his arms. I didn't know what Terry looked like when he arrived at this place, but right now I could see his ribs. I could see bruises on his face and bare chest. I could see the fear and hopelessness in his green eyes, as well as the tears.

And I felt rage.

I stepped into the room and quietly closed the door behind me just as the orderly whirled back around. "Why are you still here?" he asked.

I put the bottle Plumb had given me under one arm and began to dig in my jacket pockets. "Sorry, I forgot I have this for you," I said, pulling a slip of paper from my left pocket. The orderly snatched it from me and unfolded the note as I pulled the stun gun from my right pocket and jammed it up into his nutsac. He wouldn't be in a rush to show anyone that wound.

The big man went rigid, his eyes rolling back in his skull. I held it there for a bit longer than necessary, I must admit, but I stopped when I noticed how frightened Terry looked. The orderly dropped to the floor, and I rushed to Terry's side.

"It's okay, Terry," I said softly. "I'm not going to hurt you. I'm here to help." I grabbed the bottle and gave it a few hard shakes. "This is to help you feel better. It'll rehydrate you and help your body heal itself, okay?"

He shook his head even as he eyed the bottle with longing plain in his eyes. "I'm on punishment," he croaked. "I haven't changed yet. I can't have anything." His tongue darted out, trying to wet his cracked lips. "Not until I give up these... feelings."

I blinked at him. He was kidding, right? "Terry, what feelings? Liking boys?"

He nodded slightly, tears spilling from his beautiful green eyes.

I closed my eyes and tried to steady myself. Jesus Christ! "Terry, I know this is tough to hear, but you are fine just as you are, just as God made you." He started shaking his head even before I finished the sentence.

"Mama—"

"Fuck your mama!" He cringed, and I felt like a dick. "I'm sorry. I'm sorry," I said, patting the tiny cot he was lying on. "I know you love your mother." I sighed. "Please drink this, because, if you don't, you're gonna die, and your mother will never forgive herself. Trust me. I know."

He slowly reached out and took the bottle.

"Drink it slowly, but finish it all, you hear me?"

He nodded and began to sip.

"Listen, Terry. I'm gay. I'm gay and I'm happy and I'm in love with the most wonderful man. I've known him all my life, and I've loved him since I was eighteen years old. I can't imagine my life without him at this point—don't even want to imagine it."

He watched me as he drank, watched and listened to me. Whether it was sinking in like the minerals in that drink, I had no idea.

"As much as you love your mother and as much as she loves you, she is wrong about this." He started to protest, but I stopped him. "I know she'll point to the Bible as proof, but you need to remember that throughout history the Bible has been used to persecute blacks and women *and any group another group doesn't like. They were wrong before, and they're wrong about this.*

"I'm sure she'll say she's just trying to do what's best for you and, I'm not gonna lie, it won't be easy living honestly and accepting who you are, but you'll be healthier and happier for it." I looked into his eyes as he continued to drink. "I'm sorry if it sounds like I'm preaching, but I had someone tell me these things at a time in my life where I was this close to ending it."

"The man you love?"

I nodded. "If you remember nothing else about today, remember that you are unique, you are beautiful, and you are worthy of love just as you are." I heard voices in the hallway coming toward us, and I saw Terry tense up. "Nope," I said, pointing at him. "You finish that, while I take care of this."

He nodded and sipped some more. He was nearly done.

I grabbed a chair by a small desk in the room and dragged it over to the middle of the floor before digging out the cigarette lighter from my front jeans pocket and climbing onto the chair. I had to stretch a bit and hold the flame steady, but after several seconds, alarms sounded, and the sprinkler system came on, drenching us.

I dropped to the floor and searched the orderly's pockets as the water began to bring him around. Discovering his cell phone, I called 911 and, affecting my best Tennessee accent, said, "Yes, I see smoke at the PHIL campsite."

Covering the phone, I turned to Terry and asked, "How many kids are here?"

"Fifteen, I think."

"I think they've got about fifteen kids there. I sure hope they all get out. Better make sure to check all the rooms." The operator asked my name. "Jack Bauer." I smiled and winked at Terry, who returned it, despite the confusion in his eyes. "I don't trust that place. I think I heard some kids over there screaming the other night. Please hurry." I ended the call.

"Hey," the orderly mumbled from the floor. He was having trouble getting to his feet. I sidestepped him and went to Terry's side.

"The firefighters will find you and anyone else here who needs help."

He nodded in understanding and drained the bottle. "Thank you," he gasped. "What's your real name, mister?"

I shook my head slowly and placed a finger to my lips. My watch alarm sounded, and I was reminded of that day behind the market when Charleston had first vanished on me. I'd heard that sound then too. "Stay strong, Terry." I took the bottle from him and found myself standing in the massive TRD room, the Portal at my back.

CHAPTER 29

Bend, Oregon - November 2020

CHARLESTON CHECKED his reflection in the full-length mirror and straightened the tie of his tux… again. His longish blond hair was brushed back and hanging neatly over his collar. He turned sideways and checked himself out. He cut quite a fine figure, if he said so himself. It had been nice of Barnaby to invite him to the charity art show tonight, especially since they'd only just reconnected weeks ago at Barnaby's new show.

That night, the looks on the faces of Barnaby's friends had been priceless. How often does a person you consider a figment of a friend's imagination walk up to you and ask to see said friend? He thought that Rossom person—Barnaby's ex, it turned out—was going to choke on his champagne. Coral and India had seemed like a lovely couple, and having gotten to know them a bit better over the past few weeks, he learned they were, in fact, a very lovely couple.

Charleston grabbed his keys and left his room. The night after Barnaby's art opening, the two of them had met for drinks. The next couple of nights they enjoyed polite dinner dates. Then Barnaby took him on a tour of the town and explained the reasons he loved living in Bend. That evening had ended with them holding hands and kissing by Mirror Pond.

The next night they'd spent together in Charleston's room at the bed and breakfast, releasing all the pent-up desires they'd accumulated from their aborted encounters over the years. Despite the nightmarish décor, the B&B had been a good choice, offering comfort and a friendly staff, with all the modern conveniences. But ever since that night, Charleston had slept at Barnaby's house.

He now knew where Barnaby kept his sugar, extra paper towels, furniture polish, and toilet cleanser. He knew Barnaby's shampoo made his hair smell like oranges and fresh linen, somehow making Charleston hungry and comforted at the same time. He was learning how to touch Barnaby, learning that he often liked to be manhandled but was fully capable of handling his man right back.

The desk clerk wolf-whistled when Charleston headed for the exit. "Have a nice evening, Mr. Meeks," she said with a wink.

"Thank you," he said, chuckling. He hopped behind the wheel of his rental and made the short drive to Barnaby's place on the edge of town. During their weeks together, he had expected a lot more questions from Barnaby about how he had appeared throughout his life to rescue him repeatedly, but once it was explained how RPP used to work, Barnaby seemed satisfied. *Strange.* Most people would call Charleston a lunatic if he showed up talking about time travel.

He parked and skipped up the walk to collect his date. *My date.* He grinned but fought down the giddiness rising in his chest. The door opened, and his smile fell from his face.

He couldn't believe what he was seeing. "Your... your hair...."

"Oh," Barnaby said, rubbing his hand over the buzzed hair left on his head. He appeared embarrassed, almost as if he'd forgotten about the haircut, but he couldn't stop grinning. "You don't like it?"

"It's just... just... drastic, I guess." *Drastic doesn't even cover it.* Charleston blinked rapidly, trying to clear his vision. Back when he had stopped the wedding, Barnaby's lustrous brown hair had been cut short, but after seven years, Charleston was delighted to find it had grown back to its sexy, wavy abundance. Now... now it was gone, all gone, practically shaved. "Did you join the Army since last night?"

"Ha! Hardly," Barnaby said, not meeting his eyes. He joined Charleston on the porch, then closed and locked the door behind him. Barnaby turned to him and gazed up into his eyes. "It was just time for a change." He furrowed his brow. "Do you really not like it?"

He stared down at Barnaby, taking in the tailored gray suit he wore, his pale skin, the trimmed stubble on his jaw line, and the way the porch light illuminated his eyes, which appeared even larger now and had taken on a warmer brown hue behind his thick, black-framed glasses.

"You look magnificent," he said softly, then leaned in, pinched Barnaby's chin between his thumb and finger, and kissed him gently, lingering over his sweet lips and running the tip of his tongue along the seam. Barnaby opened for him, sucking his tongue deeper and playing his own against it. Charleston drew his hand over Barnaby's head and grinned at the way what was left of his hair tickled his palm.

"Let's go, babe," he said, taking Barnaby's hand.

WHEN THEY arrived at the gallery, the place was hopping, which pleased Barnaby because it meant good things for Senator Collard-Joyce's LGBT advocacy group, Part of the Fabric. In 2020 a lot of advances had been made for the community, but there were still places where improvements were needed.

Despite marriage equality reaching nearly every state, researchers rolling out an AIDS vaccine, antibullying laws across the country including sexual orientation, and a majority of religious organizations preaching acceptance instead of hatred, LGBT teens were still catching hell in small-town USA. Homelessness, substance abuse, and suicides were not yet stamped out in those places, and the senator wanted to make sure that happened. Bend was just the latest stop as he traveled to various states, hoping to spread awareness and raise money for the Fabric group.

As Barnaby greeted people, he searched the crowd for familiar faces. He saw his usual trio of friends: Coral, India, as well as Ross, who stood with his latest bookish-looking conquest. And he waved. He saw Charleston's parents, who had flown in from Kansas for the event, partly to meet him and partly to support an organization their son supported. There was a story behind Charleston's coming out that Barnaby still hadn't worked through, but they'd get there.

"I'll be right back," Charleston said, moving to greet his parents, but Barnaby tightened his grip on his hand, stopping him. Charleston glanced down at their joined hands and then into Barnaby's eyes. "What is it, babe?" he asked.

"Oh... n-nothing. I just.... Don't go too far, okay?"

Charleston frowned briefly, searched his face, then smiled. "I promise. I'm right over there," he said as he slowly slid his hand free of Barnaby's.

Barnaby watched him go, his swagger, his broad shoulders, the way the suit hung on him all combining to excite him with thoughts of *later*.

"Don't worry, buddy," Jeri said, sidling up next to him.

"Hey!" Barnaby embraced her. "I wasn't sure you'd come to the show."

"Wouldn't have missed it." She stared into his eyes, searching. "How are you feeling?"

"A little confused. Light-headed a couple times today."

"That'll pass. It's just your mind reconciling memories."

"I remember him dying," Barnaby whispered.

"You will for a while, but eventually it will feel like a dream."

Barnaby nodded. "A nightmare, you mean."

"Yeah."

"What about his parents?"

"Chuck's mother wasn't in the Portal room, so she's not aware of the other timeline," Jeri explained.

"What about Leaundra, you, everyone else involved?"

"We've all got varying degrees of recall," Jeri said, shrugging, "but from the data we've collected over the years, the older a person is, the sooner the other memories fade. No idea why."

"You're younger than all of us, so…."

"I've had a headache all day. Fainted this morning and scared the shit out of Marva."

Barnaby examined the crowd. "Is she here? I'd love to meet the woman who can put up with you."

Jeri chuckled. "She's… there she is." Barnaby followed Jeri's finger and saw a tall, willowy Scandinavian beauty speaking rapidly with India as Coral looked on.

"Uh-oh."

"Nothing to worry about there. They're not each other's types… clearly."

He had to agree with that. "So," he said, glancing around, "is the senator here yet?"

"Should be here soon. Hope the speech isn't too long."

"You and me both."

Slightly raised voices near the entrance followed by a smattering of applause drew their attention, and both turned to see Senator Collard-Joyce walk in, security marching on either side of him.

"WHEN I was sixteen years old, my mother couldn't handle the fact I was gay and sent me away to be 'fixed.'" The senator cast his intense green gaze around the room as he shared his story. "I almost died hating myself, because the fact that my mother couldn't love me just as I was must have meant I was unlovable, unworthy."

"Ooh, he's lovely," Ross cooed in Barnaby's ear.

"Shush!" He focused again on the senator.

"I was forty pounds too thin and too weak to get up and turn the doorknob to escape the room where I had been brutalized and tortured by men who claimed to be saving my soul, who said they would make a real man out of me."

"Downer," Ross teased, and Coral, who had joined them, conked him on the head playfully.

"Luckily, I hung on until a rookie firefighter named Daniel Joyce—that's the handsome fella over there—kicked in that door and saved me. He and his colleagues saved a lot of other kids that day, and ten years later, when we met up again, we fell in love. Today, he's my husband, and I have a life I couldn't have imagined at sixteen, a life that was nearly cut short by ignorance and intolerance. We need to stop that from happening to other kids."

The crowd applauded as Barnaby gazed in wonder at the handsome, accomplished man Terry had become. He felt a swell of pride that he'd helped make that possible. His goal in stepping had been selfish, to restore Charleston, but seeing Terry before him now… well, he felt the world had received a gift.

"Now, I'm not claiming my mother changed her beliefs totally, but she and I reached a point where we could continue to love and respect each other, and I like to think I even made her proud again before her death two years ago."

"Hunting accident," Jeri whispered to Barnaby.

"I'd like to make sure other LGBT kids and their parents get that chance," the senator said.

The speech went on for a few minutes more, and then the senator entered the crowd to mingle, look at the artwork, and speak with some of the young artists. He eventually made his way over to Barnaby, Jeri, and

Coral. Ross had gone to talk with India and Jeri's girlfriend—the lovely people again orbiting each other.

"I've purchased one of your bio-generated pieces, Mr. Rosenthal," Daniel Collard-Joyce said, shaking Barnaby's hand, "and one of your hand-painted works as well."

"I'm pleased you've enjoyed my work."

"Good to meet you, sir."

The senator was next to shake Barnaby's hand. He began to speak, but then he froze and simply looked into his eyes.

"What's wrong, sweetie?" his husband asked.

"You seem familiar to me, Mr. Rosenthal. Have we met before?"

"Uh... well...."

"Oh, you probably saw him in an interview online or something," Charleston suggested as he appeared behind Barnaby. He wrapped his arms around Barnaby, then shook Terry and Daniel's hands and introduced himself. The Collard-Joyces eventually mingled away from them, and Charleston turned Barnaby in his arms and kissed his cheek.

"You wanna get outta here?"

"Very much."

On the way out, they stopped to say good night to Charleston's parents. "Please stay and enjoy yourselves," Barnaby said. "We'll see you both for dinner tomorrow night at Elliott's."

"I look forward to it, young man," Dr. Meeks mumbled gruffly.

"This was a lovely event, Barnaby," Charleston's mom said. "Thank you for inviting us."

"I'm so glad you could come," he said.

"I was hoping to meet *your* parents," she said, gazing around the gallery.

"Mom...." Charleston warned.

"It's okay, Chuck," Barnaby said. "I'm sorry, ma'am, but my stepfather still isn't up to traveling, or they would have been here. And you could have met my baby brother Nelson too."

"I'm sure he's delightful if he's half as dreamy as you are," she said, with a pinch to Barnaby's cheek.

"Mother!"

"Oh shush, dear. You boys have a lovely night. As it is, I'll be steering your father back to the B&B soon. He didn't sleep well last night."

After some hugs and kisses and shaking of hands, Barnaby followed Charleston to the exit, eager to get him alone. He turned at the last minute and waved to Jeri, who stood across the room unwrapping a cherry lollipop. They shared a smile.

EPILOGUE

BARNABY LAY in bed and watched Charleston sleep. He traced a finger along his forehead, down his nose, and then along his lips and chin.

"What are you doing?" Charleston asked, smiling, his eyes still closed.

"Mapping you, studying you."

"Why?"

"I'm… I'm trying to convince myself you're really here."

Charleston sighed and rolled over, pinning Barnaby to the bed. "If what we just did doesn't convince you, I don't know what will." They kissed, and Barnaby let himself sink into it desperately, but Charleston pulled back. "Really, what's going on? You're being weird."

"We've only know each other a couple weeks. You can't possibly know when I'm being weird yet. This"—he pointed back and forth between them—"is new, Chuck."

"Don't call me Chuck."

"See?"

"What?"

"Nothing."

They were quiet for a few moments, holding each other and rubbing their favorite naked bits together.

Then Charleston said, "My dad says he had a nightmare that I died." Barnaby stopped rubbing. "Creepy, huh?"

"Yeah… creepy." Barnaby tightened his arms around Charleston and buried his head against his shoulder.

"What is it, babe?"

"I love it when you call me babe."

"Good to know." Charleston stroked his back. "Tell me. I'm here for you. Just tell me what the problem is."

"I'm afraid I'm going to lose you, and there will be no way to get you back."

"First, you're not going to lose me, and second, that's life... *and* death. It's the way the world works."

Barnaby abruptly sat up in bed. "No! No it's not. You brought me back four times."

"Yeah, but RPP is gone, Barnaby. There's no more coming back."

"That's what terrifies me."

Charleston blinked at him. "I have no response to that."

"I had the same dream."

"What are you talking about?"

"That you died, Chuck. I dreamed you were shot and killed by Senator Collard."

Charleston laughed. "Why the hell would he shoot me?"

"No." Barnaby shook his head vigorously. "No, not him... his... his mother."

"Barn—"

"No, listen to me before it's gone, okay?"

Charleston nodded and sat up next to him, and Barnaby proceeded to tell him everything he could remember, everything that remained clear to him. It was fading fast, spilling over the edges of his thoughts like water he was trying to hold in one hand. He told him their story, their other story: how Charleston had saved him yet again and been shot, the meal they shared at Coral's, meeting Handal, saving those children, making love, fighting off Katch and Kaan, the crash, Ramirez, their reunion at the firefight, Collard's death... all of it.

After Barnaby finished, Charleston sat staring into the dimly lit room with an arm around his shoulders.

"Well? Say something." Barnaby nudged a rib with his knuckle.

"That was some... nightmare."

"Chuck—"

"No, babe," Charleston said, "that's what it was. That's all it will ever be now." Charleston rolled over on top of him again, apparently trying to instigate some action.

"But there's a record of it all, right? The alternate timelines, I mean."

"Yep. TSS or temporal-safe storage. Why?"

"How does that work, exactly? Sounds a bit… well, it seems a bit tenuous."

"I don't know about that. Pop developed it, and I don't really understand how it works, but basically it's a containment field that prevents the records from being exposed to our timeline. What are you getting at?"

"What if there were some kind of *accident*, some electrical power-surge thingy? All those records, accounts of everything the Restore Point Program has done… they could just get fried, couldn't they? Wiped out?"

"Sure. In fact… well, I have no proof of this, but I believe Jeri engineered something like that to delete my unauthorized step to your wedding." Charleston went back to nibbling at Barnaby as he fought to maintain his thought processes. "Can we stop talking now?"

"I bet there are some ugly stories in there," Barnaby continued.

"Guess not," Charleston muttered before sucking Barnaby's nipple.

"N-n-nightmares…," Barnaby said, grinning and writhing, "but, I'm thinking, with temporal-safe storage not being EMP safe…."

Charleston froze, and Barnaby knew he'd finally engaged his mind instead of just his body. When their eyes met, he tingled at the broad smile on Charleston's face. "I'll speak to Jeri tomorrow," he said, nodding. "She'll make those bad dreams go away."

Barnaby laughed out loud, rolled Charleston over on his back, and straddled him. "So, you'll stay with me, Chuck?"

"As long as you want me."

He ran his fingers through Charleston's hair, fanning it out over the pillow. He stroked his handsome face, drawing a thumb slowly across his bottom lip. "I've wanted you so long, I don't know how not to. You've always been there, supporting me, believing in me… loving me. You're the one constant in my life."

DAWN KIMBERLY JOHNSON is a native of West Virginia. She earned a BA from the Marshall University W. Page Pitt School of Journalism and Mass Communications and worked as a copy editor at *The Charleston Daily Mail* for eight years. She enjoys writing just after waking, after her characters have strolled through her subconscious, chatting with one another, making love, arguing, figuring out how to live their lives and hold on to their lovers.

Blog: http://kimswritingagain.wordpress.com/
Twitter: https://twitter.com/Dawn_KJ
Facebook: https://www.facebook.com/DawnKimberlyJohnson
E-mail: KimsWritingAgain@yahoo.com

Also by DAWN KIMBERLY JOHNSON

Dawn Kimberly Johnson

BUTTON DOWN

http://www.dreamspinnerpress.com

Also by DAWN KIMBERLY JOHNSON

http://www.dreamspinnerpress.com

Also by DAWN KIMBERLY JOHNSON

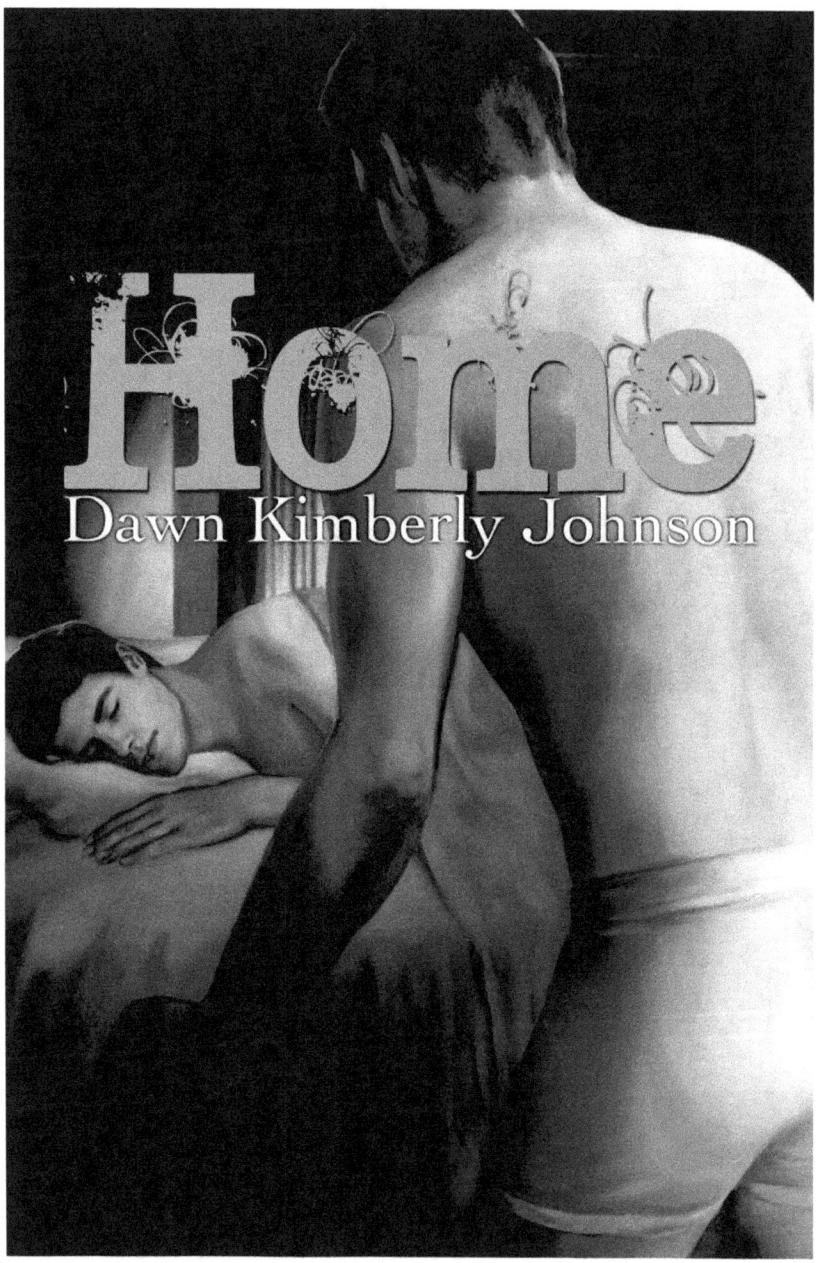

Home

Dawn Kimberly Johnson

http://www.dreamspinnerpress.com

Also by DAWN KIMBERLY JOHNSON

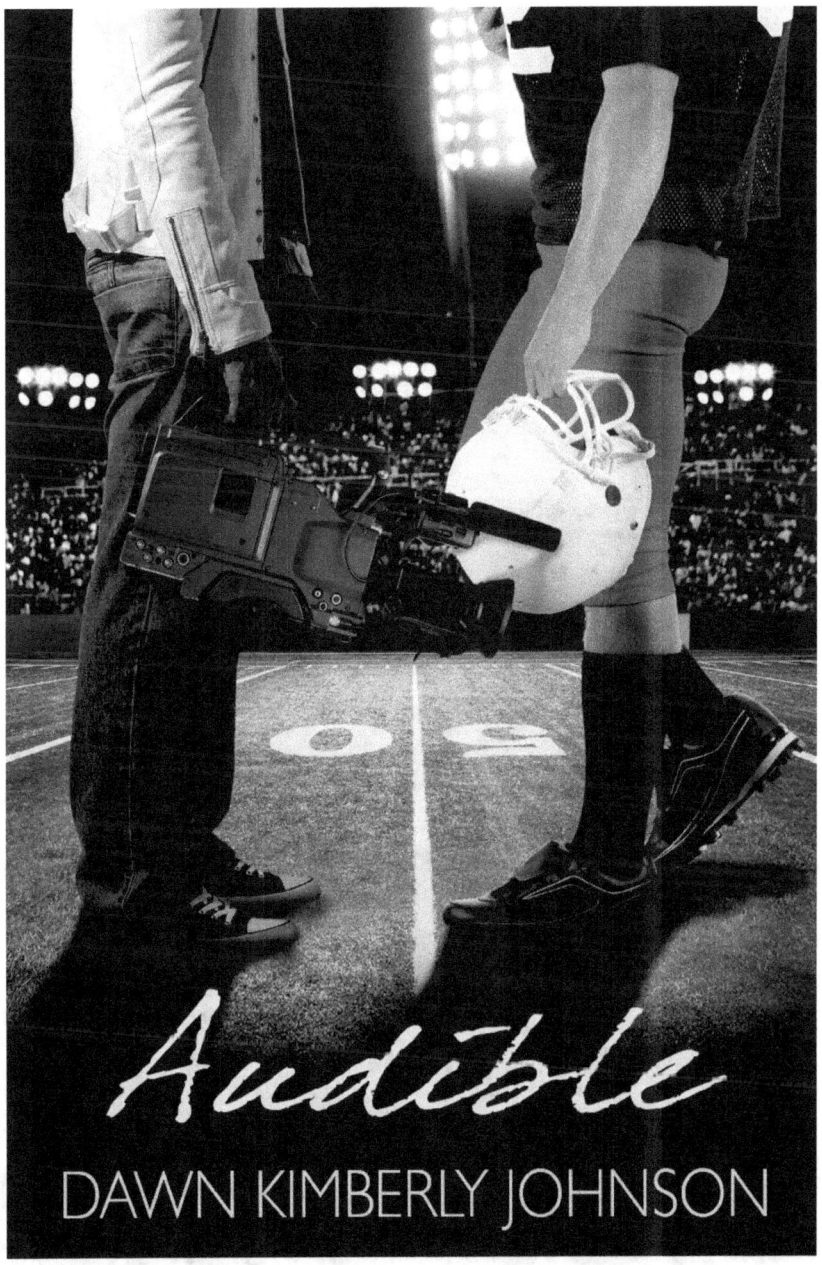

Audible

DAWN KIMBERLY JOHNSON

http://www.dreamspinnerpress.com

Also by DAWN KIMBERLY JOHNSON

GOOD
QUESTION

DAWN KIMBERLY JOHNSON

http://www.dreamspinnerpress.com

Also by DAWN KIMBERLY JOHNSON

http://www.dreamspinnerpress.com

Also by Dawn Kimberly Johnson

WHAT HAPPENED
TO LARRY ALAN?

DAWN KIMBERLY JOHNSON

http://www.dreamspinnerpress.com

www.ingramcontent.com/pod-product-compliance
Lightning Source LLC
Chambersburg PA
CBHW070122260626
47160CB00004B/1586